LONESOME MOONLIGHT

Sir Patrick Bijou

BOOK DESCRIPTION

Being uprooted from the city to the winter tundra of Lonesome Moon was a significant adjustment for Saoirse. And she made sure to make up for it with drugs, booze, and porn every single night.

But what should've been a time of freedom and "alone time" as her father leaves for a week-long work trip, turns into a night of blood-curdling terror?

When spine-chilling cries from outside seeped into the safety of her family's cabin, Saoirse tries to investigate. However, she is faced with a creature that she's only seen in her wildest dreams.

Before she realises what's happening, the creature leaves its mark on her, and she is left to die... or so she thought.

Daniel is coming to her rescue — a blue-eyed, six-foot-two knight in shining armour who nurses her back to health. But Saoirse doesn't realise that the bite mark would soon turn into a curse that Daniel and his family have been trying to keep contained.

With all her street smarts and cunning, Saoirse never saw this one coming.

What will become of Saoirse?

And more importantly, would Daniel signify her redemption or her untimely demise?

Find out for yourself in **"Lonesome Moonlight"** by bestselling author Sir Patrick Bijou!

If you're looking for handsome werewolves, gorgeous damsels, and animalistic sex, get ready to meet your next favourite book!

LONESOME MOONLIGHT

I HAVE SOMETHING TO TELL

Sir Patrick Bijou is known for his role in the United Nations as a UN Ambassador for World Peace and a Senior Sovereign Redemption Judge for the International Court of Justice and International Criminal Courts. He is also a Fund Manager and dynamic Investment Banker.

Sir Patrick is an eclectic writer who lives in the United Kingdom and was born in Georgetown and raised in London, England.

His authorship has earned him fame because his publications are not limited to a genre or theme but from adventurous, thrilling, romantic, criminal, and dramatic theme fictional novels. However, his many experiences have influenced his diverse writing prowess.

In all his academic studies, though, the true treasures he took away are not the certificates (though those are very important), but instead, the experiences he had, the people he met, the foods he ate and even the places he stayed.

"In truth, I am a citizen of the world, and this greatly influences my writing., says Sir Patrick.

"So, if you are already a fan of mine, I appreciate you. If you are not yet one, then what are you waiting for? Read a book and then read some more. I create characters that resonate with you and infuse life into all he writes".

Finding his Books

Sir Patrick has written over 25 published fictional and non-fictional books across several genres and realises the need to make it easier for his readers to find his books.

www.sirpatrickbijou.com
www.bijouebook.com

TABLE OF CONTENTS

CHAPTER 1

Dad was gone, and I was alone. He'd taken off in the truck for the town, and he was going to be gone for a week on a job helping a couple flip a house for later sale. He was supposed to be staying at the local hotel, but I knew damned well he was going to be staying with his girlfriend. He was actually working the job, but he'd give any excuse to fuck that woman.

Not that I cared who my Dad was having relations with. I was just upset that we had moved out here to the middle of bumfuck nowhere, and now he'd ditched me for a week. This area was nothing but snow and heavily wooded coniferous forest, so I felt locked up like some kind of medieval virgin.

I can't blame him, though. I've been kind of a worthless, lazy slut for the last six years, ever since I turned sixteen and drank for the first time, hit meth for the first time, smoked weed for the first time...got 'personal' with boys for the first time. Now I'm twenty-two, and my habits really haven't altered in that arena. I still like the drugs, the booze, and the boys, and they still like me, but my Dad's wised up, so here we are at Lonesome Moon, otherwise known as bumfuck nowhere.

This cabin my dad invested in belongs in the Land That Time Forgot. It took us almost two months to get it livable, and I went an entire week without running water. Now we've at least got a bathroom with a working toilet. Nothing says I love you like taking a dump in a freezing outhouse.

I still have to wash my clothes by hand, though. We haven't put in a washing machine or dryer, so...it's the old warsh thuh clothes on thuh ol' washing board routine. Jesus...Just fucking shoot me.

Whelp, Dad took off and left me here for a week, and he apologized profusely for it, but you know what? I don't mind this time. You know why? Because I am not doing a damned thing this week. I'm going to sit back, smoke some weed, drink some whiskey, and masturbate...a lot. It's a miracle that we have internet out here, and though it may be slow, and though I may only have my dad's laptop, that is all I need to vegetate.

My name's Saoirse Lennon, and that's pronounced 'Ser-sha' if you were wondering. Yes, I'm of Irish descent, and no, I don't have red hair. My hair is brown, brown as bark, just like my eyes. Long, curly brown hair that falls down to my shoulders. No red hair and green eyes for me.

As you already know, I'm twenty-two, twenty-two going on forty. I'm supposed to be working toward an end goal, like getting my GED and getting a job somewhere, but...ever since Mom died when I was fifteen, I haven't done much of anything. I just...never felt like it.

Dad's old, he's tired, and he's upset with me, but he's never even thought about kicking me out. No, I think his move here to Lonesome Moon was a passive-aggressive way of telling me to get the fuck out and get a life. I will...eventually. I need to have some motivation, though. As it is, I do most of the housework for him, so...it's not like he complains a lot.

Of course, he's probably going to be pissed when he comes back and finds that nothing's been done, but he shouldn't have just ditched me. He didn't even ask if I could start learning construction, or carpentry, or whatever the fuck it is he does; I have no idea, but that's not the point.

I thought about this as I breathed deeply into the joint I was holding in my right hand. I blew out a smoke ring and felt that mellow peace wash over me. Dad had left in the morning, so right now I was having a little 'me' time.

I leaned back in my dad's dark-brown comfy chair and placed one barefoot on our little oak-trunk coffee table. The laptop was on the table in front of me, and on the screen was a video of a muscular-looking troll of a man with a ring-beard and tats on his arms fucking a brunette with piercings in her nipples. I don't know why I was watching this, probably because it popped up first and I was too lazy to look for anything that was more to my tastes.

I was fully nude, of course, naked as a jaybird, sitting right smack in the middle of what constituted our 'living room' for this log-built dump, but I didn't care. It was in the middle of the night out in the middle of some bumfuck nowhere woods. No one was going to walk in on me, anyway.

I looked down at my naked body, and that turned me on, which was the point of the porn I was watching. I was five-eight, one-hundred and thirty-seven pounds, with nice C-cup breasts and pretty-in-pink nipples, and I had a nice butt, not too big, not too small. I was attractive in the face, though I looked like my dad; square jaw, you know. Still, I was good-looking. I wasn't into other girls, but I'd fuck me.

I reached over to the little wooden stand on my right, rested my joint in Dad's green ashtray, and picked up my bottle of rye whiskey. I had my ways of getting what I needed, even out here, but Lonesome Moon had not made that easy. Even so, I had enough to last for a week.

I took a swig of whiskey and shook my head from the burn of it. It didn't take much for me to get lit, so this was going to be a happy experience until morning hit. The morning was going to suck.

I put my bottle down, picked up my joint, took a puff, put it back down, and slid the fingers of my right hand down between the lips of my already wet snatch. My fingers ran through my thick brown pubes as I rubbed my whole pussy in anticipation of the orgasm that was to come...cum? You know what I mean.

I stroked my small pink clit, let that sensation sink in, and thought about fucking, just fucking, fucking like a wild animal in heat. I stroked myself slowly at first, rubbed my whole pussy in between strokes, and stuck two fingers inside myself in the occasional heat of pleasure.

"Yeah," I whispered. "Fuck me like that...Mmm...Suck on my big titties..."

Titties. Titties is such a stupid word for breasts. Who thought of that, anyway?... It's retarded...Nevertheless, just saying it, feeling the dirtiness of it, turned me on even more.

"Yeah, suck my titties," I breathed out. "Mmm...Fuck my pussy like that. Give me that great big fucking cock...Oh, I want to suck that big fucking cock...Rub that big fat cock on my titties...Fuck my pussy...Fuck it...Fuck my cunt hard with that big fat cock..."

I reached over, grabbed my bottle of whiskey, took another pull, and shook my head again from that shock that only strong alcohol can give. I set the bottle down, took another puff from my joint, set that backdown, and went back to stroking myself.

"Yeah..." I breathed out. "Fuck my pussy...Fuck it hard, bitch...Give me that cock...Let me lick those big balls...Mmm...I want to suck on those balls..."

I pulled lightly on my clit and savored that magic electricity as I bit my lower lip, pulled hard on my left nipple with my left hand, felt that pleasure build, that slow explosion building in my lower belly, oh, sinking in, feeling it down in...

A loud cry from outside startled me, and I gripped the arms of the comfy chair out of reflex.

'What the fuck!" I said in surprise.

A loud bleating erupted once more, a terrible sound, like some animal being brutally murdered, and it was loud, like really fucking loud. I didn't know what the fuck was going on.

"What the fuck?" I said again, this time in a whisper.

I got up from Dad's comfy chair, grabbed my jeans, and shimmied into them. I didn't even bother to put on my panties; I was wet, anyway. I put on my red flannel shirt and quickly buttoned it up, and no, I didn't bother to put on my bra, either.

A loud thump hit the south side of the cabin, that side to my immediate right, and the pictures on the south wall rattled.

"What the fuck!" I hissed, this time in anger.

I pulled on my thick, black, winter socks, pushed my feet into my black winter boots, slipped on my grey parka, zipped up, and proceeded to grab Dad's twelve gauges, taking them off their mount on the north wall. I went into the kitchen on the west side of the cabin after that, opened up the box of shells that Dad had left on the kitchen table, and quickly loaded the shotgun. I held it up and readied it to fire as I headed toward the backdoor in the kitchen.

"Ruin my night, will you!" I hissed out. "I'll ruin your balls, motherfucker!"

I was pissed. I didn't know what was going on outside, but I was going to give someone a bad hair day; that was a fact. It was never cool to interrupt someone's alone time. That was a dueling offense. An offense worthy of calling someone out on the street at high noon.

I opened the backdoor and walked out into the freezing cold, my boots crunching down upon packed snow. I watched my breath freeze in the light of the moon, realizing at that moment that I'd forgotten to bring a light, but that didn't matter, obviously. The silver light of the full moon above me blanketed everything with a soft glow and made the white of the snow glare in my vision.

I carefully walked around to the south side of the cabin where the 'thump' had occurred, my boots crunching into the snow. It was deathly quiet out here, spooky, but I had a loaded twelve-gauge in my hands and whiskey in my blood, so I didn't care about that.

I discovered the source of the thump. It was a deer, a mature doe, in fact. It was ripped open, entrails everywhere, hot steam rising from the bloody carcass, the snow black from its blood.

"Oh, shit..." I said nervously.

This was bad. This was probably the work of a bear, and...I didn't know if a twelve-gauge could stop a charging bear...I suspected it couldn't unless I was very lucky.

"Fuck," I whispered.

There was the sound of crunching snow out near the large woodshed that existed on the property. My dad stored some tools in that thing, but it was pretty much falling apart. He was either going to have to tear it down or fix it up, one or the other.

Regardless of that, the sound of crunching snow made me anxious, fired up my adrenaline, so I readied my twelve gauges and headed over to the shed. If worse came to worst, I could shoot a bear in the face and then make it back to the safety of the cabin before it could retaliate. Then I could shoot at it from an open window.

The bears were mean fuckers, especially grizzlies. They liked to get revenge on anything that pissed them off, so if a fight was coming, I was going to have to kill it, not let it go. I wasn't stupid.

I walked up to the old woodshed and readied my shotgun at the shoulder for firing. The light of the moon shone up from the snow around me, but the side of the shed was shrouded in shadow, so the whole thing was creepy as fuck, and this finally creeped me out, creeped me out whether I was loaded full of whiskey and weed or not.

"Fuck this," I breathed. "Go back inside, Saoirse."

I turned to head back toward the cabin, but the bleating cry of a flying animal startled me into inaction. Another deer, a large eight-point buck, flew past me and slammed into the side of the woodshed, cracking the old boards of that side of the wall through sheer force.

"What the fu...!" I started to say.

Massive pain stabbed into my right shoulder and cut short my startled cry. Hot blood, black in the moonlight, spurted up from my grey parka as a large animal's fangs sank into me, sank into my skin and muscle.

I screamed, my mouth as wide open as it could go, and the shotgun went off in my hands because I must have pulled the trigger by reflex. The gun bucked out of my hands from that force, and then I was flying through the air a second later, tossed like a ragdoll.

I hit the side of the woodshed and crashed right through the wall, the boards splintering upon impact, crashed through it, and rolled across the wooden floor to stop in the middle of the darkness of that shed.

I was all in pain. I was bruised and battered from being thrown through a wall, but that was nothing compared to the absolute burning agony in my shoulder. My tongue was lolling out of my mouth, and I tasted the red copper of blood; I must have bitten it when I was thrown.

I rolled over to see the big buck wobble past the woodshed in front of me; it wobbled on unsteady legs in the moonlight, its head bobbing this way and that as if it were seriously addled. It took five steps through the snow, but it never made it any farther.

A beast, a big fucking thing over six feet tall, tackled the deer, and its great jaws clamped down upon its neck, spurting steaming blood everywhere. This buck bleated once before it was dragged at a running lope out of my vision, leaving a trail of bloody black snow behind it.

That thing had walked on two angled legs, like a dog's legs. It had great big paws that almost looked like clawed hands, and its head didn't look like a bear, not like a bear, not like that at all.

There was no time for me to think; I just acted. I stood on two battered legs and hobbled through the snow back to the cabin; I didn't even think to grab the shotgun. My right knee was fucked up and my left ankle was twisted, but I hobbled back to the house without looking behind me. I was scared shitless at that point.

I got through the kitchen door, shut it behind me, and quickly locked it.

"What was that? What was that? What the fuck was that...?" I babbled.

I was in shock. I unzipped my parka and cried out from the stabbing, burning pain in my right shoulder. My grey parka was shredded at the top, stained dark red with blood, my blood, and that realization didn't hit me until I saw my savaged shoulder.

I let out a high-pitched whine at the sight of my bloody shoulder. There were large, bloody holes in it where each fang had sunk into my tender flesh, and it was so gross that I couldn't look directly at it.

I ripped off my flannel shirt and went topless in order to attend to this wound. I threw my shredded shirt to the kitchen floor, hobbled into the living room, grabbed my bottle of whiskey, and poured some over the wound without thinking, but that was a serious mistake. It burned like someone was pushing a blowtorch into my skin.

"OH GOD!" I screeched.

My eyes watered over with tears as I set the bottle down and sat down in my dad's comfy chair. The pain was so intense, so terrible, that I didn't move. I just whimpered and cried and shook in that chair for an entire minute.

There was so much blood. I was bleeding a lot. Just red blood running down my skin and over my bare right breast.

I don't know why, maybe it was because of the shock I was in, but I reached over and picked up my still lit joint, took a drag, breathed out that smoke, and set it back in the ashtray.

I looked down and noticed for the first time the large dark piss stain on the crotch of my jeans. I must have pissed myself at some point, but when that was, I had no idea.

I slowly, painfully unbuttoned my jeans and pulled down the zipper. I used my right boot to kick off my left boot, then used my left foot to kick off my right boot, and then I pulled off my jeans.

I took another drag off my joint, set it back down, picked up the whiskey bottle, cried out from the pain of moving my right arm, took a deep pull of whiskey, and set the bottle back down.

I stretched out, fully naked except for the pair of black winter socks on my feet, and tried to steady my breathing. I leaned back in the chair and just laid there staring up at the sloped ceiling, the overhead lamp shining down from above, and then I closed my eyes, closed them as I took in a deep breath. The pain in my shoulder was a deep and throbbing ache, so I just laid there and breathed in and out, in and out, in and out, until darkness took me.

*****

I awoke from a nightmare, a dim memory of fangs and claws and fur still clinging to my psyche as I struggled to shake off my lethargy. It was morning, and morning light streamed through the windows of the cabin.

I reached up and rubbed the crust from my eyes, but my right shoulder felt stiff as fuck. It hurt with a throbbing ache, so I inspected it, and that's when the horror of what had happened the night before sunk in. My naked chest was covered with crusty, dried brown blood. My shoulder was the worst in that respect, but the wound on it had sealed somehow, scabbed over by some miracle I did not understand.

Even so, I was hurting all over. It felt like I'd been run over by a truck and then thrown off a cliff. My throat was so parched that I'd swear I'd been swallowing desert sand, so my first order of business was to get up and get some water. Maybe later I'd go and get in the tub, wash off this wound of mine, and stop looking like a horror movie victim, but without some water first, I wasn't going to be doing much of anything.

I peeled myself up from out of my dad's chair and whimpered as every injury screamed at me at once. My left arm was bruised and battered, the left side of my face felt fucked up, and my left ankle felt sprained...You know, I'm thinking I hit the side of that woodshed with my left side, but...that's just a guess.

My right knee was also fucked up, but the worst was still my right shoulder. All in all, I looked like a Goddamned mess, and if anyone saw me like this, they'd be rushing me to an ER, but considering where I was, that wasn't going to happen.

I dragged myself into the kitchen, took a glass with yellow flowers on it out of one of the kitchen cabinets, filled it up with tap water, and gulped it down. Gulping it down had not been a smart idea, however, because the world wobbled and wavered a second later like I was on a ship at sea, and I saw little stars as I went lightheaded.

The kitchen door clicked as the knob turned and the door pushed in from the outside.

Oh, good. Dad was home. There was no way in hell I was going to be able to explain to him why I was naked and covered in blood, but...at least he was home. He'd know what to do.

Only it wasn't my dad. A young man walked in; he was only a little older than me, maybe by two or three years, very cute, six-foot or so, white with short black hair, blue eyes, average weight, and he was wearing a tan winter coat and dark blue jeans, light-tan hide leather gloves on his hands, light-brown outdoorsman boots...

He stared at me in complete surprise, but I wasn't so much surprised as I was about to pass out. I dropped the glass in my hand, it shattered on the kitchen tiles beneath my feet, and then I pitched backward as the world started to fade again.

The young intruder in my house rushed forward and caught me in his arms before I completely lost consciousness. I can remember staring up into his blue eyes before everything went totally dark. He really was cute for an intruder...

*****

I dreamed while I passed in and out of consciousness, though most of my 'conscious' periods were nothing more than fleeting moments of blurry vision and soft light. No, most of my time was spent in the dream world, somewhere I did not need to be while an intruder was in my cabin.

I found myself running through the woods. I was completely naked, running through the brush on my bare feet, on the snow, my toes crunching into that packed frost, and I was following a wolf, a big thing with brown fur.

I stopped running as the large animal turned and stared at me with a vivid pair of bright golden eyes, and somehow I knew it was female, and that it wanted me to follow it further into the large pines, but I got scared, not because it was a wolf, no, but because wherever it was going, I wasn't sure if I wanted to follow it into that dark place.

We stood and stared at each other, our breath crystalizing in the freezing air around us, and it looked at me with those golden eyes, wanting me to follow.

I briefly awoke from my strange dream to find myself spoon-fed some chicken noodle soup. I was in my own bed, and I had on my blue flannel shirt, this one not shredded, thankfully, and the intruder that I had seen earlier was trying to get me to eat something. I was covered by my bed's thick brown quilted cover, so I was warmer for the moment, and that cute boy had my head lifted in his right hand with his left hand holding the spoon.

"Who..." I choked out.

He forced me to sip some chicken noodles, and I swallowed them, and then I closed my eyes again as I lost consciousness one more time. Passing out was getting really inconvenient, especially when a stranger was invading my home.

*****

I awoke to walk through the snow, only this time I was on the edge of the forest. I could smell pine in the crisp winter air, and before me was the thick of the woods, but I could not see very far into that darkness.

Golden eyes looked at me from out of the thickness of the wooded park, and then the snout of the great brown wolf appeared, and then its full head. It looked upon me with sad eyes, its breath and my breath visible in the cold air, and it backed into the forest as if it were beckoning me, only this time I wanted to follow it.

I moved carefully through the snow-covered brush on my bare feet, feeling the cold on my soles, the crunch of that snow between my narrow toes. I stepped forward into the darkness, intent on following the mysterious she-wolf into the heart of the forest.

I felt alive in my nudity, my nipples so hard in the cold air that they were like sharp pink points, and I wished to be warmer but still naked, to be liberated from the constraints of the clothing humanity had inflicted upon me so that I could truly be free. It was my lack of body hair that attacked my sensibilities and made me angry at my own limitation.

I stepped into the darkness, the cloying atmosphere of pine and chill all around me, and I sniffed once, twice, and smelled something unfamiliar upon the breeze. The great she-wolf stared at me from out of the darkness of the pines, and in its jaws was a young hare. I could smell the blood on it, and that scent quickened my pulse.

The great brown wolf laid the dead hare at my feet, and I accepted the gift without hesitation. I sniffed all over the carcass, taking in the smell of fresh blood and its gamey scent, and then I bit deeply into its soft belly, tasting that hot blood filling my mouth.

That rush of blood filling my mouth excited me in a way I had not felt before. I grew wet between my legs as my eyes rolled up in the whites, and I crunched down into sinew and bone with my teeth, tasting the richness of muscle and blood and flesh, a taste that turned me on and caused me to shake in excitement.

*****

My eyes fluttered open to the darkness of my own bedroom. The only light in my room was coming from the soft silver glow of moonlight casting through my bedroom window.

I laid there in my bed, still in pain, still unsure of what was going on anymore, but this did not last long. A shape rose out of the darkness, a massive thing, the beast that had savaged me, a hulking monstrosity that I could only see in outline due to the shadow of night and moonlight. It rose up from all fours and stood on two angled legs, and I could feel the heat from it as it loomed over my helpless and prone body, its shape all fur and rippling muscle and bestial power.

I was way too out of it to know fear. I was simply there, not really thinking, not reacting as a long and low growl surfaced from the beast's throat. It bent down toward my face, and I could feel its hot breath upon my flushed cheeks. It smelled like death, but not like a corpse, no. It smelled like hot blood, like a fresh kill, as if it were the embodiment of the hunter over prey.

It looked like a wolf up close, but unlike any wolf, I'd ever seen before. It had golden eyes that stared directly into mine, golden eyes that held an intelligence I was not familiar with in any animal I had ever seen.

It raised its left paw, but that paw was more like a hand, four long, clawed fingers and an opposable thumb, and its claws were long and black hooked things it used to pull up my thick brown quilted cover. It moved my cover aside, pulling it down to reveal my helpless figure.

All I had on was my blue flannel shirt and a pair of white panties. It ran its claws along the top of my shirt, popping off the little blue plastic buttons one by one. I was still out of it, however, so I didn't feel fear like I should have.

It opened my shirt to reveal my bare breasts, and then it took one claw and lifted my panties at the upper seam. It bent down, its massive head in full view, and it took in a deep breath of my crotch, then let go of my panties, ripping them at the top. Its long, reddish-pink tongue slithered over the bare skin of my belly, slathering me with its hot saliva until that tongue slid over my right breast and large pink nipple.

That tongue slid along my bare throat, over my chin, and into my open mouth. I tasted it right then, the raw power of its animal essence, something that called to me from deep within the recesses of my subconscious.

It pulled its tongue back into its maw as it reached down with both hands and slid them under my back to lift me up just a little. I whimpered, a high-pitched, pathetic moan as the pain in my shoulder lanced through me, and it released me, let me fall back into the softness of my bed.

It stared down at me before backing away into the soft and silver light of the moon, and I could see its huge penis hanging down from between its legs, a thick rope at least eight inches long flaccid, the thing circumcised, which was weird to me, because animals weren't typically circumcised, and I stupidly pondered this as it backed away out of my room and into the shadows of the cabin living room.

Darkness took me again, but this time I was glad for it.

*****

I awoke in the morning. This time I shook the fog from my head, rubbed the crust from my eyes, and sat up. My shoulder was still stiff, but it didn't hurt nearly as much as it had hurt before, and that was good.

I was in my bed, and I was wearing my blue flannel shirt, though it was open in the front. A quick inspection of myself revealed the buttons popped off of my shirt, some still in my bed, and my panties were ripped at the top. This, of course, sounded an alarm in my head.

"What the..." I groaned.

I'd awoken from that strange dream of the beast, that dream still fresh in my mind, but I knew it had only been a dream because such a creature would have ripped me to shreds if it had been a reality.

I heard footsteps, and then the young man I had seen earlier appeared in my bedroom doorway. He was dressed in dark blue jeans, a light-blue, long-sleeved work shirt with a white undershirt, and tanned work boots, and on his handsome face was a look of deep concern, but that was not what held my attention. It was the fact that there was a Goddamned stranger in my home that held my attention.

I immediately covered my bare breasts by closing my shirt, holding the two sides together with my right hand.

"Who the fuck are you!" I said in an angry response to this intrusion. "What the fuck are you doing in my house!"

The young man turned away and stepped back, looking to the side to avoid staring directly at me.

"Oh, shit..." he breathed. "I'm sorry...I didn't know you were awake."

Was he stupid? Oh...This...This pissed me off.

"That's not an answer!" I hissed. "Why are you in my house!"

"I...My name is Daniel," he said quickly. "Daniel Christianson. My parents owned this property, and my dad sent me to check in on the new owners. Mr. Lennon just has a couple of more things to sign, and then I'll be on my way."

"My dad's not here," I frowned. "He won't be back for a few days...What the...Why in the fu...Why did you just walk into my house?"

"I knocked on the front door, but there was no answer," said the boy, this 'Daniel'. "I walked around to the kitchen door, and I saw someone through the window, so I was just going to step in and say 'hello', but I saw you standing there and..." 'You saw what?" I asked in sudden horror.

I was pretty sure at that moment what he'd 'seen'.

"You were pretty badly injured," he said meekly. "I got you to your bed and...and cleaned you up...bandaged your...uhhh..."

Yep. He'd seen everything.

"Wha...Why...Why didn't you call an ambulance!" I stammered.

"I hiked here," he said sheepishly. "It's a twelve-mile hike to our..."

I cut him short.

"Why in the fuck did you hike here!" I cried. "Why didn't you call an ambulance!"

"I hike all the time," he said uncertainly. "I hiked out here without thinking about it. It's not really a big deal, but...when I got here...you...you had drugs laid out everywhere. It looked bad...I just...I didn't want any trouble with the police..."

Okay, I understood that, but still...

"I could have died, you idiot!" I hissed. "Why didn't you call somebody! 911! My dad! Your dad! Anyone!"

"My dad's a vet," replied Daniel. "Veterinarian. I've got some experience with wounds like that, and it didn't look that bad, so I used the emergency kit to stitch you up. I had some antibiotics and bandages...I...I panicked. I didn't want to get in trouble with the police...I didn't know if you were going to...I just..."

Okay, this was making more sense. It was clear that he was kind of stupid, or maybe...he just really didn't know what to do. I was pretty fucked up when he saw me for the first time...but still...what the fuck? He'd obviously seen me naked, and he obviously dressed me, but...my clothes are fucked up...Makes me wonder...

"All right, shut up," I said unhappily. "Just be honest with me, and I want an honest answer...Did you do anything to me while I was out? I need to know, 'Daniel' because if you did, the police are the last thing you'll need to worry about."

He looked straight at me this time, but his eyebrows furrowed as if he didn't understand.

"Do anything to you?" he asked. "What do you mean, do anything...?"

His blue eyes widened as his face turned beet red. He waved his hands in front of himself and emphatically shook his head no.

"No, no, no!" he said. "No...I didn't do anything bad. I just cleaned you off, stitched you up, put on that bandage, and...and dressed you. I didn't...I didn't do anything...I mean...I tried to feed you, but that was a little difficult. In fact, I was about to call someone, because you were thrashing around in your bed like you were having a seizure, and I...I didn't know what to do. Maybe I should have called someone...Oh, fuck...This is all so fucked up."

Okay, it was clear to me that he hadn't done anything, but Jesus, he's kind of stupid. He should have called somebody. I mean, I'm glad that he didn't; I lucked out on that, but...what the fuck?

I decided to deescalate this and contain the situation.

"Tell me about it," I grimaced. "This is fucked up...Look...I won't mention this to anybody if you don't. My dad doesn't have to know anything about this, okay? You already got a free peep show, so...consider that my thanks. We can both just forget about this and pretend as nothing happened."

"Oh, I..." stammered Daniel. "It's not like...You haven't got anything I haven't seen before..."

"What?" I glared at him. "What!"

"No, it...it's just..." stammered Daniel. "I...I've seen naked women before, okay? You were hurt...It's not like I was going to...Who does that, anyway? You were hurt..."

Okay, he didn't do anything. I was a thousand percent certain now.

"All right, all right," I frowned. "It's not a big deal. As long as you don't mention the booze and the weed, we're cool. My dad doesn't need to know about either."

This 'Daniel' let out an exhale of relief.

"Okay," he nodded. "That works for me."

I chewed on my lower lip as I thought about all of this.

"How long was I out?" I asked.

"Well," replied Daniel. "I walked in yesterday morning..."

My brain came to a screeching halt.

"Y...Yesterday!" I choked out. "I've been out that long! What the...Why in the hell...Won't your family think you're missing!" "No," replied Daniel with a shake of his head. "After coming here, I was going to hike out to a small hunter's lodge my family owns. It's about three miles north of here...They know I'll be gone for a few days...Oh, and....I found your shotgun out by the woodshed, by the way. I brought it inside."

"Thanks," I said unhappily.

"I don't know what happened to you, but..." shrugged Daniel, "it looks bad out there. There's blood everywhere, a deer carcass near your front door, and...bear tracks all over the place."

"Bear tracks?" I asked.

That thing hadn't looked like a bear to me. Not...at...all.

"Looks like a bear dragged off another carcass into the forest," said Daniel. "I'm surprised that one's come this far south, but...it's not unheard of. I'm really surprised it didn't kill you. Did you shoot it? I had to pop an empty shell out of your twelve gauges."

I thought about this some more. It was clear that he would never believe me if I told him what had really happened...what I think had happened, anyway.

"I don't remember," I said warily. "I remember getting attacked, and the gun went off, but then the...the 'bear' went after the buck it had wounded, so I dragged myself back inside and passed out on the living room chair."

"Well, you're lucky," breathed Daniel. "It took another kill and left."

"Yeah," I replied, but I was still unsure about all of this.

It didn't matter at the moment, though. What mattered was getting up and getting something to eat. This 'Daniel' had said he'd tried to feed me, but he'd said it was difficult, so I probably needed to eat something in order to help heal this nasty shoulder wound of mine. I was bruised up, sure, but bruises couldn't get infected. At least, I didn't think they could.

I got up from my bed, this time unconcerned about whether he could see my nudity. He'd already seen me naked, and I must have been the one that had torn my clothes while I was thrashing around in my sleep, so...I decided to be a little bit of an exhibitionist. He struck me as too much of a weenie to come onto me, forthright as he was about patching me up.

"Well, let me throw on some clothes, and I'll make us breakfast," I said.

"Oh..." started Daniel.

His eyes went wide as I took off my shredded shirt and shimmied out of my torn panties. I found this really amusing, especially the crimson color of his cheeks, but he'd already seen me naked, up close, I might add, so...what the hell.

I dug around in my dresser drawers as he stood there at the doorway gawping. It gave me a little giggle to think that I could give this boy a hard-on, but I played it cool, nonchalant so that I was in control. He was cute, and cute boys were hard to come by out here in the middle of bumfuck nowhere. Plus, he hadn't molested me while I was out, so that took him up a notch in my eyes. At least, I don't think he'd molested me. I was going to hope for the best on that one. And he was cute. Did I mention that?

I felt a little flushed at the thought of being alone with this boy. Hmm...Now there's an idea. I thought that perhaps a little breakfast was in order, and then maybe...Oh, yeah...Sausage sounded good to me.

"You got a girlfriend, Daniel?" I asked innocently as I pulled out a pair of panties. "Uhh...no..." he said after some hesitation. "I had someone a year ago..."

"Oh," I replied as I shimmied into my panties. "Just wondering. Didn't want to make anyone jealous. My name's Saoirse, by the way. It's an Irish name, so the spelling's kind of fucked up on it, but that's neither here nor there."

I pulled out a white T-shirt, one that was somewhat see-through. I wanted his eyes to wander toward my nipples for the time being. It would make easing into his pants, less awkward, smoother. I had to make him think like it was his idea, though. That way, any guilt about it was solely on his shoulders. Boys were my specialty, after all.

I slipped on my shirt, turned, and made sure he could see my front as I adjusted my shirt's hem. I wasn't going to wear anything else for now...No, I needed the blood to rush to his other head. The trick with boys was to make sure that there was more blood running toward their penises than to their brains. This 'Daniel' was a little slow and a little shy, but he was cute, and for some reason, I was both hungry and horny, and this was in spite of the fact that some motherfucking monster had put me in a coma for a day. I wanted sausage, dammit, and I wasn't going to let my injuries pass up this opportunity for some meat in my mouth.

"Come on," I said as walked toward him. "I'll make us breakfast."

He backed up as I walked through the door, though I could feel his eyes on my tits. Yeah, things were a little different now that I wasn't passed out and helpless. He was one of those 'good' boys, not the kind that fingers you when you're in an alcoholic daze. I've known plenty of that kind. Now that I was up and running on full steam, however, that meant he wasn't trying to fight his 'urges' anymore, or at the very least, he wasn't fighting as hard.

I led him into the kitchen and motioned for him to sit down at the table. He took a seat closest to the backdoor and clasped his hands in front of him.

'You like sausage?" I asked him as I opened the fridge. "I know I do.

Uhh...sure," he said quietly.

I pulled out the pack of sausages and a dozen eggs, closed the fridge, and set them on the table. I could feel his blue eyes roaming over the curves of my butt, but I liked that...Yum. I was definitely hungry, and in more ways than one.

"Sit back," I urged. "Relax. I'll make us some breakfast. You patched me up, so...I'm happy to service you in return. I'll get that sausage sizzling hot for you."

"Uhh...umm...uhhh..." started Daniel.

I couldn't help but giggle at his reticence. He was going to be fun; I could tell.

I took a pan down from the hanging rack above the kitchen sink, filled that pan with water, and started the kitchen stove burner, that white stove right next to the sink. There was the click, click, click as the electric spark hit the gas, and the flame ignited a moment later. I opened up the sausage, took in a deep breath of that delicious scent, and waited for the water in the pan to start boiling.

Oh my God, that meat smelled good. I wanted to take a bite out of the raw meat in front of me, but I wasn't that desperate for food. Still, my stomach growled, a loud and embarrassing sound in front of my guest, but I played it off.

"Oof," I said. "I am starving. Don't you hate it when your stomach does that?"

"Just means you're hungry, right?" asked Daniel. "I could barely get you to eat anything at all while you were out."

"You're lucky I didn't die," I chastised him. "You would have been in deep shit if I had."

Daniel's handsome face wilted in embarrassment and guilt. I think by now he was figuring out just how much he'd fucked up. He should have called someone, but I'm really glad he hadn't. I can think of better activities than spending my days and nights locked up in jail due to drug possession.

"That's okay," I said in reassurance. "You did me a massive favor, anyhow. Now I'll return that favor."

"Oh...that's fine," replied Daniel nervously. "I...think I should change that bandage, though."

I dropped the sausage into the pan, all of it, the entire pack, and what can I say? I was really hungry. I took down another frying pan, got it started on the stove with a little olive oil, took two eggs from the egg carton, cracked open those eggs, and dropped them in the pan.

Fuck it. Fuck making him think fucking me is his idea. I'm hungry and horny, Goddammit. It was time to be a little more obvious with my intentions.

"You're cute, you know that?" I said as I dug out a spatula from the top kitchen drawer. "Oh...uhh...thanks," said Daniel.

"I don't think I believe you, though," I said.

"About what?" asked Daniel.

"About you not having a girlfriend," I said. "Guy like you should have a girl on each arm, don't you think?"

I...I never thought about it..." stammered Daniel.

Oh, I like him. He's not only cute, he's vulnerable. I can have fun with that.

"Well, you did me a massive service by not turning me in," I said nonchalantly. "I've never been caught with drugs, and I'd like to keep it that way."

"I...I don't do drugs," said Daniel.

"I don't consider weed a drug," I replied. "Now the meth I have, that's another story. Even so, I'm not nearly as bad about it as I used to be. I don't want to end up with sores and missing teeth and all that other stuff, so I've been sticking to weed lately. It's better for you, you know?"

"I wouldn't know," said Daniel, and I could tell that he was nervous.

"My dad went into town on a house flipping project," I said. "He says he's staying at the hotel, but I know he's shacking up with his girlfriend. I don't really care, though. As long as it makes him happy, right? That's all that matters."

"Yeah..." replied Daniel.

The eggs were done much faster than the sausage, but I wasn't interested in them. I put them on a plate and handed them to Daniel along with a knife and fork.

"Thank you," said Daniel.

I went back to breathing in the delicious fumes of the sausage I was still cooking.

"Not a problem," I said. "So...when are your folks expecting you back?"

"In three days," said Daniel. "That's the normal timetable." 'You could stay here, instead," I said.

"What?" asked Daniel.

"I think you should stay here," I said, this time more firmly. "I don't know how to change this bandage or anything...Maybe you should stay here and make sure I don't get an infection?"

"Oh...well I..." said Daniel hesitantly.

"It'll be nice to have some company," I said. "I'll fix you some meals as payment. You can sleep in my dad's bed...or mine...if you want."

"Umm..." said Daniel.

"Why don't you just eat breakfast and think about it," I said. "You can change my bandage after we eat."

"Oh...Okay," replied Daniel has marked uncertainty.

I took some orange juice from the fridge and poured him a glass, then finished cooking the sausage. I gave him a couple of links and then dumped out the rest onto my plate, sat down across from him, and looked down at my breakfast. Staring down at that pile of meat, however...Goddamn, was I hungry.

That first bite was so juicy and so delicious that I just tore into the rest of the links on my plate. Daniel ate slowly, patiently, but I was like some preschooler eating Jell-O for the first time. I ignored him completely during that time, scarfing down that pile like it was my last meal.

I finished a little after he did, but the look on his face...I can't really describe it. He was either impressed or horrified; I couldn't tell.

"That was good," I said as I picked up our plates and put them in the sink. "Now you can change my bandage. That's not too much trouble, is it?"

"It's probably a good idea," said Daniel.

"Let's go, then," I replied.

I led him into the living room and waved a hand toward the comfy chair in the center of the living room floor.

"Sit," I ordered.

"Uhh...okay," he said nervously.

I stood in front of him, brushed my long curly brown hair back with my hands, reached down, and pulled off my shirt. Daniel's eyes went wide as I tossed my shirt aside and shimmied out of my panties, tossing them aside as well.

"What...What are you...?" he started.

I leaned forward and placed my right index finger across his lips, and then I got down onto my knees before him, fully intent on having a little more sausage for my breakfast. I pushed his knees apart and unzipped his jeans, and he said nothing in response to this.

He sucked in his breath as I reached into his jeans, reached through the hole in his underwear, and pulled out his cock. He was already partially erect, and his penis was a good six-and-a-half inches long, circumcised, just like I liked them. I took the head of his cock into my mouth and sucked up and down the shaft, and his breathing went ragged and erratic as I did so.

I tasted some salty precum as his cock hardened in my mouth. It was a thick thing, his erect penis, definitely enough to satisfy my urges, so I popped it from my mouth and straddled his lap, ready to take it in.

I breathed out in relief as I slid myself over his hard rod. That head moved up my wet tunnel, spreading me open, and it was like scratching an itch you just couldn't quite reach, a relief of something I needed so badly that I couldn't resist the urge if I tried.

I adjusted my knees and legs so that they were comfortably positioned next to his, and then I bent down and kissed him lightly on the lips.

"Now you may change my bandage," I said in a husky voice.

I took his hands in mine and guided them up the sides of my bare ribs, and then I picked up his hands and moved them up toward my shoulder. His breathing was ragged, hard, but he said nothing as he undid the medical tape he had so diligently put on me yesterday morning. I slid up and down his cock as he did this, slowly, sinuously, making him feel every inch of my pussy, and oh, I could certainly feel every inch of him at the same time.

He pulled off my bandage, and a rough breath of surprise escaped his lips.

"Your stitches came out..." he breathed.

I looked over at the wound on my shoulder, but the bite mark was pink with new scarring as if I'd been bitten a month or more ago. The discarded bandages were stained yellow and brown, the black stitching stuck to that nasty coating.

"Whoa," I said as I continued to slowly fuck him. "What the...? Is that normal?"

I moved up and down his thick dong as he stared me right in the eyes, a look of strange shock on his handsome face.

Nothing about this is normal," he said, and he sounded weirded out.

"Oh," I breathed.

I shut him up by taking his head in my hands and kissing deeply into his mouth, sliding my tongue over his. He tasted like eggs and sausage and orange juice, but I didn't care. I open-mouthed him as I slithered up and down his cock in animal passion, feeling him inside me, that bulbous head up near my cervix, feeling my soft wet muscles gripping it, massaging it.

I rubbed my clit and hood on his jeans as my own juices flowed down the shaft of his penis, and I reveled in that wet sensation.

"Mmm...mmm..." I moaned as I sucked lightly on his tongue.

He dropped the bandages to the floor and gripped me around my waist, running his hands up along the smooth skin of my back.

Yes...Now he was into it.

I pulled away from his mouth and hugged him tightly, my arms pushing back around his shirt to trap them between his back and the comfy chair. I nuzzled my left ear into his left ear, and then I pushed aside his shirt to lick into the bare skin of his left shoulder. I nipped lightly into his skin and held my teeth there for a moment, licking a bit into what little flesh I had pulled up.

"Oh...Oh..." breathed Daniel.

I let go of his skin and then sat erect, my back straight, and moved his head down toward my left nipple, urging him to gently suck on it. He suckled it with the finesse I was hoping for, and I moaned in response to that, a loud moan that surprised even me. I pushed my hips into him while angling my back, pushed out, then in, then out, then in, enjoying the sheer pleasure of his thick dong inside my happy wet tunnel.

"Oh, you'll stay, yes," I breathed out. "Yes, you will. You'll stay here and protect me...Protect me from any monsters..."

I moved his head over to my right breast and felt his lips across my right nipple, his tongue curling around it to stroke it in a gentle caress. I moved my butt from side to side, feeling my clit move back and forth across the cloth of his boxer briefs.

I wasn't thinking about talking dirty. I wasn't thinking about saying titties or cunt or anything like that. All I did was concentrate on the fullness of his cock inside me, that round head up near my cervix, my small pink clit moving across his underwear.

"Don't go," I whispered as I closed my eyes. "Stay with me. Tell me you'll stay with me."

I didn't give him a chance to answer. I gripped the sides of the comfy chair and pulled up, slid off of him to stand, slowly, carefully. I balanced on the chair to keep it from falling over as I moved my throbbing wet pussy toward his lips. I wanted him to taste me, taste all of me so that he wouldn't leave.

He may have acted like a schoolboy, but he was no virgin. His tongue slid up into the folds of my wet snatch, licking up my juices and slithering into my open hole. I brought my left foot up to stand it on the right arm of the chair, my left knee right beside his head, reached down, and gripped the back of his head as I pushed his face in a little more. I wanted to smear my cream all over him, let him smell me, smell my wild scent, even when he was out of my reach.

His tongue licked over my large pee hole and then up, up onto my clit. I shivered in excitement, my butt jiggling a little as I bit my lower lip.

"Mmmm...fuck..." I breathed out. "Oooh...Oohh fuck...Mmm...Keep doing that...Mmm...Suck it a little...Mmm...Yes...Mmm...Yes..."

I pushed in a little more, felt the breath from his nostrils stand my pubes on end, and I shook as I felt an orgasm building in my lower belly, spreading out from my clit to enter me, spreading out and up like a burning liquid flame of desire and want.

"Mmm, yes...Mmm, yes..." I moaned. "Mmm...Right there...Mmmn...nng...Oh...Oh fuck...Oh, fucking God...Mmm...Mmmnn...Nnng...Unnng...Oh...Oh...Don't stop!...Nnng...Oh...Oh my God!...Mmmn...Nngg...NNNNGGGGG!"

I came, shivering and shaking on his face, that explosion of release inside me, cumming like a little bitch in heat, and I loved it, loved that shaking nudity and ass clenching spasm that made me grin wide and wonderful in that moment of pure sexual energy. My juices spilled out onto his face, down his chin, and his shirt, but I didn't care. I'd never had sex like this before, and I wanted more.

I didn't give him any time to think about it. I straddled him again and licked across his lips and chin, licked up my own pussy cream, and savored its strong, wild taste. My tongue was pressed wide and flat against his wet skin as I licked across it, and he shook in my arms, a helpless prey in the jaws of a fearsome predator.

I got down from his lap and onto my knees upon the wooden floor again, took his thick cock into my right hand, and studied it as I stroked it up and down, the shaft still wet from my pussy juices.

"Oh, yeah," I said softly. "Oh, that's a big piece of meat...Mmm...I like big pieces of meat...Big juicy sausages...Mmm..."

I stroked him like this as he closed his eyes and sucked in his breath, and then I took that big dick into my mouth, sucked it in as my eyes rolled up into the whites from it. The taste of his precum was much stronger now, much saltier, and I breathed through my nose as I sucked hard on his tip.

"Mmm...Mmm..." I breathed out as I slurped up and down his thick shaft.

I reached into his underwear and pulled out his balls. I popped off his cock, licked across his big balls, and then sucked both of them into my mouth. The musk from his balls flooded my mouth, and I licked up and down the sack with my tongue before releasing them and taking his dong back into my mouth.

"Oh...Mmm...So good...So fucking good..." I said as I continued to slurp him up and down.

His breathing picked up as he pushed out more and more ragged breaths. He clutched the sides of my head as I slurped faster and faster, but I couldn't control myself. There was a need inside me to unleash everything sexual about me, so I did.

"Oh...Oh...Oh...OH...OH...OH...OOOOOH GAWWWHD!" cried, Daniel.

White-hot semen squirted up into my mouth in a glorious ivory fountain of salt and lavalike heat. His whole body shook as he spurted up into the back of my throat, his hands clutching my head as if he were holding on for dear life.

I waited until every last drop of semen squirted in to my mouth before pulling off him. His cock plopped down onto his jeans as I quickly got up and straddled him again, pulling his face toward mine. I opened-mouthed into him, semen spilling from the sides of my lips as it spilled into his mouth at the same time. My tongue ran across his as semen and saliva exchanged in that impassioned kiss, and then I swallowed what I could, so that his spore was with me from now on, the taste of what was him so that I could track him wherever he went, wherever he might go.

I was not going to lose him. I wanted him, and he was mine.

My name is Saoirse Lennon. I moved out to the town of Lonesome Moon with my dad, though 'town' is a relative word. We moved out to the middle of bumfuck nowhere, out into the middle of snow and pine trees. The town is forty minutes away through rough country, and the roads out here consist of little more than backwood dirt and gravel that cuts through heavy forest. This cabin we're at is the real Lonesome Moon, 'lonesome' being the keyword, here.

I'm twenty-two, a white Irish girl with long, curly brown hair and brown eyes, and my name is Irish, pronounced 'Ser-Sha' if you didn't know. My dad moved us out here to 'start a new life' probably on account of the fact that I've been a burden to him for the last six years, seven really, ever since my mom died when I was fifteen. I think he got tired of my lifestyle, the drugs, and the booze and the boys, so now we're out here in the middle of bumfuck nowhere, probably to keep me on the straight and narrow.

He's away for a week, busy flipping a house for a couple that wants to sell it, and so I'm up to my old tricks, drinking and smoking weed. At least, I was, until...It's difficult to explain.

I was doing my thing that night after Dad left for town. I was drinking, smoking pot, playing with myself to porn...but then things got crazy...and violent. I almost died. Something attacked me outside the cabin when I went out to investigate a disturbance. It bit me in my right shoulder and threw me through the wall of our old woodshed. I was lucky, though. Whatever it was grabbed an injured buck, a big male deer, and ran off with it into the woods.

I dragged myself back inside and passed out in the living room. I was pretty fucked up in the morning when I came to, naked and bloody from the attack, and that's when Daniel showed up, Daniel Christianson. Apparently, his folks owned the property before my dad bought it, and he found me just before I passed out again.

Daniel was a hiker, and he was on his way to his family's hunting lodge when he stopped by to have my dad sign some additional stuff, but that all changed when he found me. He didn't call an ambulance or the police, because he was afraid of getting in trouble, so he cleaned me up, stitched up my wound, and bandaged it. He took care of me until I woke up the next morning, though it took some serious explaining to get me to trust him.

To make a long story short, I had my way with him. Daniel's cute, very cute, and cute boys are hard to come by out in the middle of bumfuck nowhere. Still, this isn't normal behavior for me. I've had some really weird dreams ever since I've been bitten, and I've been hungry and horny as fuck for some reason, so I jumped on him like he was a juicy piece of meat, and I had my fill of that.

Now as for me...I'm five-eight, and I weigh one-thirty-seven, nice C-cup breasts with beautiful pink nipples, great butt, at least I think so, and I'm good looking, though I have my dad's square jaw. I can get boys when I want them, but like I said, just jumping a guy is not my style. I like to get to know them a little bit before I do that.

Now Daniel...there's something about him that makes me...possessive. I want him, want him like a gambler wants a jackpot, so I can't keep my hands off him. Yeah, I fucked him this morning, and I didn't just fuck him, no. I was insane, like...like some kind of wild animal. It was weird, it was freaky, but it was also awesome.

Daniel's white, about six-foot, the average weight for a guy his height, with short black hair and blue eyes, and his cock is...whuff...six-and-a-half inches long and thick...Mmm hmm. He is yummy, and that's a fact. Still, I've never had sex like what I did to him. It never even occurred to me to have sex as I did with him.

Now we've just finished our wild little fuck, but truth be told, I was the one that fucked him, not the other way around. Now we're at that awkward stage of 'did that just happen?' So...yeah...that just happened.

I got up off of Daniel's lap, removing myself from our position on my dad's dark-brown comfy chair. I stood in front of him and stretched, arms toward the ceiling, brushing my hair back as I did, showing him everything my naked body had to offer, though he'd already seen it when he'd first patched me up yesterday morning.

"Oooohhnnn..." I moaned out as I stretched.

My shoulder was still a little stiff, but it was looking so much better than yesterday, so that was one less thing to worry over. Daniel, however...I didn't know if he was going to stay or not. I was hoping, really hoping, that he would.

I turned my back to him, put my left hand on my hip, and leaned a little to my left to cock my butt to the right, giving him a little more incentive to stay. He was supposed to be holing up in his family's hunting lodge three miles north of here, but...I wanted him to lodge with me, instead, hole up in my hole for the next three days.

"I could use a bath," I said nonchalantly. "Are you coming?"

I turned to see Daniel stuffing his thick cock back into his underwear, only to zip up his dark blue jeans a moment later. He was still wearing his light-blue long-sleeved work shirt with the white undershirt, and his jeans, of course, but I was going to get him out of those clothes, take off those tanned work boots of his, and get him naked, so I could see all of him, taste all of him.

He looked at me with a confused expression on his handsome face.

"I...Maybe...I think I should get going, Saoirse," he said uncertainly.

That was exactly what I did not want to hear. Still, I knew how to play it cool. I could get him to stay.

I put my left foot upon the dark-brown comfy chair he was sitting in so that my legs were spread and he had a full view of my pussy, but more importantly so that he could smell the heavy scent of my open wet snatch.

"What's it going to take to get you to stay?" I asked. "Do you want me to sing the 'My Pussy' song? Is that what you want? Because I'll sing the 'My Pussy' song."

I stepped back from the chair, making sure I avoided hitting the oak-tree coffee table in front of us because my dad's laptop was on that table. If I was going to shake it for him, I didn't want to damage that laptop.

I raised my right arm in the air and spun my hand in a circle as I turned around to shake my bare butt for him.

"My pussy!" I sang. "Oh! Oh! My pussy! I put it in your mouth, oh, it squirts into your mouth, it is my pussy! Oh! Oh! My pussy!"

I turned to see the wide-eyed look of slight horror on his face, and I cracked up, laughing hard as I picked up my panties to shimmy back into them.

"It's a joke, Daniel," I chuckled as I slipped my white T-shirt back on. "No girl in the history of ever has sung that song. It was made up by some dateless pervert that probably spends his time yanking off to pictures of his waifu...Don't you know what I'm talking about?"

"I...uhh...no..." he stammered in confusion.

"It was a nasty meme for a while," I smiled. "It started with that anime girl spinning in a circle, singing about her pussy?...No?...Well, you're lucky you missed it."

Oh..." breathed Daniel. "Oh...I just thought...you know...because you actually did that...

What?" I asked, and this time I was the one that was confused.

"What you did..." stumbled Daniel. "You know...When you stood on the chair..."

Ooooh. Thaaaat's what he meant.

It was my turn to go red with embarrassment.

"Oh...I guess I did..." I said sheepishly. "I normally...I don't normally do that kind of thing..."

He gave me a cute smile, obviously amused at my own cluelessness.

"That...That's okay," he said slowly. "I think, maybe, though...I should be on my way." No, no, no. I couldn't let him get away.

"Oh, please don't go," I begged. "Please? Stay with me for just one more night? We'll have fun, I swear."

"I don't know, Saoirse," he said as he took in a breath. "What if your dad comes back?" "He won't," I said with a shake of my head.

"Even so..." breathed Daniel.

Oh, God, he was one of those 'good' boys, and I forgot about that. Maybe it was my 'habits' that were turning him off.

"Is it...Is it the weed?" I asked. "I'll get rid of it. I'll get rid of the booze, too...Please? Please stay with me? Isn't it dangerous to hike out there right now, anyway? That thing might come back and catch you...It's still out there somewhere."

That was actually a viable concern. I didn't want him to leave and end up getting ripped apart by that thing that had torn into me. For some reason, I wanted him, wanted him bad, and I'd never wanted a boy like this before. It was tearing me up inside to think that he was going to leave already.

"I stuck around because you were hurt," he said, and I could tell that he was being honest.

I panicked and started asking questions, all of the questions you're not supposed to ask.

"Is it me?" I asked. "Did I come on too strong? I'll behave, I swear...I mean, I'm good-looking, right? You like my body, right?... You liked what I did to you, right? Oh...Oh, no...Are you...Are you gay? Tell me you're not gay!"

"I'm not gay, Saoirse," said Daniel, and I cringed when he said my name.

When a boy says your name like that, it means he's not interested.

"I'm sorry, but I have to go," said Daniel.

He got up to leave, and ooooh, that hurt. It hit me right in the chest. I think it hurt worse than when that thing outside bit me and threw me through a wall.

"Daniel..." I whined. "Please? Please, don't go..."

Okay, this was getting out of hand. I'm not some Goddamned eighth-grader with a crush. I needed to have some fucking dignity. I needed to get my hooks in him without sounding desperate.

I...I'll go with you," I said.

He looked upon me with supreme confusion etched across his handsome face.

"What?" he asked me in audible surprise.

"I'll go with you," I repeated.

"I can't do that," he said with a slight frown and a shake of his head.

"Then stay one more night," I begged. "Just one more...Please? I swear to you...I swear that I'll let you go tomorrow morning...Do it for me? Please? Nothing bad is going to happen...I promise. I just...I got attacked, and...I really need you here. I'm scared..."

His handsome face buckled in, twisting with some kind of internal moral dilemma, but what he said in response to my offer gave me an inner smile.

"Just one more?" he asked. "You...You promise?"

"Yes," I nodded eagerly. "Stay with me today and tonight, and I'll take care of you. You took care of me, so I'll do the same for you. Then you can go tomorrow morning."

"Oh, I don't...Fine...Okay," he breathed out, but I could tell he was conflicted.

He stared down at the wooden floor of the cabin, stared down at his tanned work boots, and frowned. He looked back up at me, stared me in the eyes, and cast forth a strange expression.

"Just don't sing that song again," he said. "That...freaked me out."

I snorted out a sharp laugh and nodded in agreement.

Deal," I said. "Come on. Let's get in the tub.

"Saoirse..." began Daniel, but I wouldn't have it.

I grabbed him by the front of his shirt and pulled him toward the bathroom. That room was north past the kitchen, down the hall past my dad's bedroom.

"Come on, come on," I grinned. "Let me clean you up first. Let's get clean."

He closed his eyes, sighed, opened his eyes, and gave in to my insistence.

"All right," he said in a tired voice.

This attitude of his bothered me. I didn't know if he was angry with me or not, but that didn't make sense, since he was the one that had walked in on me while I was naked. Of course, he may have saved my life, but that was beside the point.

"Are you angry with me?" I asked, and I mentally kicked myself for sounding so whiny and needy.

"No, it's not that," he said unhappily. "It's just...I really shouldn't be here."

"You'll be fine," I urged him. "Everything'll be fine, you'll see."

I coaxed him back to the bathroom and urged him through the door. Our bathroom was just a small white room, just a toilet, a sink, and a tub, and the tub didn't even have a shower, but I didn't care. I wanted him all alone to myself in here, and the small size of this room only enhanced the feeling of being close to him.

I closed the door behind us and started the hot water for the bath. He stood there, staring at the clear water filling the old white tub, and I studied him at that moment. He really was cute, and I couldn't wait to see him naked. I'd experienced his cock before, but that I had taken directly from his pants, so I wondered what his butt looked like. It made me foam inside thinking about grabbing that tight muscular ass, or so I imagined it to be.

"Hold still," I said.

I undid the buttons of his work shirt, and he slipped out of it to set it on top of the white wicker hamper next to the sink. His arms were corded with good muscle, natural muscle, something earned by outdoor work, not lifting weights. I had nothing against weightlifters; they were sexy in their own way, but Daniel's natural physique lit my candle, and made it flare up again without effort.

He wore a white cotton tank top under his shirt, and oooooh that made him look even more delicious. I pulled up on the hem of that undershirt and helped him take it off. His chest rippled with natural muscle, something I had suspected but had only now just confirmed.

I ran my fingers along his chest, down his six-pack abs, and around to the small of his back. I clasped my hands around him, pulled him in close, and ran my hair along his chest.

"Saoirse," he said quietly.

"You just...You just get undressed and get in," I said in an equally hushed tone. "I'll be right back. There are some bath salts in the kitchen. I'll be right back with them."

"Okay," sighed Daniel.

I left him there and closed the door behind me. I was shaking in my skin, feeling that powerful animal lust hit me from deep within. Oh my God, was he hot. He was far hotter than I'd first thought him to be.

I took off my shirt and tossed it to the hallway floor, skipped a couple of feet to pull off my panties while still walking, and hustled down toward the kitchen, completely naked once more. I felt more comfortable this way, odd as that was, to be completely nude, to be free of any restrictive clothing.

I was not thinking at all as I skipped to the front door, unlocked it, and opened it wide. The cold air hit me like a sheet of knives, but I ignored it and stared out into the white glare of the snow in the late morning sun, oblivious to the fact that I was fully nude.

I pissed into the snow right at the entrance to the doorway, a yellow stream that splattered across those packed crystals to leave the strong smell of urine in my nostrils. I shook my head out of that daze and quickly shut the door, unsure of what just happened.

"What the fuck did I do that for?" I asked myself.

Maybe the attack had fucked me up in the head, I don't know.

I locked the door and headed to the kitchen, weirded out by what just happened. What had just happened was not normal, not in the slightest, and I had done it automatically, not a thought in my brain as it had happened.

"Why did I do that?" I asked myself.

I bent down, opened the cabinet doors under the sink, and grabbed the large carton of bath salts from that small space. I turned to move around the kitchen table, saw the kitchen door, walked to it, opened it wide, and was once more hit with the chill of winter air.

I pissed a stream into the snow right at the entrance of the kitchen doorway, and that strange action, that automatic and odd behavior coupled with the strong scent of my own urine, snapped me out of yet another temporary daze.

'What the fuck!" I hissed as I shut the door.

I was weirded out now. It had happened again, and I hadn't the faintest clue why. "What is wrong with me?" I asked myself. "Why did I do that?"

I stressed over this as I made my way back to the bathroom. What I'd just done was not normal, and I'd done it without even thinking about it. People just didn't open their doors and piss on the steps. It wasn't right.

I walked into the bathroom and shut the door behind me, and one look revealed a very naked Daniel sitting in the tub, waiting for my return. I should have been excited to see him, especially naked, but I was shaken from my pissing incident, and he immediately picked up on this.

"Is something wrong?" he asked, his brows furrowed in concern.

"I...I just..." I started to say as I turned back toward the bathroom door.

Fuck it. Don't tell him. It was counterproductive to weird him out again. He was already naked and in the tub, so...fun time.

I decided to let it go. He was reluctant, anyway, and I wanted him to stay, wanted him all to myself, wanted to make sure no other bitches got ahold of him. He was mine, Goddammit! Mine!

I opened the carton of bath salts and gave a liberal sprinkling into the hot water around Daniel, that hot water still filling the tub. I set the carton down on the toilet lid, turned off the running water, and then I joined him, sitting down upon his lap, happy to feel his cock between my legs again.

I reached down, held Daniel's hands in mine, and slid them up over my wet skin to cup them under my breasts. He gently held my breasts as I held his hands, and I leaned back into his muscular chest, the left side of my head caressing his right cheek.

"Saoirse," he said softly.

"Mmmm..." I purred as I nuzzled into him.

"What do you want from me?" asked Daniel.

"I want you to stay," I said softly.

"I can't," he replied.

I reached down between my legs and tugged on his penis, massaged it, and felt it harden in the crack of my ass and between the hairy lips of my pussy. I sat up a bit while still gripping his cock, and then I sat back down, slipping his thick penis into my wet hole. He filled me once more, and I eased into a comfortable position on top of him, moving my butt a little to enjoy that living rod inside me, enjoy its warmth and power within my own living tunnel.

"You said you didn't have anyone," I breathed. "Why can't you have me?"

"I don't know you," replied Daniel. "I don't even know why I'm letting you do this to me." "Because you want me," I said. "You want me to be yours, that's why."

"I...I don't think..." began Daniel.

His hands had moved down to my waist, so I moved them back up to my breasts and had him run his fingers across my large pink nipples. I leaned back into him again and stroked his right cheek with my hair, purring away as I did.

"It's instinct," I replied. "It's natural selection. I want you. You want me. There's nothing else to it."

"There's getting to know one another," said Daniel.

"I already know you," I replied.

"You do, huh?" he asked. "What am I like, then?"

"You're a good boy," I said. "You took care of me, and now I'll take care of you. It's instinct."

"What do you know about instinct?" he asked.

"I know you're inside me," I purred. "Right where I want you."

"We don't know each other, though," he said unhappily. "There are things about me...You shouldn't...This is a mistake."

"No, it isn't," I said firmly. "Is this because of your last girlfriend? Did you have a bad breakup? Is that why you're afraid to get close to me?"

He took in a deep breath and sighed.

"I had to break it off with her," he said unhappily. "It was just too...Never mind. I couldn't be with her. Let's leave it at that."

That wasn't any kind of an answer, but that didn't matter to me. I wanted him, and he'd had a bad breakup, even if he wouldn't admit it. In order to secure him, I was going to have to convince him that I was the right one for him. I had never wanted a boy like this before, and the thought of some other bitch rubbing her pussy on him made me bristle inside, sparked fury in me that I had to push deep, deep down within myself.

"I'll change your mind," I said firmly. "I will."

I pulled off his cock and moved forward in the tub, some water splashing over the side to the black and white tiles below, but I didn't care. I positioned myself in front of the faucet and got on my knees, offering my ass and pussy to him without any embarrassment or fear of reprimand.

"You want to know me?" I asked with a smile. "Smell me."

"What?" asked Daniel in confusion.

"Smell me," I commanded. "Bend over and smell my ass and pussy."

"Saoirse," said Daniel in frustration.

I don't know why I'd told him to do that, but the thought of him doing it seriously turned me on.

"Do it," I commanded. "Just trust me. You'll like what you smell."

I turned and looked over my shoulder, waiting to see if he'd do it. The look on his face was...interesting. He didn't look disgusted, no, just surprised, and with that surprised face, he bent down and took a sniff of me, right over my big pink asshole. To his credit, he closed his eyes after that and took another whiff, breathing in deeply this time.

"Now take me," I commanded. "Take me, and this time fuck me. Fuck me hard."

He sucked in his breath, his pecs rippling in excitement. Apparently, my scent had done the trick, and he was excited, though I could tell he was fighting that feeling.

Oooh, what am I doing?" I heard him mutter under his breath.

He grabbed my bare ass and plunged his cock into my waiting pussy a second later. I cried out as the entire length of his thick dong speared me all the way up to my cervix, and my own hot white juices gelled and congealed around his throbbing cock, smearing it with that ivory love sauce, greasing it for ramming, and repeatedly.

He pounded into me, a savage burst of thrusting and splashing water, and I cried out with each spearing of that cock, enjoying every inch of my impalement.

"Oh, God, yes!" I cried out. "Oh, fuck me, Daniel! Make me your bitch!"

BAM, BAM, BAM! he rammed me, grunting and huffing as he did so, his fingers digging into the soft skin of my ass, and I loved it, every ass-shaking second of it.

"Oh, fuck, yes!" I cried. "Oh, that's what I need! Fuck me hard, Daniel! I need it! I need it!"

My pussy clenched and creamed all over his cock during this accepted violation of my privates. I was not thinking with a full deck; there was no thought in my head about pregnancy or disease or anything like that. No, Daniel's thick penis was the only thing on my mind, the only thing running through me at that moment, literally and figuratively.

I gritted my teeth as a low growl erupted from my throat. My fingers clutched the slick porcelain at the lip of the tub, and my shoulders tensed as I felt my own muscles ripple beneath my skin.

"Oh, God!" I cried out again. "Oh, yes, Daniel! Oh, make me your bitch!"

Daniel responded by hammering into me even harder than before. Water splashed all around us and out of the tub, and I was going to have to clean that up later, but that didn't matter right now. What mattered was the orgasm building inside my lower belly, that explosion waiting for a timely release.

"Pussy fuck me like the bitch I am!" I screeched. "Do it, Daniel! I need it! I need it!"

Daniel's fingers dug deeper into the skin of my ass as he groaned from the strain of fucking me so hard. I looked back over my shoulder to view him, his eyes closed, his teeth gritted as he pounded into me. That look, that look of pure sexual power, launched me over the tipping point, and my pleasure built to an explosive finale.

"Oh, oh, oh, oh, oh, oh, oh God..." I cried out.

My eyes widened as my jaw dropped from the intensity of force inside me, that thick cock hammering my cream-soaked pussy. My tongue lolled out of my mouth at first, and I licked up, and I'm sure it was just my imagination, because there's no way it could be possible that this happened, but...I felt my tongue lick up over the tip of my nose before pulling back down into my mouth. The feeling was so odd, so Goddamned weird, that I came right then, howling as I did.

"Oh, oh, oh, oh, oh!" I moaned. "Oh, oh, oh, fuck, oh, oh, oh...What the fuck?...My tongue! Oh, OH, OH, OH, OH, OOOOOWOOOOO!"

My pussy burst hot white gel all over Daniel's wet cock and balls, splattering all over his crotch, spreading over my pussy and ass as well. I was not one of those girls that squirted, but this was the second time it had happened, and both of those times had been with Daniel.

My pussy clutched Daniel's thick dong as I came, my big pink asshole winking up at him at the same time, and he grunted, groaned, and pulled out of me, his cock spraying my winking anus with his hot sperm.

He clutched my ass as both of us shivered and shook from trembling aftershocks. My pussy squirted one more time, spurting my hot white juices into the roiling bathwater beneath us. I felt the last few squirts of his burning semen on my asshole, and then he let go of me to fall back into the water into a reclined position.

I was disappointed that he had not cum inside me, but he was right…We didn't know each other well enough to risk pregnancy. Nevertheless, I reached back with my right hand and dipped my fingers into his semen, that love juice thoroughly pocketed in the folds of my big pink asshole, and I brought my fingers up to my mouth, savoring the salty taste of everything that was him.

"Mmmm…" I moaned as I sucked upon my fingers.

"You are crazy…" puffed out Daniel.

"Crazy for you…" I huffed. "You're a Goddamned beast, Daniel. I love it."

"This is crazy," said Daniel. "I shouldn't be doing this."

"But you want to," I said as I turned around to face him.

The bathwater we were in had our cum mixed into it, and I had no problem with this whatsoever. I moved my hands around in the water and grinned at him, no longer shy about what I wanted.

Daniel's face twisted into an expression of worry mixed with guilt, and this bothered me, bothered me a lot.

"I...I need to make a call..." breathed Daniel.

He got up from the tub, water splashing around him, and I reached for him, but he jumped out before I could grab him.

Don't go!" I called out.

He grabbed a white towel from the outer shower rack, wrapped it around himself, and opened the door to leave, no thought of grabbing his clothes.

"I need to make a call," he said forcefully. "I need to make one now."

I sulked in the water as he shut the door behind me. This was not turning out as I had planned.

I got out of the tub, grabbed another white towel, and dried off. I was chilly from getting out of the hot water, but I didn't want to put my clothes back on, not just yet. My shirt and panties were out in the hallway where I'd left them, anyway.

I took a look in the mirror and inspected my own nudity. I really was good-looking, but there was something about me that made me even more attractive now, and I could not put my finger on it. It was an aura of natural beauty, wild and electric energy I was giving off, but I liked it. I was finally coming into my own.

I raised my arms to run my hands through my hair, and I noticed the thick line of hair growing within my pits. I'd shaved them not three days ago, so this was an unwelcome surprise for me.

"What the fuck?" I asked myself. "Fuck...I hate shaving."

Oh, well. I'd do it later.

I looked down and raised my right leg to see the hair growing back there as well. I grunted in unhappiness at this, because shaving was a pet peeve of mine, but I definitely looked better shaved than hairy, so...whatever. I'd get to it eventually, definitely before I started looking like a Sasquatch.

I quietly opened the door and walked out into the hallway, but my sensitive ears could hear Daniel talking in the kitchen. I peered around the corner to spy on him, but his back was turned to me, so sneaking around didn't matter that much.

He stood there, his towel wrapped around his waist, talking into a smartphone that he'd produced from somewhere, probably from the large green rucksack he had laid out upon my kitchen table. His gear didn't interest me, however. No, it was the conversation he was having that interested me, mainly because it didn't make sense.

"No, I screwed up," said Daniel.

I could dimly hear a female voice on the other end of that call, but I couldn't make out any words.

"Yes!" hissed Daniel. "She's all over me now...What do you think I mean?... She's got all of the signs...I know I should have, but you can't expect me to just...How do I know? Mom, she's marked the doorways...Yes!...No, don't tell Dad...No...What?...Why do you want me to...No! No, I don't want to do that!...No, please, don't tell Dad. There has to be another way...Well, yeah, she's pretty. Wait, why does that matter?... Oh, for fuck's sake!"

I sauntered into the kitchen and laid my hands on the muscles of Daniel's exposed shoulders, and he stiffened at my touch. He turned and eyed me with suspicion, but I just gave him a quiet smirk and took the phone from him. I ended the call and handed him back his phone.

"You can talk to Mommy later," I said as I ran my right index finger across his luscious pecs. "You have a very naked and very viable female right in front of you. You don't need anything else right now."

Daniel closed his eyes, took in a deep breath, and then gave me a stern look.

Saoirse," he said firmly. "You and I have to talk.

"I'm right here," I shrugged. "So talk."

"You..." he said hesitantly. "You may...I think we have a problem."

I could read the fear and worry on his face, and that...that worried me, too.

"What's the problem?" I asked. "Does this have to do with your parents?"

"Something like that," he grimaced. "It has more to do with my dad."

"What about your dad?" I asked.

"He..." started Daniel.

He closed his eyes, reached back, and ran his fingers through his hair, an anxious effect that I picked up on immediately. His anxiety made me anxious, and I had a bad feeling strike me, an omen of sorts.

"What is it?" I asked, and this time I really was worried.

"My dad's a hunter," frowned Daniel.

"Ooookay," I drawled out, thoroughly confused.

"He hunts...things," said Daniel.

Things?" I asked in confusion. "What do you mean 'things'?

"I mean..." said Daniel hesitantly. "Look. You know what I mean. Those tracks outside...Those aren't bear tracks."

My breath caught in my throat. He knew something, and I needed to find out what.

"What do you mean?" I asked, and my heart began to race in fear. "Do you know something, Daniel? What are you not telling me?"

"You know what I mean," he repeated. "You saw it, didn't you? You saw what attacked you, right? It wasn't a bear."

"N...no," I said in a shaky voice. "No, it wasn't."

"Well...I'm just going to say it," said Daniel. "Monsters are real, and you got attacked by one."

I knew it. I fucking knew it. I knew that wasn't a bear.

"Okay," I said nervously. "So your dad hunts these things. What does that have to do with me?"

Daniel took in a deep breath, released it, and gripped my arms so that I couldn't move. "What are you doing?" I asked fearfully.

"I'm just holding you, so that you don't freak out," he said.

"I'm already freaking out," I blurted. "You're scaring me."

"I'm not trying to scare you," said Daniel. "I'm just...I'm trying to help you. Just listen."

Okay..." I said nervously.

If my dad finds out you've been bitten," said Daniel slowly, "he's going to...to kill you.

"What!" I spat in disbelief. "What the fuck for! What did I do!"

"That creature that bit you..." explained Daniel. "That creature was a werewolf. What happens when a werewolf bites someone and that person lives? What do you think happens?"

Ooooooh. I'm an idiot. Now everything made sense. I should have put that together on my own. What a fucking retard.

"So thaaaaat's what's been happening," I said, more to myself than to him.

"Uh, yeah," grimaced Daniel. "You have a serious problem now."

"No shit," I said, but I was in shock over this news.

I looked back toward the living room, looked back at Daniel, and nodded toward the direction of the living room.

"I...I'm going to go sit down and smoke some pot," I said without thinking. "I...I think I need to smoke some pot right now."

"Okay," breathed Daniel. "You just...You go ahead and relax. I'll get dressed, and...we'll have a discussion about this."

"Yeah," I said, but I wasn't really listening. "Yeah, we'll...we'll uhhh...we'll do that."

He left me to go back to the bathroom and fetch his clothes.

I wandered into the living room, sat down in my dad's comfy chair, pulled open the small stand's drawer next to the chair, and took out my plastic baggie of joints. I took one out, put the baggie away, lit my joint with a lighter, and inhaled. I sat there and puffed away on that joint, trying desperately not to freak out. I knew with one billion percent certainty that what Daniel had said was true, so that meant...Oooooh. I was pretty sure lycanthropy was going to screw with my life choices.

I sat fully nude on that comfy chair and smoked my joint. Terrible thoughts came to me as I tried to relax, but my anxiety overrode the pleasant mellowness of my weed. Was it going to hurt when I changed? Was I going to kill anyone? Would I go after my dad? What was I going to do now?

"Fuck...Fuck, fuck, fuck," I muttered to myself. "What am I going to do now? This can't be good for a resume...Sure, Miss Lennon, we'd hire you, but I'm afraid your condition isn't suitable for waitressing. The last werewolf we hired ate our lead cook."

My own humor did nothing for me, and I held my face in my left hand as I started to cry.

"This can't be real," I whined. "It can't be..."

I didn't get a chance to wallow in my pity. I felt a sharp prick in the side of my neck, and the injection that entered my bloodstream went straight to my brain, slowing down time in my vision. I looked up to see Daniel, fully dressed in his clothes again, the syringe in his right hand, an apologetic look on his face.

"Daniel...?" I asked.

"I'm sorry," he said in a sad voice. "I have to leave. I need time to think this out."

The joint in my right hand fell to the wooden floor beneath us as my vision faded into a blurry mess, and then darkness took me again, but this time from drugs, and not the good kind.

*****

CHAPTER 2

I awoke to the light of the full moon, and the first thing I noticed was that I was in my bed again. I had not dreamed this time, probably because I had been put into a drug-induced coma, but that was not what bothered me. What bothered me was the fact that it was night, and Daniel was gone.

"What the fuck?" I said, and my voice was garbled, my tongue thick like it was swollen.

I pulled off my brown quilted cover, but it was difficult because my muscles were slow and lethargic. I groaned and then blinked to get the crust out of my eyes, and even though it was dark, I could still see somewhat due to the light of the full moon.

I sat up and immediately wished I hadn't. I had the worst hangover/headache, and I felt like throwing up.

A quick inspection revealed an envelope on my pillow right next to where I'd rested my head, and picking it up revealed my name across it, it is lightweight slightly heavier due to the waiting letter inside.

"That son of a bitch!" I said in a shaky voice.

So that was his game, was it? Just run when the going gets tough, huh?... Motherfucker. Motherfucker!

My tears came to my brown eyes as I futilely tried to wipe them away.

"You were supposed to help me, Daniel..." I bawled into my right hand.

I didn't get the chance to cry for very long. I felt a presence nearby, and the hairs on the back of my neck stood up. A long and low growl rumbled from beyond my open bedroom doorway, and I froze, too frightened to move.

A shadow arose from out of the darkness, the shadow of the beast, and my breath caught in my throat. I looked down at myself and realized that I was still naked...Daniel had not bothered to dress me in anything this time. That would make me extremely easy to eat, and not in a good way. I was unwrapped for easy snacking.

"Oh my God..." I choked out.

The creature walked forward on two large, muscular, angled legs, and as it moved into the silver cast of moonlight streaming through my window, I could see its great head in clear detail. It was indeed the head of a great black wolf, the head of a great black wolf atop a man's body, the head of a great black wolf with beaming golden eyes, and I froze in that stare, too terrified to even piss myself.

Instinct struck me, and I laid back down out of reflex, and this saved my life, though I wouldn't realize that until later. I moved my head up and to the side, resting my right cheek upon my pillow, baring my throat for it. I had no idea why I was doing this; the urge to do it just overwhelmed me at that moment, so I offered it my bare throat, and I was sure it was just going to crunch those huge jaws down into it, and that would be the end of me.

The creature bent over me, and my life flashed before me. It was an old cliche, but it happened, and it was a bitter disappointment to me that I hadn't done much that was worthwhile during the time that I'd been alive in this world. That stabbed into me worse than the realization that I was about to be brutally ripped apart.

The great beast bent down and took in a deep breath of my bare crotch. It sniffed once, then twice, breathing in deeply, and then its long and sinuous tongue licked into my exposed vulva, licking across my clit to give me a brief jolt of strange sexual excitement before its tongue ran up the sweaty skin of my belly and chest.

I whined in terror as that long tongue made its way up to my offered throat, and then it opened its jaws, only to close them lightly down upon my neck. I closed my eyes, fully expecting my head to pop off my neck, but that clamping of deadly fangs did not occur.

The bed creaked as the full weight of the creature bore down upon it, straddling my naked body, for what reason, I hadn't fathomed yet, but that purpose was revealed to me a moment later when the stiff head of its monstrous cock touched my exposed pussy.

I raised my legs out of instinct and held them up as if I were riding a horse. I choked out a gasp as my hole spread wider around than a golf ball for the glans of its circumcised penis, and ten inches of long, ebon-skinned cock entered me. The creature rode into me, spreading my pussy wide and bulging my belly with each thrust, and I lay there helpless in the grasp of its fangs, wondering if it would clamp down and end me at any moment.

My pussy creamed all over the beast's thick dong, and I moaned out of unwanted pleasure, breathing in the rich scent of its wild musk as it violated me. It pumped into me slowly, enjoying my forbidden torment, enjoying doing this to me in my bed.

I did not know what to do, so I did nothing at first. The creature's cock was so large that it was indescribable; I had never had anything that big inside me before. It thrust in over and over again, and I felt incredible pleasure, even though I didn't want to.

My breathing quickened as my body began to enjoy the unholy violation happening to me. I couldn't help myself, so I slowly reached up with both hands and ran my fingers through the black fur of its massive arms. It let forth a long and low growl at this intrusion, but I stroked it slowly, softly, petting it with great care.

I wrapped my legs around its back as its growl died down, as it had figured out that I had submitted to it. My throat was still locked in its jaws, but I had given in, and it knew this, so it continued to fuck me without further threat.

I dared not make a sound as it fucked me, and I decided to enjoy the violation instead, because this monster had decided not to eat me, at least for the moment, and that was a positive outcome in my book.

I pet the ebon fur upon its arms as it plunged deep inside me, and its cock could not fit all the way in, so my cervix was pummeled over and over again as it pumped into me.

"Oh...Oh..." I moaned quietly.

I was afraid to make any noise, but I couldn't help it. This thing was all power and muscle, and the scent of it drove me wild. My pussy creamed all over its long, thick cock, and its scent plus mine flooded the room in a heat of wild, unnatural passion.

"Oh, oh, oh, oh, oh..." I huffed out.

My sounds of pleasure caused the beast to pick up in its own heat, and it thrust into me harder and faster, pounding into my cervix, causing me to moan even louder in both ecstasy and slight pain.

Its cock was so large that I felt an odd, light pain in my bladder, and I peed without wanting to, but that release felt incredible, increasing my pleasure just by that primal sensation alone.

"Oh, oh, oh, oh, oh fuck..." I moaned. "Oh fuck, oh fuck, oh, oh, oh, oh, OH, OH, OH....!"

I was crying out now, but I couldn't help it. I was fully expecting the creature to clamp down and behead me, but it only thrust harder and faster upon receiving my loud cries of building pleasure. The explosion building inside my lower belly was more powerful than anything I had ever experienced before, and it was coming, and quickly.

"OH, OH, OH, OH MY GOD...!" I cried out. "OH, OH, OH, OH MY GOD...OH...OH...OH, OH, OH, OH, OOOOOOOWOOOOOOOO!"

I howled without wanting to as the whole lower half of my body volcano in an eruption of white-hot juices and body trembling, butt shaking orgasm. My pussy clutched the beast's cock over and over again as all of my muscles spasmed at once, and my own juices spurted and creamed and sluiced over the monster's giant penis.

The great beast released my throat, raised its great blackhead, and howled as it came, a sound so deafening in that small room that it hurt my ears. Lava-hot semen filled my long wet tunnel, spurting all over my cervix, coating my inner orifice with that primal seed.

The great beast stared down at me as I stared back at it. I felt lost in those golden eyes, but this did not last. It opened its maw to lick out its long tongue, and I received that tongue in my mouth, tasting this creature's raw essence, and it sank deep into my soul.

It pulled out of me after that, its penis coming out with a loud POP! Hot juices gushed from me onto my bed, and then the creature was gone, padding out of my room to find other game to hunt.

I laid there without moving for some time, wondering what it was I had become. I had enjoyed that violation, enjoyed it to the point where I wanted more, and I was hoping that the creature would return to ravish me yet again.

There were two more nights left of the full moon, and...I couldn't wait for that silver glow to rise once more.

My name is Saoirse Lennon. Saoirse is an Irish name, which is why it's pronounced 'Ser- Sha', and I'm of Irish descent. I'm a twenty-two-year-old white girl, five-eight, one hundred thirty-seven pounds, with long, curly brown hair that falls to my shoulders, and I have brown eyes, though I suspect those eyes will change to a golden color soon.

Let me explain. Me and my dad moved out to Lonesome Moon two months ago. Lonesome Moon is the nearby town's name, but the cabin I'm currently in is out in the middle of bumfuck nowhere, smack in the middle of a snow-covered, coniferous forest. There is nothing out here but snow and pine trees...oh, and the occasional werewolf.

My dad moved us out to this snow-covered shithole to keep an eye on me, and let me tell you, he's done a bang-up job with that. He went into town for a week for a house flipping project, and when the cat's away, all hell will break loose. I got bitten by a werewolf on my first night alone here, the cute boy I had wild, wild sex with has a dad that wants to kill me, and...oh, yeah...I just got fucked by the same werewolf that bit me two nights ago.

Yep. I just got pounded back to the Stone Age by the creature that bit me, and it did it to me in my own bed. Not that I'm complaining, mind you. It didn't eat me, so that's always a plus, and the sex was...holy shit...like nothing I've ever experienced before. I'm still reeling from it.

On my first night alone at the cabin, I went out to investigate the sound of an animal being murdered, and that's when I got bitten and thrown through the wall of my dad's woodshed. The creature ran off with a large buck, a male deer, so I got spared a gruesome death. What I didn't get spared was lycanthropy, because according to Daniel, I'm 'showing all of the signs'. Jesus, you fuck a boy like a wild animal, and suddenly he thinks you're going to sprout fur and pop claws...which is probably what's going to happen to me, but that's beside the point.

Daniel. Daniel Christianson. He stopped by on the second morning and hiked here on his way to his parent's hunting lodge, that lodge located three miles north of my cabin. His parents owned this cabin before we did, so he was going to have my dad sign something my dad forgot to sign, but...he found me, naked, bloody, and fucked up from that initial werewolf attack.

Daniel's one of those 'good' boys, or so I thought. He cleaned me up, stitched up my bitten shoulder, and bandaged me, but he didn't call an ambulance or the police, and now I know why. His dad's a veterinarian, but his dad is also a 'hunter', one of those people you hear about in B-horror flicks, the people that hunt monsters. If his dad finds out that

I've been bitten...he'll kill me...At least, that's what Daniel told me.

Daniel's a hottie. A grade A, luscious pecs, ass-to-die-for hottie. That's one of the reasons I jumped him as I did. The other reason I fucked the bejeezus out of him is because of my growing 'problem'. I've been bitten by a werewolf, so I've become a horny bitch all of the sudden, and I mean 'bitch' in the literal sense.

But he betrayed me. After he told me what the score was, that I was becoming a werewolf, Daniel stuck me with a needle and injected something into me that made me pass out. When I came to, it was night, and he was already gone. That's when the werewolf struck again, only this time...this time it didn't bite me. Oh, no. It did something else, something I'd prefer it to do again if it shows up here tomorrow night.

I lay in my bed in the light of the full moon and stared up at the wooden sloped roof that was my ceiling. I was fully nude, stretched out, my legs spread, my open and fucked pussy hole still leaking a mix of my cum and werewolf semen. I reached down and touched the wet curls of my pubic hair, brought my fingers to my lips, and sucked on them.

The taste of the creature's semen overwhelmed me and gave me a rush to my brain as flashes of images struck me. My eyes fluttered into the whites as I experienced a series of ancient scenes in my head, one of the soldiers in banded mail sacrificing a young woman, a virgin, sacrificing her by tying her naked in the cold to a stone mound, and above that mound was a great stone statue of a mother wolf nursing two male human babes.

This poor young woman suffered tremendously in the cold, but she did not die. No, the soldiers walked away to let her freeze to death, to let the wolves have her tender flesh, but that's not what happened. No, the full moon arose after the soldiers abandoned her on that stone altar, the moon's light washing over her like a silver waterfall. The great stone statue bled from its lupine mouth into hers under the light of the full moon, and then she burst from her bondage, all fur and fangs, and fury, and the new she-beast tore through the soldiers' camp, leaving some alive and slaughtering the rest.

This new pack, these ferocious hybrids of wolf and man, spread across the globe, spreading their curse and their gift wherever their roaming took them.

I shook in my bed over this, my muscles spasming without my control. It did not last long, however, because that violent shaking stopped once the images faded from my mind's eye.

"What the fuck?" I breathed.

I was really shaken this time. This was some supernatural shit going on, and I didn't know what to make of it. I didn't even know any of this shit was real until two days ago.

"I am so fucked," I whispered to myself. "Ooooooh, yeah. Dad is not going to like this...Hey, Dad...uhh... a funny thing happened while you were out. Umm...I'm, like, a werewolf now, so...you'll have to lock me up every full moon, or I'll rip your fucking face off. Just warning you now...oh...and we're out of milk."

I smiled at my stupidity. It didn't lessen the gravity of the situation I was in, but it certainly helped.

First things first, though. I needed to talk with Daniel. He had some explaining to do. Which reminds me...

I groaned as I rolled off my bed and stood on two wobbly legs, but I immediately regretted that action.

Oh, shit..." I said quietly. "Mother...fucker...

Oh, yeah. I was feeling it in my nethers now. That beast had done a number on me.

I grimaced as I hobbled over to the wall switch and flipped on the light. The light of the overhead lamp glared down at me, and I had to cover my eyes for a moment. It was a hassle to get up and do this, but...I needed to read Daniel's letter. He'd left it next to my head on my pillow.

I hobbled back over to my bed, that bed now a terrible, cum-stained mess from the freaky lycanthropic sex I'd just had on it, and I snatched up Daniel's letter. I opened the envelope, took out the single page of notebook paper with his penned handwriting on it, and diligently studied its contents.

"Dear Saoirse," it read. "I just wanted you to know that I like you, and I like you a lot. I know you may be angry and confused because I left you for now, but I have my reasons. I have to break the news of your existence to my father, and then I have to convince him not to harm you. If you want to continue seeing me, then you'll have to play by my rules. It's for your own safety. Right now, things are complicated, but I'll get back to you in the morning. I have something I have to do first...Daniel."

"Oh, you'd better explain this one, bucko," I grimaced. "I got hammer-timed tonight because you weren't here. Of course, if you had been here, you'd have probably been eaten, but...that's not the point. Drug me and leave me as wolf-bait, will you..."

Still, this was good news. Daniel would be back in the morning. Of course, I needed to tell him about...well...maybe not. I don't know. I don't know what I want to do with that. Part of me wants to...oof...run my hands all over Daniel again, but another part of me...the wilder, untamed part of me...wants to let that beast come again tomorrow night.

I wasn't sure what I was going to do.

I'll just wait till he gets back," I told myself. "See how it goes.

That was the best I could hope for right now.

I had a sudden urge strike me, a need to do something weird, even for me. I bent over the wet spot on my bed and sniffed all over it, breathing in the wild musk of the creature that had violated me, taking in my strong and wild aroma as well. Doing this caused my breathing to quicken and my heart to race.

"What the fuck am I doing?" I panted.

I was hot, super hot, like burning up inside with desire. I really wanted that thing to come back, and I knew this was a bad idea because there was no guarantee that it wouldn't rip me to shreds. Still, as sore as I was down below, I wanted that huge dick back inside me, because a deep and primal part of me knew that's where that monstrous penis belonged.

I was stroking myself without even realizing it. I felt my nipples harden, and I knew that biological reaction was not from any cold temperature, but from desire, unchained, unfettered desire.

"Ooooh..." I moaned out of frustration.

I laid back down in order to masturbate. I masturbated regularly, but this was different. This was a need to satisfy this sexual hunger inside me, so I was going to do that before going back to sleep.

I stroked myself with my right-hand fingers, my index and middle fingers, plunged those two fingers into my cum-soaked hole, reached up, and plunged them into my mouth to savor that incredible, supernatural taste.

Mmm...mmm..." I moaned.

I reached down and rubbed my whole pussy, spreading wet cum all over my fingers. I rubbed hard and fast, wanting to curb this insane desire, but also enjoying the pleasure inherent within it.

"Ooooh, fuck..." I moaned.

I so wanted to suck my own clit. I was not limber enough to do that, and believe me, I had tried in the past, but now...

I groaned as I pulled my butt up toward my face and locked my legs against the wall behind my bed, right beneath my moonlit window. I pushed down on my butt cheeks to lower my cum-soaked pussy toward my lips, hoping, just hoping for once...

I felt my spine adjust as I moved my wet snatch closer and closer to my lips. My stomach compressed as I strained my neck, and I felt pain in my lower back, but Goddammit, I wanted my clit in my mouth, so I pushed myself harder than I'd ever pushed before.

My pulse quickened as my extended tongue licked into the folds of my hood and over my clit. I'd never gotten this close before, and holy shit, it felt good.

"Nnnnngg..." I moaned out in both pleasure and pain.

I could taste the creature's semen spilling over my clit and hood and into my mouth. That taste, that wild and unnatural flavor, made me shake uncontrollably in excitement. My fingers dug into the soft skin of my ass as I pushed even harder, and my small, pink clit was suddenly in my mouth.

My eyes rolled up into the whites as I sucked hard on my own little magic button. My legs shook uncontrollably as I sucked it like it was a tiny little dick, and oooooh...I couldn't begin to describe the absolute light show going on between my legs.

"Mmm...nnngg...mmm...nnngg..." I moaned as that pleasure built and built.

I slurped out my tongue and felt it extend, felt it lengthen and slither across my open wet pussy hole.

I had thought I'd imagined my tongue licking my own nose when I had been fucking Daniel in the bathtub, but I was wrong, because I could clearly feel its extension now, and it had to be at least six inches long out of my mouth. No, it was definitely not my imagination this time.

I slurped into the wet and cum-filled folds of my lower lips, ran my tongue across the wet curls of my dark-brown pubes, and lapped up those juices, my juices, my own pussy cream mixed with the leftover semen of the beast.

"Nnnng...mmm...nnnngg...mmmm..." I moaned.

I knew that dogs could lick themselves to get clean, and wolves were the ancestors of dogs, but it had never occurred to me to try licking myself now that I was a werewolf. I pushed my tongue out even farther on a whim, and the strong and pungent taste of my own big pink asshole flooded my mouth, but this only heightened my excitement, turned that dial up to eleven and snapped it off.

Hrmm. There were some definite benefits to lycanthropy.

I licked down across my whole pussy as my tongue slithered back into my mouth, and that long and sinuous organ slid across my large pee hole, feeling the slight bulge of that little hole as my tongue made its way down and over my clit and hood. Feeling and tasting all of my lower parts, all of them, turned me on so much that I was shaking on the inside as well as the out.

"Nnnng...mmmnnng...nnngg...!" I cried out.

I went back to sucking my clit, taking light strokes across it with my tongue as I did. My fingers dug even deeper into the soft skin of my ass, and the pain in my lower back, my neck, and my compressed belly did not bother me at all as a powerful orgasm built up inside, a drumbeat of slow progression to a magical, orchestral ending.

"Mmm...nnngg...MMMM...NNNNGG...!" I moaned into my own pussy.

My clit felt like it was pulsing with electricity. I could feel that pleasure sink in, ride down into me and up, or down was the case, toward my bladder, and I felt my pussy start to spasm, that long wet tunnel convulsing to a climax.

"MMMM...NNNGGG...MMMM...NNNGGG..." I moaned in a muffled suckling of my little bead. "MMMM...MMMM...NNNGGG...NNNNNNGGGGG HHHGG!"

I came, and I came hard, a body rocking orgasm that caused me to straighten my legs, lock them at the knees, and have them tremble without control. My toes pushed into the wood of my wall, and my butt shook without any volition on my part. My pussy contracted over and over again, and hot white cum, that hot delicious gel, squirted up and out of me in a line to splatter all over my face and into my long, curly brown hair.

I was rocked, once, twice, and then a third time by the powerful explosion in my nethers, my pussy squirting onto my face and hair with each incredible squeeze of orgasmic force from between my legs.

I popped off my clit and slammed my legs back down onto the bed, the whole bed rocking from that impact, my spine expanding all at once, my belly released from its cramped position. My neck hurt and was stiff, and my back felt like I'd just pulled out my spine and whipped it around a couple of times for good measure, but the calm and relief that waterfalled over me made all of my muscles melt together, had me feeling like jelly as I sighed out in intense relief.

I had my own cum all over my face and in my hair, on my pillow, on my bedsheets, but I didn't care. I closed my eyes and smiled, because whatever was happening to me...it was fucking awesome. Maybe being a werewolf wasn't so bad after all.

I drifted away into sleep after that, drifted away while still soaked from my own juices, breathing in that wild and heady scent with each pull of air through my sensitive nostrils.

*****

I dreamed of the forest again. I was in the thick of it now, in the heart of it, and the great brown she-wolf that had led me in waited for me in the center of a clearing, a large grove of dark and standing pine trees, their strong aroma wafting all around me in a stiff winter breeze.

I could see in the casting of the silver light of the full moon, and the great brown she-wolf waited before a huge stone statue of a mother wolf suckling two male human babes. I had seen this statue before, lived it in my semen-tasted vision, but I was not scared, no. I was curious, because I wanted to know, needed to know, what this wolf desired of me.

I walked forward toward the brown she-wolf, and she padded towards me, and as she did, she stood upon two legs, and then she was human, a female just like me, naked just like me, nude under the moonlight just like me.

I looked at her face, studied it past the frigid, crystalizing breath she exhaled, and it was like looking into a mirror. She was me, and I was her, only her eyes were golden, not brown like mine.

She stepped forward and embraced me, and I embraced her in return, and then we kissed, I kissing my own doppelganger without so much as a hint of hesitation, our sharp and erect pink nipples rubbing against each other's skin, our tongues gliding over one another.

She tasted of wild passion, of unspoken and arcane secrets, of pure animal magnetism and lust and desire, everything that my hedonistic side screamed at me to reach out and grasp and pull in close to my heart.

*****

I awoke due to the freezing temperature in my room...only I wasn't in my room. One look around me showed dark pine trees and crisp, packed snow beneath my bare feet. It was still night, and the light of the full moon still shone down from above, but I could sense that morning was coming soon, though how I knew this, I could not fathom.

I was still fully nude, my hairless human body shivering in the frosted air, and in my mouth was a large hare, the blood of it still running down my chin and dripping into the white crystal powder all around me.

I dropped the hare into the snow, the gamey taste of its blood and flesh still assaulting my sensibilities as I tried not to freak out.

"Wha...What the..." I choked out in a panic. "What? Where...Where am I?"

Okay, this was getting out of hand. This whole lycanthropy thing was definitely getting out of hand. It's one thing to be hungry and horny, but it's entirely another to wake up naked and afraid, outside, in the freezing cold, with a dead hare in your mouth. What the fuck?

I stood up and clutched myself, wrapping my arms around my chest as the absolute freezing chill of the outside sunk into me.

"What th...th...the fuck?" I stammered as my teeth chattered.

The dawn light crept over the trees as I looked around in wild-eyed confusion and swiftly growing fear. I had no idea where I was. There were pine trees all around, chilling, numbing snow underneath my bare feet, and that was it. I had no idea which direction to go in order to get back to the safety and warmth of the cabin before I froze to death.

"Uhn...uhn...uhn..." I whined.

I chose a direction and started moving. The sun was coming up behind me, so that meant I was facing west, but I had no idea whether or not I should go north, south, east, or continue west, so I just started walking north. If I was north of the cabin, then I might eventually run into Daniel's hunting lodge, and if I was south of the cabin, then I would see it sooner or later.

I took one step after the next upon packed snow, frozen grass, and bits of twigs and this and that. Walking on bare feet in this was murder, but I did it, though I was truly scared, because the odds were pretty good that I was going to freeze to death before I made it anywhere.

My large pink nipples were steel fucking points in the cold. I could have opened a can with them like this, and they hurt, so I just covered my breasts with my arms and kept moving north, keeping an eye on the rising sun.

"Oh...ho...ho...ho...my God...!" I chattered as I kept walking forward.

The sun lit up the area I was in, but I was slowing down, feeling really tired and sleepy, and I had not traveled very far through the spread of pine trees around me. My fingers and toes were starting to hurt, a throbbing, burning sensation I could not ignore. I was no doctor, but I knew hypothermia was setting in, and I'd be a frozen little popsicle soon. No more Saoirse.

"P...Please...Somebody...help!" I called out. "S...Somebody HELP ME!"

I stumbled as my bare foot caught on frozen brush. I fell to my hands and knees, and that hurt, but what hurt worse was the absolute chill numbing me right down to my bones.

Oh...Oh G...God..." I chattered.

I raised my head and sniffed as a familiar scent picked up on the stiff and murderous breeze blowing around me. I took in a deep pull of frozen air through my nostrils, and I smelled sweat and musk, a strong scent of masculinity that I was most definitely familiar with, that scent belonging to...

"D...Daniel!" I cried out. "DANIEL, HELP!"

He appeared off to my left, out of the western line of trees. He was still his cute and unbearably hot self, six foot, white with short black hair, blue eyes, all natural muscle under those winter clothes. He was wearing his tan winter coat and dark blue jeans with his tanned hide-leather gloves on his hands, and on his feet were his tan outdoor work boots, those boots crunching through the snow as he approached me. He carried his dark green rucksack upon his back, and he had a hunting rifle slung by a strap over his right shoulder.

"D...Daniel!" I called out.

"Saoirse?" asked Daniel in surprise.

He ran to me as I picked myself up from off the ground. I stumbled into his arms, and he held me there as our breath crystallized and mixed together in a little cloud of shared steam.

"What are you doing out here?" he asked. "I was just at the cabin, and you weren't there..." "N...N...No sh...shit," I chattered.

"You're going to freeze to death out here like this," he said in open concern. "You can't walk around outside naked! Are you crazy?...Come on, let's get you back to the cabin."

It...wasn't...b...by...ch...choice," I replied.

Daniel pulled me into a tight embrace, and he led me west, one painful footstep after the next until we reached the line of trees where he had originally appeared. I could see the old woodshed ahead, and the cabin beyond that.

I was not that far from home, but if I'd continued north...I didn't want to think about it.

It was murder making it that short distance to the cabin, but Daniel got me there, back to the kitchen door, which was typically unlocked, and still unlocked now.

I stumbled into the warmth of the kitchen with him, but that sudden change in temperature made me feel like passing out.

"Come on," urged Daniel. "We need to gradually warm you up. Your lips are blue." "Y...yeah..." I replied. "All...f...f...four of them."

"Let's get you into the living room," instructed Daniel. "It's warmest in there. It's a good thing your dad replaced that old furnace we had when you moved in. This new one is a lot better at circulating heat throughout the house."

"Wh...Whatever..." I chattered. "J...Just g...give me...s...some heat."

He led me into the living room, still holding me tightly in his warm embrace. He helped me lay down on my dad's dark-brown comfy chair, and then he took off his rucksack, set it down, unslung his rifle, and set it down so that the barrel did not point toward us.

"What were you thinking?" he asked as he unzipped his coat and pulled it off. "If I hadn't found you..." "I woke up out th...there..." I said unhappily. "I w...woke up outside in the snow."

"You've got blood all over your lips and chin," said Daniel. "Did you hurt yourself?"

"No," I said with a quick shake of my head. "I w...woke up with a dead hare in my mouth."

Daniel sat down on the floor and pulled off his boots, pulled off his thick white winter socks, stood, and then unbuttoned his light-blue work shirt, slipping out of it to throw it down upon his rucksack. He undressed until he was completely nude, pulling off his white tank top and his dark blue jeans to finally slip out of his checkered-red boxer-briefs.

I stared at his thick hanging cock and the patch of black pubes above that magnificent organ. Woof, woof. If I wasn't so cold...

"Your condition is getting worse," he said matter-of-factly. "Faster than I expected...I...I think...I think you'll change soon."

He slid in next to me until he was underneath me, and he held me tightly, his naked body a nice little radiator to help thaw me out.

"I figured that out, Daniel," I frowned. "Trust me. That was a no brainer."

"Well, let's warm you up first," he said quietly. "Just so you know, I trekked back home yesterday so that I could do a little research."

"Fucker," I said unhappily. "You drugged me and left me here."

I stared up into his handsome face, and he winced from what I was sure was guilt.

"I was just trying to help you," he grimaced. "I went through my dad's old books about werewolves, but...I didn't learn anything I didn't already know." "I should be mad at you..." I frowned. "I should be...but I'm not."

I rubbed my bare butt into his crotch to make sure he got my point. His thick penis rubbed against my bare butt cheeks, and he moved a little in uncomfortable recognition of my parts against his.

"Saoirse," sighed Daniel. "I really like you, but...this is moving so fast."

"So?" I asked. "So what? I like you, too. We both like each other. It's only natural that we should hook up."

"Yeah, but...I don't know if you actually like me for who I am," explained Daniel. "I don't know if you just want me because of your new...'instincts'."

"Both," I frowned. "You're a good guy, Daniel. A little stupid, in my opinion, but still good. I'm not happy about the drugging, though. Don't do that again. Because of you, I got...I...never mind."

I wasn't going to tell him about the ten inches of werewolf dick that speared me last night. It was best he didn't know.

"I'm sorry about that," he said with an unhappy frown. "I had to go, and I knew you wouldn't let me. You'd try to follow or...I don't know."

"Yeah, yeah," I replied in equal unhappiness. "Just don't let it happen again. I only have so much forgiveness in my heart."

"I know," sighed Daniel. "I know. I'll stay here for now. That's what you want, anyway."

Good," I said, and this made me happy. "You owe me, you big dummy.

I sidled off his crotch and wedged myself in between his body and the left side of the comfy chair. I reached down, grabbed his cock with my right hand, and slowly stroked it up and down.

"Ooooh..." he breathed out. "Saoirse..."

"Shut up," I said firmly. "I just froze my tits off because you weren't here to watch me. I'm having sausage for breakfast again, and you're supplying the meat."

He said nothing as I stroked him up and down until his cock was nice and thick and hard in my hand. Cold as I had just been, I knew of an activity that would put the heat right back into my naked body, and that activity had to do with the thick link of sausage between my fingers.

"It's your treat, Danny boy," I said, and my voice had turned husky, wanton. "You owe me, anyway. Pony up."

I grew wet between my legs as I straddled him. I leaned over, reached down, and pulled on the handle of the comfy chair, releasing the lock so that the back would bend down toward the floor. I pushed forward on his muscular chest until the back of the chair tipped so that he was in a reclining position.

I sat up, my knees on the outside of his legs, brushed back my long, curly brown hair, and took his cock into myself. That thick piece of meat slid up into my wet hole, filling me full of its warmth as I sat back down on him.

"I'm good-looking," I stated. "I know I am. You shouldn't have any complaints. You get my pussy whenever you want it, and you don't even have to ask, so...shut up. Just shut up and be with me. Be mine. Be my...my mate. Let me be your bitch. That's what I want. I want to be your bitch, and you'll be my cur."

Saoirse..." breathed Daniel.

I bent down to kiss him, but he pushed upon my bare chest and turned his head to the side.

"Saoirse," he said quietly. "You've still got blood all over your face."

I'd forgotten about that. I could understand why he wouldn't want to kiss me, not with hare's blood all over my lips and chin, but this angered me, anyway. I let forth a low growl from somewhere within my throat, and his blue eyes widened at the sound of that threat.

"Oh, you'll have to be punished for that," I said firmly. "Oh, yes...I think...I think I know...just...what...to do."

I pulled off his cock, lamenting the loss of that thick dong inside me, but I had other plans. I turned around and lowered my bottom to his face until he grasped my bare butt cheeks with both hands. I balanced on my side of the chair on my hands and knees, hoping that the chair would not tip over because of this.

I looked back behind myself, but the wide curves of my naked bottom hid his face from view.

"You can lick my butthole," I commanded.

"What?" I heard him say.

"You heard me," I said firmly. "Eat out my asshole. Eat out my big...pink...asshole." "Saoirse..." began Daniel.

Do it!" I commanded. "Do it, cur!

I wasn't sure if he was going to do it, but then my blood-encrusted lips turned upwards in a smile as I felt his tongue lick over the muscled rings of my anus.

"Eat it out," I said, a wicked grin in my voice. "You drugged me and left me here all alone. You need to be punished for your insolence. Eat out my asshole until it's clean, cur, until its sparkling clean. I want it to shine in the light."

He licked into my anus, parting the folds of pink muscle I had in that little ring. This really turned me on, just the power of having this command over him, and my own cream ran down my right leg as I felt my lower lips puff in pure excitement.

"Now stick your tongue in my pussy," I commanded. "Lick deep in there and lap up my juices. I want to cum on your face again, cum all over it again."

I reached up and brushed some of my hair from my eyes, and it was stiff, matted with my own dried cum from last night. It was his turn to taste that torrent, that white current of husky wild gel that crusted throughout my hair.

He grabbed my ass as I lowered my pussy to his face, and I grinned in sinful pleasure as I rubbed my hairy twat across his lips and nose, smearing him with my own white cream.

"Ooooh, yeah," I said. "Yeah. I'll fuck your face, choir boy. Mmmm...Fuck that good boy smile you have...Oh, yeah..."

I reached back underneath myself and stroked his thick penis with my right hand, back and forth, back and forth, as I rocked my own pussy upon his lips and nose and chin. My clit rubbed across his nose and chin as I rocked like this, and it took my forward weight to keep the chair from tipping backwards to the floor.

"Drink from my pussy, cur..." I purred. "Mmm, yeah. Take it in, cur...Take it all in..."

I rocked backwards in excitement, the chair finally tipped, and then we were on the floor, still in the chair, though its base was now up in the air. Daniel was fully below me now, his legs in the air, my ass thoroughly clamped around his reclined head.

"Much better," I said as clutched the edge of the chair.

I stared at his hairy legs and his bare feet as I ground my wet pussy into his helpless face.

"Now I'm going to really fuck your face," I said. "Fuck it hard. Fuck it like a bitch fucks a cur."

His thick meat was stiff in my hand, so I kept it there as I rubbed my pussy back and forth across his handsome face, and his cock moved back and forth in my hand as I did so.

"Ooooh..." I moaned out. "Ooooh, I'm going to fuck your face...Fuck your face hard...Fuck it with my pussy...Ooooh, fuck your face with my pussy...Oh, yeah...My wild, hairy pussy...Ooooh, yeah...Mmm...Ooooh...Ooooh, my bitch pussy...Nnnngg..."

Saying the word 'pussy' over and over again really turned me on. I had to look a sight, hair wild and matted, face covered with animal blood, just pounding into this cute boy's face with my wet twat, and I could only imagine my father's reaction if he walked in on my now. He would probably think I was in some Satanic cult. Come to think about it, he wouldn't be far off.

"Ooooh," I moaned. "Oh, yeah, Daniel. Ooooh...Ooooh, my pussy...Ooooh, my wild pussy...Ooooh,yeah...Oh,Daniel...Mmmm...nnnng... Ooooh...my pussy...my pussy, pussy, pussy..."

I chanted the word 'pussy' like a mantra as I rocked back and forth across his face. I felt that orgasm build, felt it deep in my belly, and doing this to him empowered me, made me feel like a true alpha bitch.

I stopped stroking his cock, reached down, and grabbed his balls, pinching my fingers around the narrow base of them. I pulled hard on his balls, and he squealed a little into my open, cream-soaked snatch, but this drove me wild, and I fucked his face even harder.

"Ooooh, give me those balls," I said.

My voice turned to a low growl as I continued to ride his face without mercy.

"Ooooh, I want those balls, Daniel," I said. "Mmmm, yeah. I want to torture these balls, yeah...Oh, fuck...Fuck, yeah...I've got your big balls now, Daniel...Ooooh, yeah...You have to do everything I say...Mmmm, nnng...Yeah...I'll fuck your face with my pussy, yeah. Fuck it hard with my pussy...   fuck   it withmy...my...oh...oh...oh...OH...OH...OH...OHHHH H OOOOOWOOOOO!"

I came, my long wet tunnel clenching like a fist with nothing to grab, and my juices spurted from me in a lava-hot shower all over Daniel's face, squirting and spurting once, twice, and then three times to form a small puddle around his head.

I arched my back as I came, feeling the muscles in it ripple as I did, feeling my spine crack and contort a little, and I looked up toward the ceiling and howled, a long and loud ringing sound within the cabin's living room. My tongue lolled out of my mouth at the end of my howl, and my teeth hurt as they briefly lengthened, sharpening at the tips, my jaw extending slightly with the distinct sound of cracking bone.

And then it was over. I let go of Daniel's balls and l dropped to the base of the chair, resting my head in between Daniel's raised knees. I sat there on Daniel's face as I caught my breath, breathing in and out until I was ready to move again.

"Daniel?" I asked.

Mmmmfff..." came his muffled reply.

Right," I breathed out. "I should probably let you breathe now.

I got up from off his face, stood next to the chair, and stretched. I felt a lot better now, a lot warmer, looser, not stiff from the cold, relaxed, really good, in fact.

I looked down at Daniel's cum-soaked face and gave a slight giggle. That was my cum all over him, even in his hair, and I reveled in that, reveled in the fact that I had this cute boy in the palm of my paw...uhh...hand.

I pulled the base of the chair forward and pushed down until both the chair and Daniel were upright, the heavy comfy chair coming down upon the wood floor with a loud THUMP!...Wow...I've got some serious strength in this little body now. Cool.

Daniel blinked twice before staring at me as if I were a creature from outer space.

"I'm not sucking your cock this time," I grinned. "I don't think you want my bloody lips on your sausage, at least not until I clean up...However...that does not let you off the hook, big boy. This she-wolf wants you to stroke that thick meat between your legs."

"What?" asked Daniel in dazed confusion.

"I said stroke your cock," I commanded, pointing at his still firmly erect dong. "Stroke that big dick until it squirts. I want to see semen shooting out of it...Don't look at me like I'm crazy. Do it."

He stroked his penis up and down, up and down upon my command. I enjoyed controlling this boy, but another urge struck me, and this time I knew what that urge was for.

Keep stroking yourself," I said. "I'll be right back.

I walked to the front door, unlocked it, and opened it to the chill morning air of the snowy outdoors. I stood with my hands on my hips as I pissed a yellow line in the snow, this time fully aware that I was marking my territory. I shut the door, locked it, and proceeded to the kitchen, but not before chastising Daniel one more time.

"I'd better not come back to find you slacking off," I said firmly. "I want you jacking off, not slacking off, comprende?"

I left him there, walked into the kitchen, walked to the backdoor and opened it, and pissed another yellow line into the snow. I knew now that I was marking my territory, ensuring that any other bitches out there understood that this cabin was mine, as was the handsome young cur within it. I would not let any other female touch him.

"I'll rip their fucking tits off," I muttered as I closed the door and walked over to the sink.

I took a hand rag and washed off the crusted blood upon my lips and chin, then dried myself with a paper towel, throwing that spent paper into the trash can near the fridge.

I walked back into the living room to continue my fun, but I was supremely disappointed at what I saw. Daniel was pulling on his red-checkered boxer-briefs, and his smartphone was up to his left ear, held there by the crooking of his head into his shoulder.

"All right, I'll be there," he said into the phone. "I love you, too. Yeah...Bye."

He snapped his briefs into place, set his phone down upon the small wooden stand next to the comfy chair, and turned to look at me, a sad and guilty frown upon his lips.

I placed my hands on my hips and gave him the evil eye.

"What is this?" I demanded.

I have to go," he said firmly.

No, you said..." I began, but he cut me off with a shake of his head.

"I have to meet my mom at the hunting lodge," he said firmly. "It's to talk about you. She hasn't said anything to my dad yet. If my dad finds out I haven't been at the lodge...Damn...If I don't go now, then..."

I sighed and nodded my head in unhappy agreement.

"Fine," I grimaced. "Just do it, but...when will you be back?"

"I don't know yet," said Daniel, and I could tell that he was being honest. "I'll get back to you as soon as I can."

"You'd better," I frowned. "My dad comes back in four days. If this isn't worked out by then..."

"I know," replied Daniel in a worried tone. "We're both having trouble with our dads. I get it. I'm going to work this out, one way or another."

"Good," I said, but I didn't feel confident in that reply.

*****

I sat in my dad's dark-brown comfy chair, completely nude, watching porn on my dad's laptop. Night had fallen, and I'd done nothing but get something to eat, clean myself up, wash my hair, and wait for Daniel to return. I had not even bothered to throw on any clothes. I felt more comfortable now being naked, and...that was something I was going to have to get used to.

I reached over and picked up my lit joint from my dad's green ashtray resting on the wooden stand next to my chair. I took in a puff of that weed, blew out a smoke ring, and set it back down in the tray. I reached over, grabbed my bottle of rye whiskey, took a long pull from the top, and set it back down on the stand.

Normally, I liked to watch regular porn, nothing weird or freaky, but tonight I had flipped through monster porn, watching various young women get ravished by a variety of different creatures. It turned something inside me, a key of sorts, and I couldn't help but watch those videos with fascination, hoping to learn something new, though I knew that to be a fantasy in itself.

I had the lights turned off in the cabin, and the only light generated from inside was from my dad's laptop and the lit joint still burning away in my dad's green ashtray. The light of the full moon cast a silver sheen through the windows, but that was what I wanted. That moon's light comforted me just as much as the whiskey and weed did because I was anxious and afraid for my situation, unsure of what was going to happen to me.

"Daniel..." I whispered to myself. "You'd better come back..."

I shed a small tear from my right eye as I took another pull of whiskey. I could drink more than I could before, and it was taking me longer to get lit and crispy as I wanted, but I could only blame that on my lycanthropy; there was no other explanation.

I set the bottle back down and wiped that tear from my eye.

I sniffed the air as a familiar scent floated before me. It was a strong and wild scent, one of untamed, unnatural passion and musk.

"I know that smell..." I whispered.

A loud and ringing howl erupted from outside the front door. It caused me to grip the chair out of reflex, and my belly tightened in both anticipation and fear.

I sucked in my breath and gulped my own saliva, steeling myself for what was going to happen next, and...well...I knew what I wanted. What I wanted was unnatural, wrong on so many levels, but I wanted it, nonetheless.

I got up, walked to the front door, unlocked it, and threw it open to reveal darkness lit by glaring white snow, snow reflecting the light of the full moon.

In the snow, in the distance, was the shadow of the beast, that great black wolf's head upon a man's black-furred body, that huge circumcised cock swinging between its legs.

My breathing quickened as my pulse picked up at the sight of it, and I grew wet between my legs as my lower lips puffed in excitement. My belly quivered as the beast walked forward on two large, muscular, angled legs, occasionally padding forth on all fours, then standing up to walk again.

I turned, walked to just in front of the oak-tree coffee table that held my dad's laptop, and got down onto my hands and knees. I laid my head down on the wooden floor, rested it upon my right cheek, my long, curly brown hair spilling all about me, and I did this out of instinct because this was the pose of a submissive female, submissive and waiting for her alpha male. I waited in this position, my ass and pussy in the air, and I was already wet, my snatch dripping my juices to run down my inner thighs, my sex organ ready and willing for violation.

I could hear it walk through the open doorway, but I could smell it long before that. It was that incredibly heady, musky scent of primal lust, and I whined a little as I breathed it in, because my body was so excited that I could barely contain myself.

I heard the door creak shut behind me, and then the click of the lock as its tumblers turned in place.

So it could shut and lock doors, huh? That meant it could open doors, too. That...explained a lot. That explained a hell of a lot. I probably should have locked the kitchen door those last two nights, but I was completely out of it during those times, so...yeah.

I could feel its massive presence directly behind me. It bent down, its slightly wet nose directly in my open wet snatch, and it breathed in, sniffed in my scent before licking up and into my dripping hole.

"Oooohnnn..." I moaned and shook from the feel of its long and sinuous tongue.

It gave a low growl, a deep and guttural rumbling that terrified me, so I shut my mouth and tried not to make any more sounds, but it was difficult. The last thing I wanted to do was piss it off.

Its huge, black-furred hands reached down and grasped me around the waist, and those long and curved claws raked lightly across my sensitive skin, but not deep enough to draw blood. The floor creaked as it lowered itself, and then ten inches of thick, sable, circumcised cock entered my wet hole, stretching me out and causing me to gasp in both surprise and slight pain.

It pumped into me, a THUMP, THUMP, THUMP as it worked me over, and I took it, enjoying every hit of its monstrous crotch against my bare bottom. My right cheek slid back and forth across the floor along with my arms and knees, and it was uncomfortable but not as uncomfortable as being ripped apart by this thing if I pissed it off. My ankles turned inward, my feet up upon my toes, and it humped into me, over me, plunging deep within me to where it felt like the head of its cock was up in my belly.

"Oh...Oh, nnng..." I whined.

I didn't want to make any noise, but it was almost impossible not to. I was this thing's bitch whether I liked it or not, so there was nothing I could do but let it ravish me, and I had no problem with that. It was preferable to be eaten alive, and I know I've said that before, but I repeated that in my mind because I needed to hear it in my own head to justify what was happening to me at the moment.

"Oh...nnngg...Oh...Oh fuck..." I panted. "Oh fucking shit...Oh...Oh...mnnngg...Oh..."

The sound of my whining and panting must have done something to it, because it picked me up a second later, picked me up as I weighed next to nothing. It stood with me still impaled upon its long, thick cock, and I bowed my legs and locked them around its muscular, angled legs. It lifted me up and down, using my pussy to jack off its huge dick, and this was so surreal, so bizarre, that my eyes widened like round saucers.

I could see everything clearly within the living room, even though there was virtually no real light around us. Everything was covered in a soft reflective glow as if my eyes were picking up every spark of light possible in order to see.

I stretched up and back to loop my arms around its thick, fur-covered neck. It let forth a low growl, but I tempted fate and leaned my head back to where my long hair spilled around its huge left shoulder. I licked up and out, and my tongue slapped out across my right cheek, so long in its extension that there was no possible way that it could be human anymore. I drew my tongue back into my mouth, tasting the salty sweat of my own right cheek, all the while the beast moved me up and down upon its monstrous cock.

The creature moved its head down next to mine, and I nuzzled my hair into its furry cheek, whining as I did.

"Mmn...mmn...mmn..." I whined, and I sounded like a dog that had disobeyed its master.

I licked up and to my right to lick my long tongue across its lower jaw. Its tongue licked out in return, slapping across my right cheek to lick up across my eye. That long tongue returned to its mouth, and that simple action, that action of licking me, was the signal that I was truly its bitch.

The beast set me down upon the floor once more, and I resumed my submissive position, head on the floor, ass in the air. It gripped my sides and then pummeled into me, fucking me much harder and faster than before.

"Oh...Oh...Oh...OH...OH FUCK!" I cried out.

The creature hammered into my pussy, and my own juices creamed around its monstrous cock, spilling out and about that dong and over its huge, ebony balls.

"OH...OH...OH, OH...OH!" I cried.

This pounding of my pussy was torture, but torture in such a way that I wanted more, needed more, so I took it, and I took it willingly.

"OH...OH...NNNNGG...UNNNGG....!" I moaned.

BAM! BAM! BAM! it fucked me, and I took it, and I loved every second of it. My breasts bobbed wildly back and forth as it pounded me, my belly quivered, and my feet turned inward at the ankles. This thing's cock was spearing deep inside me, and it felt so wild and natural that my orgasm struck from out of nowhere, no real buildup to warn me.

"OH...UNNGG...OH...NNGGG...AH, AH, AH, OOOOH...OOOOOOWOOOOOO!" I howled.

I raised my head and howled, but this time my voice was deeper, unnatural in its reverberation. I came in an amazing, pussy-squeezing burst of hot cream, spraying the creature's cock, crotch, balls, and my own ass with that magic love juice. My white gel splattered down upon the wood floor beneath us, and then the creature matched my howl with its own, raising its head to join my voice with its.

The both of us together sung a wild song as we came, and then my belly bulged with the liquid heat of its semen, those two huge balls beneath its monstrous cock working in tandem to fill my bitch pussy with its life-creating, alabaster seed.

It pulled out of me after that, all ten inches of its huge, circumcised dong pulling back and out of me with a POP! Burning semen spilled from my open fucked hole to join the puddle of my cum beneath my ass and between my legs.

I panted hard like a vacuum formed in my pussy, my sex organ pining for the loss of that massive dong inside me. I laid there in the submissive pose, but the creature backed away, its padded feet sounding out softly upon the wood floor. There was the click of a lock opening, the swivel of the front door, a cold chill breeze on my cum-soaked ass, and then the sound of steaming piss on the snow of my front steps.

And then it was gone. It had marked its territory, and...it was gone.

I breathed in and out as I tried to collect my wits. I was going to have to get up and close the door, but that could wait. My insides hurt a little, and my pussy felt stretched to hell and gone, so...I needed a little breather.

This...This thing coming in at night...This...was a problem. I now had two lovers in my life, one I had to control over, and the other that had control over me. I needed to make a choice, and that choice was going to be difficult. I had to choose between the man...or the beast...and that choice was not a clear-cut one.

CHAPTER 3

My name is Saoirse Lennon, and I am a werewolf. At least, I will be soon. I got bitten by one a few nights ago, bitten and thrown through the wall of my woodshed, and I was pretty fucked up after that attack, but now...things are happening to me, and almost none of them good.

Sure, I can eat myself out now, and licking my own privates was fun, but that guilty pleasure doesn't make up for the murderous change that's bound to happen every time the full moon rises, and it will happen. According to Daniel, I'm showing all of the signs of the curse, so it's only a matter of time before I sprout fur and pop claws...That'll be fun...Oh, I am so fucked.

And speaking of fucked, twice now I've had the beast that attacked me come into my home and ravish me, fuck the ever-living bejeezus out of me, and the only thing I can think of, the only conclusion I can come to on that is...I'm its bitch now.

Let me explain. My dad and I moved out to Lonesome Moon over two months ago. I've been kind of a lazy, worthless piece of crap for a long time now, about seven years, ever since my mom died when I was fifteen. I've been into the drugs, the booze, and the boys since I was sixteen, so this little move out into the middle of bumfuck nowhere was my dad's way of passive-aggressively telling me to straighten up.

Lonesome Moon is the nearby town, but that town's over forty minutes away from this little cabin, and this little cabin is out in the middle of bumfuck nowhere; there's nothing out here but snow and pine trees. Dad's gone for the week on a house flipping project, and he left me here to watch over things, and...that's not gone well. Not at all.

But let me tell you a little bit about myself. I'm a twenty-two-year-old white girl of Irish descent, and my name is Irish, so it's pronounced 'Ser-Sha'. I'm five-eight, one hundred and thirty-seven pounds, and I have brown eyes and long, curly brown hair that falls to my shoulders. I have nice C-cup breasts, beautiful pink nipples, a good-looking ass, and...Goddamn. I've been naked about ninety percent of the time since Dad's been gone. What the fuck?

This is all so fucked up. After the initial attack three nights ago, four if you count tonight, I've been going through changes, and I've had really weird dreams with strange urges on top of that. I was always kind of a hedonist, but...this lycanthropy business has made it even more difficult for me to control my impulses. I mean, I fucked the hell out of Daniel the very same morning he introduced himself, and I've been pussy-whipping him ever since that first fun encounter.

Now Daniel Christianson, Daniel...is a hottie. He's six-foot, has short black hair and blue eyes, very, very cute, with all-natural muscle and a ...grrrrowwwlll...a thick, six-and-a-half inch long circumcised cock that I love to have in my mouth and pussy. Mmmm hmmm. He is delicious...Is it wrong that I feel like eating him sometimes? He is just so tasty...I'm pretty sure that urge is wrong...Ugh.

Daniel's dad is a veterinarian, but his dad is also a 'hunter', one of those people that hunt monsters. Daniel's made sure that I understand that...if his dad finds out I've been bitten...that man is going to kill me. That's why Daniel's been dealing with his mom lately, setting things up so that his dad doesn't shoot him with a silver bullet or something.

Daniel came around the morning after my attack, and I was pretty fucked up when he showed up, so he took care of me, stitched me up and bandaged my wound, and watched over me when I was in a monster-induced coma. He saved my life again when I woke up outside in the forest, naked, afraid, and in danger of freezing to death. Daniel's a decent guy, though he did stick me with a needle that first day I met him, put me into a drugged-out coma for a few hours, but I already punished him for that, so...I've let bygones be bygones.

Still, this creature that bit me...it's come by every night, walked right into the cabin, and had its way with me twice now. When I was fucked up and out of it the second night of the full moon, I had a dream that it had come in and stood over my bed, but...I'm pretty sure now that wasn't a dream. This thing has marked me as its bitch, and I've...I've stupidly given into it. I want it to come in...I want it to fuck me like a bitch, so I've let it.

So that's my current problem. I like Daniel, and I like him a lot, but...the wild and unnatural part of me, the part that's turning into a monster, wants the beast instead. Ooooh...I really don't know what to do about that. The rational me wants Daniel, and the hedonist me wants the creature, so...fuck. Here I am, and I have no idea what to do.

I groaned as I pushed up from the wood floor of my living room. It was still night, the full moon's silver light was still casting over everything in here, the front door was still open, and I was still buck naked, werewolf cum leaking from my open fucked pussy. The creature had just come in and ravished me yet again, and I let it. I didn't even try to fight back. I just straight up enjoyed that unholy union.

My nethers hurt a little as I walked to the front door and stared out into the moonlit snow. I was getting used to this beast coming in, or maybe it was part of my 'condition', but my privates didn't hurt as much as they had after last night's fucking. Was it wrong that I wanted this? Ooooh, I am just...I am so fucked.

I took a sniff and breathed in the heavy scent of the creature's piss upon my front step. It had marked its territory, so I drew in its scent, a wild, heavy, unnatural aroma that spoke to something untamed in my soul. I pissed a line of yellow out into the snow on my front step in response to its marking, and then I shut the door, locking it behind me.

I'd say this was getting out of hand, but this got out of hand a long time ago. Dad would be back in three days, and he was sure to notice some 'changes' going on with me. I'd say my frequent nudity and exhibitionism were a dead giveaway.

I thought about the creature, thought about its power and presence, and this made me let forth a low growl from somewhere within my throat. I stretched, arms over my head, and I heard and felt my bones crack a little as I did so. I could still see everything so clearly within the cabin, a soft silver sheen lining everything around me as if my eyes were picking up every speck of light possible.

I felt energized, pumped full of adrenaline, and I knew something was off, so I made my way to the back of the cabin to the bathroom, intent on looking in the bathroom mirror.

I felt strange, wild, and wired, so I covered my eyes as I flipped on the bathroom light. It took my eyes a moment to adjust to the blinding glare, but after they did, I gave myself an inspection in the mirror, and...whoa.

I looked like me, but pumped, muscular, my physique filled out as if I'd been lifting weights for a long time. I still had my long curly brown hair, but I was covered in brown fur, the same color as my hair, and I could tell that my skin had turned that same color of brown. I had sharp fangs instead of canines, and my eyes were that rich golden color, and...whoa...I was taller, too, by at least four inches; I was at least six feet tall now.

"Fuuuuuck..." I growled.

Even my voice was a low growl...Wow...I was...holy shit. I'd changed, but not like the creature, not all the way, yet. I was still me inside, but I felt wired, hyper, like on meth but without having actually smoked it.

My biggest surprise was my breasts. Those two symbols of womanhood were bigger now, no longer C-cups, but double D's, and this excited me as well. Maybe that's why the creature's dick was so big, because everything about you grew when you changed, and...good God. I was fucking hot, even as this furry she-bitch. Apparently, getting fucked by this thing tonight did something more than just give me an incredible orgasm. It did a lot more than just that.

I felt so pumped that I wanted to run, just run, just pick up my feet and run. I felt bursting with energy, and I growled from deep within my throat because I also felt like hitting something, smashing something to bits. It was weird to have this...this...fury inside me. I don't know how to accurately describe it. It's like you're angry, but not angry at any particular thing, just feeling nuts like you need to beat on something to release your bottled steam.

I made my way back to the kitchen, made my way to the back door, flung open that door to feel the winter chill of the outdoors, and pissed a yellow line in the snow, marking those steps.

I walked out into the moonlit snow, my bare and furry feet crunching into that packed, crystallized powder, and I closed the door behind me. This fur acted like a winter coat, and I didn't feel the cold sink into me like I had earlier in the day when I had awakened from sleep, naked, out in the forest. Besides, this wired and wild fury inside me filled me with heat of its own, making me ignore the cold through sheer rage and lust.

I sniffed the air around me, and breathed in that frigid chill until I picked up a scent, the scent of my primal lover, the beast that had done this to me.

I raised my head and howled, a long and pining sound in the moonlit dark, one that I instinctually knew was a mating call, and my call was answered by a deeper, more guttural and ringing howl from out of the trees south of the cabin, south of the woodshed.

I took to running toward the source of that howl, and my hands reached down to have me lope on all fours, standing to run, then lope, then run, and I somehow picked up speed this way, all the while sprinting toward my unnatural lover's estimated location.

The howl in the distance rang out again, and I answered it, called back to it as I sped through the trees toward my preferred destination, that destination beneath my wild lover's fearsome loins. I wanted him like my human self wanted Daniel, but I was not human right now. No, the beast inside me drove me toward the beast of the outside, and I wished to be filled by his long, thick, sable cock once more.

I could see perfectly well in the moonlit darkness of the coniferous wood, a light sheen of silver covering everything around me, a silver glow that reflected off of everything, allowing my golden eyes to see in the dark as well as I could see in daylight. I had no trouble whatsoever finding my ferocious lover by scent and call, just as I had no trouble seeing my new lover with my new golden eyes in the thick of the southernwood.

It...He...for he was male, and I saw him as more than a monster now...He was crouched over the carcass of a mature doe. I cautiously approached him, and his bloodstained muzzle turned toward me, his large black nose sniffing the air as his golden eyes stared into mine. He growled, a long and low rumble, and I growled in return, crouching down into a threatening position, because a bestial urge had come upon me, one I could not resist. This was a battle for control, and that primal part of my soul forced me into that fight, though I did not want this.

He rushed me as I jumped at him in return, and we collided in mid-air. As strong as I felt, as strong as my new physique was in muscle and fury, and as wild and untamed that this power was, this power coursing through my veins, hitting that wall of muscle and rage changed my mind in a hurry. His massive, sable jaws clamped around my throat, and I was thrown upwards and over his back, slung around through the air like a toy, and then to the ground, hitting the packed snow with a nasty slamming and sliding off my furry body on my fur-coated back.

I rolled over, ass in the air, and squealed out a series of high-pitched whines from this loss, afraid that my ferocious new lover was going to kill me, but he did not close those bloody jaws down on my throat, no. His massive, black-clawed hands picked me up by my muscular, brown-furred waist, and he thrust his ten-inch long, thick, ebon-skinned cock into my pussy, plunging deep into me to where I barked out a sharp protest.

My protesting did not last long. My pussy creamed over his massive penis, and he humped into me and over my back as he had done mere minutes before. He pounded into me, thumping my fur-covered bottom with his black-furred crotch, and I took it, enjoying every inch of him once more.

"Ah...Ah...Ah...Ahg!" I whined as I was mercilessly fucked by his giant dick. "Ung...Mmnn...Mnnng...Mmmnnn..."

He picked me up by the waist and ran me forward, and I was forced to run while he was still inside me. We skipped a few feet forward to plow back into the packed snow, frozen grass, and ice-encrusted twigs. He pumped into me harder, my fur-covered face mashing down into the packed crystal, and his cock felt like it was digging into my belly, pummeling my cervix like a pneumatic hammer. My pussy creamed all over his massive dong, my ivory love juice sliding down his two big, ebon balls to drip into the snow beneath us.

He picked me up and ran me forward again, right into the nearest pine tree. I hugged the coarse bark of that tree, my muscular arms wrapping around it, and my breasts, once C- cups, now bigger double D's from the animal change, rubbed against that pine bark. My once pink nipples, now brown like the color of my hair, rubbed against that bark as well, lancing further pain through my sensitive chest area. I yelped in pain from this, but he fucked me even harder, pounding into me without mercy against that tree.

This was insane, wild and unholy, and I loved every second of it, painful as it happened to be.

He picked me up as he nipped into my shoulder, and that hurt, but his fangs did not draw blood. I yelped as he threw me down into the snow again, and he nipped along my shoulders and neck, pinching but not drawing blood. This was an exercise of his control over me, and he was quite skilled at it, because his monstrous dong continued to pound into me the entire time I was being savaged in this way.

"Aaaaahg!...Unnnh...Ahhhgg...Uuuuung..." I cried out from this violation. "Nnng...Ack...Ung..."

He bit down into my right shoulder, pinching that shoulder but, once again, shy of actually wounding me. He then proceeded to clamp his jaws around the back of my fur-covered neck, clamp them down in such a way that my spine was locked, and I was paralyzed in his powerful grasp.

Unnngg...Ahhhh!" I cried. "Oooooooh...

My voice was a low growl, but I was still half-human, so my female tone was audible, even in this form. My sounds of bitch pain drove my unnatural lover into a wild heat, and he drilled into me with that monstrous sable cock, the glans spreading me wider round than a golf ball, hammering my pussy until I exploded in an equally monstrous orgasm.

"Ah...Ah...Ung...Ah...Ah..." I barked out.

"Ah...Ah...Ung...Ah...Ahg...AHG...AH...OOOOOO OOOWOOOOOO!"

My pussy sprayed him as I came, sprayed him with cum and that opaque juice that shot from my pee hole, and I howled, this time a ringing, reverberating howl, that howl at its full, unholy strength.

He raised his massive black head and howled as he came in union with my cum-spraying pussy, that great wolf's head visible within the circle of the white moon above us, as if he had been drawn into a still painting for Halloween. He thrust hard into me once, twice, then three times, squirting that burning hot semen into me, filling my belly with that liquid heat.

Ooooh, it felt so good. I wanted him to fill me with his unholy, unnatural, primal seed. I needed it, and feeling that liquid heat inside me as my own juices sprayed out of me...it turned that key. I wanted this now. I wanted the beast inside me, both figuratively and literally.

He pulled out of me, slid out all ten inches of his monstrous dong, and ooooh, I felt all ten inches of it. Fuuuuck. You have no idea what that feels like, or maybe you do, I don't know, but it caused me to lift my fur-covered ass in the air and whine like the subdued, thoroughly pussy-fucked bitch I was. His cock came out with a loud POP, and my pussy squirted out his semen as if on command, a spurting of alabaster liquid in a squirt, squirt, squirt, a reflex of having so much monster-cum inside me. I felt every one of those contractions in my ravaged, cream-soaked cunt, and this caused my golden eyes to roll up into the whites as my tongue lolled from my mouth, lolling out in six inches of saliva dripping ecstasy.

Hoollly shit. Never felt anything like that before.

He loped back over to his kill, his bloody deer carcass, his huge swinging cock still dripping semen, and some of my own juices. He bent down and gorged himself on the kill, turned his great blackhead to stare at me with those golden eyes, his jaws still chewing, his fangs crunching into flesh and bone, blood dripping from his maw, and then he went back to feeding, biting into his kill once more, disinterested in me.

Typical man. Eat, fuck, eat, and probably sleep. Sounds about right.

I took my leave of him and made my way back to the cabin. I was not lost in the direction this time; I could smell my own markings, the urine I'd marked the cabin doors with. I made my way back to the cabin via my scent, went in through the kitchen door, and made my way into the living room.

I was bone-tired, and I felt beat up. The beast had done a number on me this time, throwing me around, nipping at me, pounding into my bare, furry butt. He'd fucked the hell out of me, too, and I was sore now. Ugh...I was going to feel this tomorrow. My pussy was a stretched-out, hammered, cum-soaked mess.

I laid down on the cabin floor of the living room, curled up, and closed my eyes. I needed that rest, anyway.

*****

I dreamed of the moon, and the woman within it. She had silver eyes with no pupils, and long silver hair and the moon was her chariot, driven by a long train of silver wolves. I sat, naked and tiny beside her, peering over the edge of the great chariot to view the passing world below.

Snow-covered houses and pine trees were below us, and I looked up to the giant woman who drove the moon, and I was only half her size in height. She smiled down at me with those silver eyes, brushing my hair from my cheek with her huge fingers, and I knew that I was her favorite and that she had not had one in a long time.

I smiled back at her. I felt warm inside, happy, accepted, like I was meant to be here, meant to be in her chariot since the day I was born. It was as if I was being rewarded for being a hedonist, rewarded for being my worthless and lazy self.

But I wasn't worthless. I just enjoyed life, wanted to enjoy it to its fullest, feel and experience everything, and the lady who drove the moon saw this, and she took me in, gave me a place in her chariot. I felt special for once...loved.

She placed her large right index finger on my forehead, and I felt heat burn into my skin as her fingertip shone with a silver aura. She had placed the power of the moon within me, given me an ability the others did not have, the ability to command the beast inside, and so I gladly and gratefully accepted it, happy yet again that I was special to her, that I was chosen to be her favorite.

******

I awoke to the sounds of boots on the wood floor. I rolled over, grunting, stiff from sleeping on the floor in the nude, and I looked up to see Daniel, still his hot and fuckable self.

He had on his tan winter coat, his dark blue jeans, his hide-leather gloves, and tan outdoor work boots, the same getup he'd worn every day since I'd seen him...Did he ever change outfits? What the hell? Did he at least wash his clothes?... Of course, I was one to talk, considering my 'outfit' lately had just consisted of my birthday suit. Ah, well. It was easier to fuck that way.

I was back to being my normal human and sexy me, no fur or fangs or bigger boobs...Ugh...I would have liked to have kept that last one...Ah, well. Easy come easy go.

"D...aniel..." I puffed out as I stretched and groaned from my reclined position.

The look on Daniel's face...It was odd. He looked...focused, but I had no idea why. In his hands was a big metal bracelet, but upon closer inspection, it was more like a manacle or shackle, and I stupidly stared at it, wondering why he had it at all.

He grabbed my outstretched right arm and snapped the heavy metal manacle, a shackle of some kind, around my wrist.

"Wha..." I started to say.

My right hand thunked to the wooden floor along with the shackle around my wrist. It hurt when my hand hit the floor, and I cried out from that pain, but that pain was not what bothered me. What bothered me was the incredible weakness that spread up and through me, starting at my right wrist to flow throughout me like a virulent poison.

"Uhhhnnnn..." I whined as I laid back down on the floor.

I could not get up. I felt so weak that I was like a newborn babe, my muscles atrophied in sensation, and I couldn't even open my mouth to complain about it. All I could do was just whine a little through my lips and gritted teeth. I peed a little without meaning to, and that was humiliating but not as humiliating as lying in a fetal position, whining like a whipped dog.

Daniel knelt over me and held up a small iron key to my face. I stared at it and studied it, and it was just a small, plain, iron key with a little circle on the end of it, so my eyes fixated on that, because there wasn't much else I could do except whine and piss myself.

Daniel held up my head in his hands and turned my vision toward the shackle clamped around my right wrist. This thing was just a circular metal band of partially tarnished silver, but its design was so archaic that it was like something you'd see in a dungeon from out of the Dark Ages.

"This bracelet is one of my dad's most prized possessions," he said quietly. "It's a shackle made of pure silver. It weakens lycanthropes somehow, but I don't know how it works. I just know that it does."

He pushed the small key into the large and heavy manacle on my right wrist, turned that key and the bracelet/shackle popped open. He removed it from my wrist, and it was like an enormous weight being lifted from me, a heavy cloak of invisible chains being pulled up and off me.

I sat up and stared at his handsome face in surprise, but that surprise swiftly changed to righteous and justified anger. Cute or not, this boy had pissed me off this time. Between him injecting me with a tranquilizer and now this...Oooh, was I pissed.

"Don't do that again!" I yelled, and he backed away at the fury in my voice. "Motherfucker! You son of a bitch!"

Daniel gave me a look of shock at my sudden outburst, but Goddamn, he shouldn't have done that. I swear he's as smart as a fucking pop can sometimes. It's like the boy just does shit and doesn't think at all before he does it, you know? What the fuck? Why doesn't he just torture me with silver knives next? Oh, hey, look how this works on werewolves, Saoirse! Doesn't that hurt? What the fucking, fuck! What in the hell goes on in that little brain of his?

"I...I just wanted to show you..." he started, but I cut him off.

No, I was pissed this time.

"Just don't," I said as I turned my head away from him. "Don't fucking touch me...What the fuck!"

"Saoirse...I was just..." began Daniel.

"Shut up!" I said, but my voice was a low growl. "Asshole."

I looked up into his blue eyes, and I could see the hurt in them. I think I'd made my point a little too well with my tantrum, but...he just...he's so...Sigh...I stared down at my hands and thought about this because I needed a mental breather.

Okay, I was being unreasonable, an unreasonable, angry little bitch. I think my loss of that battle for control last night pissed me off, and now I was taking it out on Daniel. It angered me that I was defeated so quickly, angered me that I was still a submissive little bitch to my monstrous lover, but...I knew I shouldn't have taken it out on Daniel. I think he was only trying to help me, so...I needed to be...gentler...with him.

"Okay, okay," I sighed. "I'm sorry. I'm just...You just...You have to warn me before you do something like that, okay?"

I looked up at him again, and he swallowed once before giving me a quick nod.

"I...just wanted to show you the bracelet," he said.

"And you did," I said as I stood.

I groaned as I stretched out, fully nude in front of him, but...eh...he'd seen me naked so many times that being nude in front of him was par for the course.

I had a little bit of pee running down my left leg, but I ignored that. I needed to address this situation with this 'bracelet', though it looked like a shackle to me. Felt like one, too.

"That thing you put on me leveled me," I said unhappily. "I couldn't move at all. I even pissed myself because of it. You can't just do something like that and expect me to be thrilled about it...Is this some kind of...What is this for? Are you trying to help me somehow?"

"Y...yeah," stammered Daniel. "I want to use it on you tonight."

"What!" I asked in slight anger. "Why?"

Daniel placed the heavy silver manacle down upon my oak-tree coffee table and then turned to address me.

I was still angry at him, a little bit, anyway, but I decided to work off that anger with a more positive activity. Thanks to my lycanthropy, I was pretty strong now for a girl my age, so...fun time. Goddamn, these urges, I swear...

I ignored what he was going to say and unzipped his coat, intent on undressing him until he was all bare skin. He talked to me anyway, he, himself, intent on telling me his plan.

"Tonight is the fifth moon," he said anxiously as I pulled off his coat. "The fifth moon is the strongest in conjunction with the cycle of the werewolf, so I think you're going to change tonight."

He did not know that I had already made a partial change last night and that I'd been getting jackhammered by the very same werewolf that bit me...I didn't want to tell him, either. I liked Daniel, and he was just trying to help me, but...I wanted to be a werewolf now. I wanted Daniel, but I also wanted the beast...Is that wrong? Jesus, I don't know. I don't fucking know anything anymore. All I wanted to do when my dad left for the town was to smoke weed, drink whiskey, and masturbate a lot. That went south in a hurry.

I unbuttoned Daniel's light-blue work shirt, pulled it off him, and threw it to the floor. He didn't fight me as I pulled up on the hem of his white tank top and pulled it up and over his raised arms, tossing his tank top to the floor as well. I wanted him naked for obvious reasons, but what I didn't want was to wear that shackle again.

"I'm not putting that thing on," I said firmly.

"You have to," said Daniel unhappily.

I ran my right index finger across his firm and delicious pecs, running the tip of my finger over his right, reddish-brown nipple. He had a dark patch of black pit hair under each arm, but my pit hair had also grown back, probably because I was a right horny she-wolf bitch now, but that was beside the point. The point was that I could smell Daniel's heady, musky scent, and I wanted that, wanted to fuck him for all he was worth.

"Why?" I breathed out.

"I'm going to have to tell my dad about you soon," said Daniel, and his breathing picked up as I undid his belt and unzipped his jeans. "If he knows I've been keeping you contained, then..."

I pushed him backward, forcing him back until he fell into my dark-brown comfy chair. I undid the laces on his boots, pulled them off, tossed them aside, and then I pulled off his white winter socks, first one, then the other.

"I understand," I said, my voice husky, my breathing heavy.

"Good," said Daniel uncertainly. "It's for your own good. You won't hurt anyone if you're...you're uhhh..."

I pulled off his jeans and smiled at the very visible bulge in his red-checkered boxer briefs. His little soldier was already standing at attention, and I wanted me some of that. Mmmm hmmm.

"I know," I breathed. "I'll put it on tonight, right before the moon comes up."

I had no intention of putting on that fucking thing. However...I still had a use for it.

I knelt before the comfy chair and pulled down on his briefs, revealing the small patch of black pubes above his thick, circumcised meat, and I practically yanked off that underwear before pitching it to the side and out of the way.

I took the bulbous head of his cock into my mouth, tasting precum, and slurped up and down that thick shaft, feeling the familiar sensation of wetness drip between my legs.

"I should do it," gulped Daniel as he closed his eyes. "I should put it on you."

I popped off his cock, leaned back, and stroked his hard phallus up and down, up and down, up and down.

He was not getting that shackle on me. No way.

"No, I don't think so," I said firmly. "I'll do it, because...because I need to get used to having that discipline. If you hadn't noticed, Daniel...I'm kind of a hedonist. If I don't discipline myself, then I won't have any control at all when I change. Do you understand?"

"Y...yeah..." he stammered.

"Good," I said. "It's time I took some control back. I need some control in my life right now.

Yeah, that fight last night wasn't a fight at all. It was a humiliating spanking, and I really needed to feel some control again. I had an idea, a plan of sorts, but I needed that shackle, and I needed Daniel out of here before the moon came up for its fifth time. He could not be here for what I was planning; he'd just get himself killed.

I took his meat back into my mouth, and slurped up and down the shaft, pushing the mushroom head to the back of my throat before sliding my lips slowly up the shaft to pop off of it again. I took his big balls into my mouth, gently sucked on them, relishing that flood of Daniel's natural musk over my tongue, and then I released his balls to take his cock back into my mouth again.

"You...You have to...ooooh..." moaned Daniel. "You have to do it, or...or you might kill someone."

I popped off his cock again, that shaft wet with my saliva, and I joined him on the chair, straddling him so that I could take his meat into my own wet hole.

"I'm not a murderer," I breathed out as I slid onto him.

I kissed him lightly on the lips as I slid up and down his shaft, my knees on each side of his legs. I leaned backward, arched my back, closed my eyes, and raised my face toward the ceiling as I fucked him slowly, gently.

"I'm a hedonist," I breathed out. "I like the pleasurable things in life, the sensations in my body, and I enjoy that, and I freely admit it. There comes a time, however, when a hedonist has to slow down and take some responsibility. I don't want to kill anybody...ever. I just want to enjoy my life to the fullest...and right now that involves my pussy and your cock."

"But..." started Daniel.

But nothing," I said firmly.

I opened my eyes, leaned forward, pressed my forehead against his, and stared directly into his own blue eyes.

"The beast needs to be controlled, and I get that," I said softly. "That is why you are going to give me the bracelet, that shackle before you leave today. I'll put it on when I'm ready, and that will be before the moon rises."

I wasn't going to put on that shackle, but he didn't need to know that. No, I had other plans for it. For one thing, the damned thing worked on me, so that meant...Oh yeah, I had a plan.

"Well, you have to," breathed Daniel. "My parents have to see that you're not a threat." "Yeah," I replied. "I know."

I pushed off of him, feeling his cock slide out of me, and that stiff wet organ plopped onto his dark pubes. I got down from the comfy chair, arched my back a bit, and then reached forward to grab a nice chunk of his short, black hair. He gave a short hiss of protest as I pulled him up out of the chair by his hair, but his slight pain was not my concern. My only concern was getting him to my bed.

"Come on, big boy," I said firmly. "You're mine for the time being, and you owe me, anyway. Let's go to my bedroom. We'll finish our 'conversation' in there."

I let go of his hair, spun him around, smacked his tight, muscular ass with one good hit of my right palm, and he jumped a little before taking a few steps forward toward my bedroom door.

"Hustle, cur," I commanded.

Yeah, I may have lost that fight last night, but I had this cute boy wrapped around my little finger. That gave me a high, just what I needed to lick my wounds and move on.

I rested my hands around Daniel's abs and pushed him forward, and we walked into my bedroom, my hands still locked around the smooth skin of his waist.

I looked down at his luscious ass and felt my mouth water.

"Oh, I don't have a dick," I said with wide eyes, "but if I did, I'd so fuck that tight, hottie - ass of yours."

"What!" asked Daniel in audible concern.

I laughed as I practically tossed him onto my bed. Yeah, he was four inches taller than me, and he was all-natural muscle, but I had the strength of the moon on my side. Oh yeah, this was going to be fun.

He lay on his stomach as I straddled the back of his legs, and I stared down at that juicy, incredibly hot, tight, tight ass of his. I stuck my right index and middle fingers in my mouth, got them wet with saliva, and then thrust them into his tight little butthole.

"Saoirse!" he cried out, but I only giggled at his protest.

"Ooooh, that's a tight little hole," I snickered. "Better hope you don't end up in prison. You'll be a squealing little bitch...Oh, yeah."

I moved my fingers back and forth in his butt, in and out, in and out, feeling him squirm underneath me. I enjoyed this for a few seconds, and then I pulled my fingers out of his butt, leveraging myself above him. I giggled, then turned him around to face me, so that he was laying on his back.

"Have some ass, little cur," I said as I plunged my two fingers into his mouth.

His expression was hilarious. I don't think he liked the taste of his own ass, but that didn't matter, because I wasn't giving him a choice.

I pulled my fingers from his mouth, grabbed his thick cock, and slid onto that fully erect dong, filling my wet tunnel once more. I positioned my butt upon his bare crotch, moved side to side a bit to rub my small pink clit across his dark pubes, and then I prepared myself for the absolute pounding I was about to give him.

"Get ready for your desecration, Mr. Christianson," I said with a wicked grin.

He looked at me in both slight horror and surprise, but this only made me giggle.

"Saoirse?" he asked meekly.

That was my cue to let the real fun begin. I let my inner beast loose upon him, because, Goddammit, he deserved it.

I placed my hands on his muscular shoulders, dug in my nails, and moved my ass up, sliding his cock through my happy wet tunnel. I dropped back down upon him, and then I pounded my butt up and down, a SLAP, SLAP, SLAP as my bare ass slammed into him over and over again, the bed rocking as if we were in a storm on the ocean.

"Ooooh, yeah, choir boy!" I cried. "Oh, take it, yeah! Oh, I'm gonna fuck that big dick! Fuck it till it squirts, yeah...Mmmmn...Fuck that big, juicy piece of meat until it squirts!"

I reached back and behind myself to pinch the narrow base of his balls between my right-hand fingers. I pulled hard on his balls, reveling in his squeal of pain as I continued to fuck him without mercy.

"Yeah, give me those balls!" I snarled. "Give me those big balls, choir boy! Mnnng...Nnnng...Fuck your big dick...Mnnn, yeah...Fuck that big dick and pull these big balls..."

I pulled hard on his balls again, listened to his squeal of pain, slapped his balls once with my open palm, enjoyed that squeal, and then I gripped his shoulders as I started into my full-on-fucking once more.

"Oh, I'll teach you a lesson, you little shit," I growled. "Mmmn, yeah...Teach you not to drug me...put a magical shackle on me...leave me alone here...Nnnng...Fucking little cur...Mmmng...Fuck your big dick...Yeah..."

BAM, BAM, BAM! I fucked him, slamming my bottom into his crotch over and over again, feeling the head of his thick dong hit my cervix again and again. Oh, it felt so good, like winning-the-Goddamned-lottery good.

I pulled off his cock and straddled his chest, smacked him across his left cheek with my right hand, and then positioned my wet, hairy snatch directly over his face. I stroked my clit hard and fast over his face, taking time to rub my whole pussy in between those furious strokes.

"Can't cum in my pussy, little cur..." I growled. "Can't cum in my wild, hairy pussy...Nnngg...Not going to...cum in me...little cur..."

I reached down with my left hand and gripped his jaw, squeezing so that his lips opened, his mouth a yawning hole right beneath my pulsing cunt. His eyes were round like blue-china plates, and he stared directly at my wet snatch as I stroked my clit and hood hard and fast.

"Fucking little shit..." I snarled. "Mmmmn...You can taste my pussy, you little shit...Nnngg...Drink from my wild, hairy pussy...Oh...Oh, you can...Mmmmn...Drink...from...Mmmnnn...Nnnng... Oh...Oh, fuck...Oh, fucking shit...Oh...Oh...OH...OH...OH...OH MY PUSSY OOOOOOWOOOOO!

I howled as I came, my juices spraying from my pee hole into his open mouth. I sprayed my magical love juice all over his face, reeling from the contractions in my happy wet tunnel. I shivered and shook and trembled in this physical ecstasy, something I was still not used to, because none of my pre-lycanthropic orgasms were ever like this, not like this.

Goddamn. I have some pent-up frustrations, you know? What the fuck?

I backed up off his chest to straddle his bare legs again as he sputtered, spat, and wiped at his face. I took his cock into my mouth, slurping up and down it at top speed. Oh yeah, I was wild and unleashed now.

I sucked his thick piece of meat with such force that he sat up and gripped my head, pulling slightly on my thick, curly brown hair.

"Oh, shit!" he hissed through gritted teeth. "Saoirse!"

I sucked up and down his cock, and I was not gentle. He squirmed in my assault of his private piece of heaven, clutching my head while digging his fingers into my scalp.

"Saoirse!" he moaned. "Oh, it's too much...Oh...Oh, my God! Oh...Oh...Oh...Oh...Fuck!...Fuck, fuck, fuck, fuck, FUCK, FUUUUUUUUUCK!"

Burning white semen exploded in my mouth, filling me with that rich, salty taste. I gulped it down this time, savoring every last drop of his delicious, ivory seed.

Daniel dropped to my bed and lay there, panting. I pulled off his cock, but not before licking the tip clean, my tongue pressed flat against that round, mushroom head.

"Mmmm..." I purred. "Woof, woof, Daniel. That's what I like. You're delicious. I better hope I put on that shackle tonight. Otherwise, I might come to find you and take some chunks out of your tasty ass."

"Yeah," puffed Daniel. "That's what I've been trying to tell you."

I leaned backward, arched my back, and felt my spine pop. I let forth a rumbling growl from deep in my throat as I stretched my arms over my head and brought them down to plop my hands onto his belly. He jumped a little and gave a slight 'oof' as my hands impacted upon him, but...what can I say? Stretching after fucking felt goooood. Relaxing.

I leaned forward, my long curly brown hair over my face, and peered through those thick curls to look down at Daniel, but he looked...freaked out.

"You...You're getting worse..." he stammered.

"Really?" I asked, slightly confused. "Personally, I thought I was getting better."

"You're out of control," said Daniel.

His shocked face was sopping wet with my juices. It was even in his hair...Hmmm...Okay...Maybe he has a point.

"I've been a little frustrated," I shrugged. "It's not typical of me. Next time...I'll go easy on you. Get in touch with my gentler, softer side."

He nodded a couple of times before wiping some more of my cum off his handsome face.

"I...Good..." he said, and I could tell that he was rattled. "I...I like you, but..." "Yeah, I know," I sighed. "Just get out of here. Go...I'll put the shackle on before the moon comes up. You have my word."

"You have to," breathed Daniel. "Once you put it on, you won't be able to unlock it, because I'll have the key."

"Yeah, yeah," I said in a tired voice. "Get out of here. Go on...I'd rather have you here, but...you know...it's not a good idea."

"Y...yeah," he said uncertainly. "I...I'll go, but...you have to put that shackle on. I really, really like you, Saoirse. You have to do this, or..."

His voice trailed off as he just looked at me in slight fear. Oh, yeah. He was rattled. I think I scared him this time.

"I will," I lied. "Just clean up and get out of here, but...for what it's worth, Daniel...you know I really like you, too...I want to be with you, but that involves trust, so you're just going to have to trust me with this...I'll do it myself...Now go on. Get along, little doggie. I need to mentally prepare for tonight...That shackle sucks ass, by the way, so you'll owe me."

"Okay," nodded Daniel. "I'll...trust you. I'll be back in the morning to unlock the bracelet. It won't be comfortable, but...it's for your own good."

"I know," I sighed, and that was the end of our 'discussion'.

Still, now that I knew he was not going to be here, that he would be safe...I could get ready to enact my plan.

*****

This was it. It was getting close to nightfall now.

Daniel was long gone, so I'd cleaned up and cooked some round steak for myself. I thawed that meat in the sink, but...I just barely kept myself from eating it raw. I barely cooked it as it was...I think Daniel was right. I was getting worse.

I was so hungry and horny all of the time. Was this what it was going to be like from now on, or was this just what it was like in the first stages of the curse? I'd sure like to see those 'books' Daniel mentioned. There had to be something in them that could help me.

I hadn't bothered putting any clothes on. I felt like something was trying to claw its way out of my skin as it was, and I had a good idea what that something was going to be. The beast inside me was growing out of control, feeding off of my selfish hedonism, and Goddamn, I didn't know if I could contain it tonight long enough for me to...I'd just have to wait and see.

I picked up the shackle or bracelet or whatever it was and inspected it. It was heavy, really heavy, tarnished a bit, so I knew it had to be silver, or at least partially silver. It had an inscription on the inside of it, but what language it was in, I didn't know. The letters were in the English alphabet, and it read 'Sit cor meum in furore alligatus est scriptor Luna lumen'. I don't know what the fuck that means. All I know is that this thing has some kind of power, though, because it worked on me, so I knew...I knew it would work again.

I bent down and slid the heavy silver shackle under my oak-tree coffee table, pushing it a little farther in to hide it somewhat. It was still open, obviously; I was careful not to close it. Once closed, it would take Daniel's key to open it.

I paced back and forth in the living room, fully naked, so anxious that I could barely hold my sanity together. The sun was going down outside, and tonight would be the fifth moon. Ooooh...I was really nervous about this. I had a plan, but...everything had to come together in just the right way, or...shit.

It was almost time. I walked to the front door, unlocked it, opened the door, and let the cold outside air stab through me. I pissed another yellow line into the snow, marking my territory yet again. It was necessary for what I had in mind.

I closed the door and went back to pacing the living room.

This was fucked. What if I...What if I killed someone?

"Maybe you should just put on the shackle, Saoirse," I said to myself. "Just put it on, and...no, no, no. I have a plan. I'm sticking with it. Stick with the plan, Saoirse."

The sun had gone down outside. The light of the last full moon for this month crept through the windows of the living room and washed over my naked body, caressing me, comforting me.

I had not bothered to turn on the lights, so I stood there in the dark, the full moon the only thing in my vision. That glowing white disc called to me, whispered to me in the dark, telling me things that upright, civilized humans were not meant to hear...

I cried out as I doubled over in pain. My stomach felt like it was on fire, and then that burning sensation spread up through my guts, up and up, all the way up to my brain. It was like napalm in my blood, and that sensation of being consumed by flame did not stop at my head but spread throughout my skin as well.

"OH MY GOD!" I screamed as I clutched my head from the crippling pain lancing all throughout me. "OH, GOD! OH GOD, HELP ME! OOOOOH, IT FUCKING HURTS! OH, OH, OH FUUUUUUCK!"

I dropped to my knees and shrieked as my jaw dropped open, the bones cracking, lengthening. My muscles bulged in my arms and legs as my spine lengthened, and my legs bent backwards, the legs angling back like dog's legs, wolf's legs.

The pain was so intense, so insanely terrible, that I wanted to die. My face warped and changed as my teeth sharpened into fangs and my jaws pushed out from my skull. Brown fur erupted all over my body, and I grew in size and mass, all muscle, all muscle, and rage and hunger. My breasts grew to triple D's; they had greatly enlarged on me, but those small melons were still covered in brown fur, and I still had my clearly visible vulva between my legs, though it was also covered with brown fur. I looked female, but also monstrous, a hybrid of animal and woman.

I stood on my new legs and looked down at my new hands, these two big, brown-skinned, brown-furred pseudo-paws of mine, big brown hooked claws jutting from my fingertips, and I rested them upon the wood floor of the cabin as I sniffed the air with my new, sensitive nose.

I was there, and yet I wasn't. It's difficult to describe. It's like being trapped in your own body like you're being forced to watch a movie through your own eyes, only that movie is your life, and you're doing things that you don't want to do, would never do if you had control of your body.

I padded to the front door, opened it, bent down, and took in the strong scent of my urine upon the steps. I left the door open as I walked out into the snow on two legs, loped forward on all fours, stood up to walk on two, and loped forward again, sniffing the air for prey.

A loud, ringing howl erupted from out of the southern woods, and I answered it in kind, raising my head to howl a mating call in return.

I did not have to wait long for an answer. The shadow of the beast appeared from behind the woodshed, and he loped around the old, falling down shed from out of the dark and into the moonlight, the padding on all fours until he was ten feet from me. He stood on two legs, stood close to seven feet tall, and stared at me with his piercing, golden eyes.

A low rumble emerged from my throat as a challenge, and he dropped into a lower stance as he growled in return. I dropped into a low stance as well, growling away, waiting to pounce.

We charged each other, both leaping at the same time, both colliding in midair. He spun me around as I snapped at his head, and he bit into my left shoulder, drawing a little blood as we clawed at each other's chests. His claws raked across my newly enlarged breasts, and ooooh, that one stung. I returned his stinging rake with my nasty bite, sinking my fangs into his left arm, tasting some of his blood, hot and salty and wild, and then I was flying through the air as he threw me off him.

I rolled in the packed snow with a yelp as he leaped atop me, and I snapped at his head as he pinned me down beneath his heavyweight, and even with my new great strength, I could barely budge him.

I rolled over in his grasp to where he was atop my back. I struggled against him as his monstrous, fully erect dong entered my cream-soaked hole. It slid up into my monstrous pussy, connecting us once again by this insane, instinctual mating. He thrust hard into me, once, twice, and then a third time before I was able to push up from the ground and drag myself toward the cabin's open doorway.

He nipped at my shoulders and the back of my neck, and I yelped from these warning bites, but I continued to drag him forward toward the open doorway, pulling him closer to my own urine-soaked steps.

He pinned me down again and pumped into me hard and fast, a BAM, BAM, BAM that made me stop and just take it for a few seconds. My huge new breasts bobbed back and forth from this pounding, and it felt good, really fucking good, so good that I huffed out a few frozen breaths before struggling against him yet again.

I pulled him forward again, but he was strong, and he refused to pull his penis from me, so I was hammered as I dragged him to the entrance of the doorway. He had a man's body, thick and muscular, ebon-skinned and covered in black fur, and he fucked my brown-skinned female body, an hourglass in comparison, with big fucking tits that my normal body probably couldn't have handled. I still had my heart-shaped bottom, still had my wet and flowing snatch, so his thick cock pounded into me, and hammered my wet pussy without mercy.

He nipped me hard on the back of my neck, and I yelped loudly this time, but I refused to give up. I dragged the beast into the cabin, squeezing us both through the tight doorframe and onto the wooden floor of the heated domicile.

I panted and yelped as he bit into my back and shoulders, all the while fucking me with that huge cock between his muscular, angled legs. Oh, it felt so good, even the nipping bites, and I wanted to stop and enjoy it, but the human part of me urged the outer beast to continue forward, coaxed it forward without stopping.

I tried to drag him forward, but he did me the favor instead. He picked me up and ran me forward to slam me down in front of the oak-tree coffee table, exactly where I wanted to be, where I needed him to be.

I panted and took his pounding cock for a few minutes. It felt so good, so Goddamned good to be hammered by that monstrous dong, and fully changing into a beast had only heightened my pleasure, made me more sensitive to the giant sable penis inside me.

He bit down into the back of my neck, paralyzing me into that submissive position I so hated. He thrust deep inside me, intent on finishing what he had started, and this time I could do nothing about it. I panted and whined as I was fucked hard in this strange, unnatural union, and then I came, a squirting and spraying of cum from my pussy over his long, thick, ebon-skinned cock.

I howled, his massive jaws still clamped around the back of my neck, and my engorged pussy squeezed his equally engorged cock over and over again. He released me, raised his head, and howled, and then he came inside me, squirting his magma-hot semen deep inside me, filling up my monstrous tunnel with his monstrous seed.

He gripped my sides and ground his muscular hips into me, ground his huge glans into my cervix, and I took it, shivering and shaking in my unholy insemination.

He pulled back his long penis, and I felt every inch of it as I had before, but this time...this time was different.

"Now!" my human mind commanded.

Whether it had been a dream or not, whether the lady in the moon had given me the power of command over the beast or not, my bestial self followed my command and did as my human mind instructed.

My bestial self, that wild and primal part that controlled my body, reached forth a brown-furred, clawed hand and snatched up the heavy silver shackle I had previously stowed beneath my oak-tree coffee table. She and I say 'she' because I was not fully in control of her, she swung the shackle around like the male beast's huge penis popped free from her, and then that shackle clamped around his ankle, the manacle locking in place with that one, timely swing.

The great ebony beast let forth a loud yelp, and he turned to escape, but he fell to his hands and knees, trying desperately to crawl to the open doorway and the snowy outdoors beyond it. I loped to the door, shut it, and then locked it, flicking the lock as easily as any human bitch could.

The great black wolf's head of the beast laid down upon my wood floor and breathed through his nose, in and out, in and out, the only action he could commit now that he was shackled by whatever ancient and arcane magics held him in place.

I loped to him, nuzzled my nose into his, and licked his great, sable-furred head with my long tongue. He whined as a dog would whine, so I laid down next to him and joined my body heat with his.

He was mine. Come morning, I would finally know who my other lover was, I would finally look upon his human face, and I would finally know who spread this gift and this curse to me. Then...Then I could make a choice. I could choose between the man...or the beast.

I laid there with him until he closed his golden eyes, looking upon this magnificent beast caged, this golden-eyed, wild and unnatural lover of mine. I fell asleep with him there, content for once that I finally had some control back in my life.

*****

I sat up in the dawn light and groaned. I had slept on the floor next to my unnatural lover, the wood floor not good for one's restful sleep, and all of the nips and bites and scratches I had didn't help my general well-being, either.

I moved my head to the right and the left, cracking my neck to pull out the stiffness of last night's monster fuck-fest, and a fuck-fest it had been. Holy shit.

"Fuuuck me," I groaned.

Okay. It was time to see who in the hell this creature was. I turned my head to investigate the shackled and sleeping nude male next to me, and...

"WHAT THE FUCK!" I screeched in a sudden rage.

Son of a bitch. That son of a motherfucking bitch. It was Daniel.

You have got to be fucking kidding me. You've got to be fucking kidding me, right? So it was Daniel who bit me? It was Daniel who came into the house each night and fucked me like a little bitch, fucked me like a bitch out in the snow, just downright fucked me over? So I'm a werewolf now because of Daniel? Fuuuuck.

My name is Saoirse Lennon. My dad moved us out to Lonesome Moon as a passive-aggressive way of keeping me in line. I've been into the drugs, the booze, and the boys since I was sixteen, a year after my mom died. Now I'm twenty-two, and I haven't changed at all since I was sixteen...until now. Little did my dad know that Lonesome Moon had a resident werewolf, and now that werewolf has spread his curse to me.

I'm a twenty-two-year-old white girl of Irish descent, and my name is pronounced 'Ser- Sha' if you didn't know. I'm five-eight, weigh one hundred and thirty-eight pounds, have C-cup breasts with beautiful pink nipples, and I have a nice ass, an ass that boys like to get handsy with. I have long, curly brown hair that falls to my shoulders with brown eyes to match, and overall, I could catch my fair share of boys, but I never felt like eating them before, as in actually eating them, you know, like steak.

Fucking Daniel. Daniel Christianson, whom I did not know at all, I only thought I did, is my closest neighbor at twelve miles away through snow and pine trees, because that's all that's out here in our little section of bumfuck nowhere. The nearest town, Lonesome Moon, is forty minutes away through heavy, snowbound coniferous forest, so...that made me an easy target for the local werewolf. Go figure.

Daniel stands six-foot with all-natural muscle, and he has short black hair, ocean-blue eyes, and a thick, succulent, circumcised cock that I've been...uhh...' exercising' quite a bit lately...Wait...How fucking old is he, anyway? He looks a little older than me, so I've assumed that he's about twenty-three, twenty-four. I have no idea. I'll have to ask him...if I don't throttle him first.

To make a long story short, my dad went into town five nights ago for a house-flipping project, so I've been here at the cabin watching over things while he's gone. All I wanted to do was smoke weed, drink whiskey, masturbate, watch movies, and dick around on the Net, you know, normal stuff. That went to hell on the first night of the full moon. I got bitten by a werewolf on night one, I was in a fucking coma from the attack all through night two, I met Daniel and fucked him twice on day three, I got fucked by the werewolf in my bed on night three, I fucked Daniel on day four, got fucked twice by the werewolf on night four, fucked Daniel yet again on day five, and got fucked one more time by the werewolf on night five, the last night of the full moon.

People who say they have no fucks to give...have never lived my life, because apparently, I had eight fucks to give. They were fantastic fucks, though, so it's not like I'm complaining about the actual sex. It's the bite plus the lycanthropy that I'm complaining about.

Let me explain why I'm upset. Daniel's dad is a veterinarian, but he's also a 'hunter', one of those people that hunt monsters. I was under the assumption that Daniel was also a 'hunter' because he knew things that only one of those 'hunters' would know. He stole a magical bracelet from his dad, a shackle of sorts, and this thing works on lycanthropes and immobilizes them with some kind of hidden power that neither I nor Daniel understands. Daniel wanted to use that shackle on me during the fifth moon because the fifth moon is the strongest in the cycle of the werewolf, but I had a plan, so I ended up using the shackle on my werewolf lover instead. Turns out that the werewolf...was Daniel all along.

I feel like the world's biggest idiot. I should have known it was Daniel. The clues were there all along, but I stupidly ignored them. Daniel was never here when the werewolf showed up, and Daniel showed up the very next day after my attack. Not to mention that the werewolf had black fur and black skin, the same color as Daniel's hair. That's significant because my skin and fur changed to the color of my hair when I 'wolfed out'.

Now that I think about it, Daniel must have had a key to the house, as well. I know I locked the kitchen door the night I was bitten, I could've sworn I did, but he walked right in the next morning, right before I passed out. His folks did own the place before us, so it figures he would have a key. God, I feel so stupid. He was playing me all along!

Now it's the morning of day six, and I've woken up naked next to my captured werewolf lover, right here in the middle of the cabin living room, but...lo and behold...my bestial 'lover' happened to be my human lover all along...I should have seen this coming. I am a fucking idiot.

So yeah...that happened.

*****

Okay. It was time to see who in the hell this creature was. I turned my head to investigate the shackled and sleeping nude male next to me, and...

"WHAT THE FUCK!" I screeched in a sudden rage.

Son of a bitch. That son of a motherfucking bitch. It was Daniel.

His eyelids fluttered open as he stared up at me with those ocean-blue eyes. Me? It's a good thing I knew what color his eyes were because all I could see was red.

"You son of a bitch!" I yelled down at him.

"Sao...irse..." said Daniel in a weak reply.

"You did this to me!" I shrieked. "How could you do this to me!"

Uuuuhhh..." groaned Daniel.

'Answer me!" I cried. "I said, answer me, GODDAMMIT!

He stared up at me and let forth a piteous whine. It was like a 'nnnnngggnnng' sound, and my brain finally put two and two together.

"Oh, right," I huffed out. "That stupid shackle."

Shit. I didn't know what to do about that shackle. Daniel couldn't move at all as long as it was on him, and only he had the key. However, my dilemma was solved a moment later.

"Key...here..." groaned Daniel.

"Here?" I asked. "Here in the cabin, here?"

"Yesss..." hissed Daniel.

This was good news. If the key was here, then I could unlock that shackle, properly chew him out, and then punish him for this bullshit. I wanted him at full steam for the hammer I was going to drop on him, and if you're wondering, that punishment will probably involve his balls in some way...Goddamn him!

"Where?" I asked. "Where is it?"

"Pil...low..." grunted Daniel.

"Pillow?" I asked. "What pillow?...My pillow? On my bed?"

"Yesss..." hissed Daniel.

I trotted to my room, flung open my bedroom door, and rushed to my bed. I picked up my pillow, and there was the key, in the folds of my bedsheet. I snatched up that plain iron key and made my way back to Daniel's prone, immobile form.

I held the key up in front of his face so that his blue eyes could properly see it, just like he'd done to me the day before.

"You see this!" I spat at him. "I'm going to unlock that shackle with this, and then you'd better start explaining, and it had better be a good one...Honestly, though...I should cut off your balls and feed them to you...Fucking...Ooooh!...You...You are in such deep shit...Never piss off an Irish girl, Danny boy. Fucking idiot."

I knelt next to him and sat my bare butt upon the floor. I lifted his left leg and swiveled the shackle around so that the lock was where I could get at it. I pushed in the key, turned it, and the shackle popped open a second later. I pulled it from him and tossed it aside, it's heavyweight landing on the wood floor with a loud thump. Daniel groaned and sat up a moment later.

"Saoirse..." he started to say.

I cut him off before he could finish that sentence.

"You bastard!" I yelled.

I slapped him across his left cheek with my right hand, and then my pent-up rage got the better of me, and I was smacking at him with both hands a second later. He held up both arms to fend me off, but I was hot under the collar.

"Stop!" he cried. "Saoirse, stop!"

"You son of a bitch!" I hissed, but I stopped hitting him.

"Why are you...?" stammered Daniel. "Why are you mad at me?... What am I...? Why am I even here? I should be at the lodge...Oh, no..." 'What the fuck are you talking about!" I yelled. "It was you the whole time!

Daniel gave me the most confused look in the world, and...my heart jumped in my throat...Did he honestly not know what I was talking about? That couldn't be right...right?

"What?" he asked. "I don't...I don't know what you're talking about. I shouldn't even be here..."

Okay, either he was an exceptionally good liar, or something funny was going on.

"No shit," I growled. "You shouldn't be here. Do you know what you've done? Do you have any idea at all what you've done!"

"No...What?" asked Daniel, and he looked thoroughly confused at my justified railing against his actions. "I should be at the lodge in the holding cell..."

My brain screeched to a halt. Yeah, something funny was definitely going on here.

"Holding cell?" I asked. "What holding cell?... And I know you're a werewolf, Daniel, so don't lie to me anymore. When you say 'holding cell', what exactly are you talking about?"

"I have a cell I'm locked in during the full moon," explained Daniel. "I should be in it. There can't be two werewolves running around out here at night...not with you already inflicted with the curse. That other werewolf is still in the..."

"What other werewolf!" I yelled, and he flinched at the sheer rage I was throwing at him. "The...The other one I've been tracking..." said Daniel.

I threw up my hands in frustration. Was he stupid, or did he not know?

"And where did those tracks lead?" I asked, my voice full of venom.

"They led here," said Daniel. "Here...around the forest north and south of here, and outside the lodge."

"Uh huh," I nodded. "Right...And what does that tell you?"

"That it's been trying to get at me," said Daniel with wide eyes. "Maybe trying to free me. It bit you, so it's been trying to get at you as well. Probably for...uhhh..."

"For what, Daniel?" I asked, my lips a tight line of angst.

"For...other things..." said Daniel as his voice trailed off.

I set my hands down upon the wooden floor of the cabin and stared at them for a moment. We were both still very naked, both still covered in scratches and minor bite marks, and he still hadn't connected the dots.

I looked up at him and gave him a nasty scowl.

"Let me guess," I said unhappily. "It's been coming here to fuck me, right?"

"Y...Yeah," said Daniel. "I've been trying to figure out who it is without telling my dad. He doesn't know about it. I don't want him finding out about you...yet...Why are you looking at me like that?"

I gave him a nasty smirk and nodded my head a couple of times.

"It's already fucked me, Daniel," I said, and my voice was laced with that previous angst.

It...It has?" asked Daniel in visible surprise.

"Yes, Daniel," I said with a sarcastic smile. "It came into the cabin and fucked me on the third night...in my own bed, I might add."

"It did?" asked Daniel, and I could tell that he was shocked at this news.

"Yes," I confirmed with a slow nod. "It fucked me that night, and then it fucked me twice on the fourth night, and then yet again last night."

"No..." said Daniel with a shake of his head. "No, that can't be...That...That's not true...is it?" "Mmm, hmm," I replied. "Let me ask you something first, though...Do you remember anything at all about the last five nights?"

"No," he said unhappily. "I locked myself in the lodge, and come morning, I would wake up in the cell...until today. I should still be in the cell. Why am I here? I don't understand why I'm here..."

"Who lets you out in the morning?" I asked because something was truly fucked up here. "I do," breathed Daniel.

"You do?" I asked.

"Y...yeah," replied Daniel. "I flip the safety latch and let myself out."

I groaned as I smacked myself in the forehead with my right hand, wiping my hand down my face in pure, unmitigated frustration. It was clear to me now what had been going on.

I dropped my hand back to the floor and gave him the nastiest look I could muster.

"Werewolves can unlock and open doors, Daniel," I said in pure unhappiness. "Did you not know that? Because I found that out when one walked into my room and fucked the ever-living fuck out of me in my own bed. Ten inches of big beast dick rammed my hole until I howled. It left me walking funny. That's not a joke."

"I...It...How...Wha...What?" he stammered.

Okay. This all made sense now. Apparently, Daniel had been locking himself away at night, but since he can't remember anything when he's 'wolfed out', then he wouldn't have known he was escaping his cell to go full beast out in the wilderness...and of course, coming over here to fuck his bitch during those times, namely me, the one he'd bitten and inflicted with a Goddamned lycanthropy curse.

"There is no other werewolf, Daniel," I said in a flat tone. "You've been following your tracks. I know, because you came here last night to fuck me again, which you did, but I used the shackle on you instead of on myself."

His expression would have been hilarious were the situation not so serious. His face crumpled up into a look of guilt or horror or a mix of the two...probably a mix of the two.

"No...No, that can't be right..." he said, and I could tell that he was in denial.

"It is," I said firmly. "You're the one that bit me on the first night of the full moon. You're also the one that plowed me with that ten-inch long werewolf dick every night for the last three nights. You've also squirted enough monster sperm in me to bear four litters...Seriously, this is fucked. You are honestly telling me that you had no idea that werewolves could open latches and unlock doors?"

"No," said Daniel, and I could tell that he was shaken now. "No...No, I didn't know..."

Fuuuuuck. I can't even be mad at him anymore. Fuck! Fuuuuuuuck!

I wiped my right hand down my face again and shook my head.

"Well, isn't this wonderful," I said unhappily. "I'll tell you what...I'm putting on some clothes, and then I'm going to eat something...then I'm going to take a bath and wash some of this monster spooge out of my massively wrecked, thoroughly fucked snatch...You...You are going to get the hell out of my house."

Daniel laid his right hand upon my bare shoulder, but I flinched at his touch.

"Saoirse," he said, and his voice was shaky, wavering in tone. "I didn't know..."

I watched in fascination as tears began to form in his blue eyes, those ocean-blue eyes set in the middle of that handsome face, that short black hair wild from last night's monster fuck-fest, his all-natural muscle rippling in those luscious pecs of his...Goddammit...Now he's making me feel like shit...and horny...Goddammit!

"I don't see how you couldn't know," I said quietly. "I remember everything. I fully changed last night, and I didn't have much control over myself...but...I remember everything."

"How?" he asked as he wiped at his own tears. "I can't...I can never remember anything afterward."

"Well, I guess I'm special," I frowned. "Look...This is all fucked up. You have cursed me, Daniel. Curr-ess-ed-me. That means, for the rest of my life, I'm going to change into a ravenous...and somehow really horny...bloodthirsty monster every full moon. I'm pretty sure that's going to fuck with my life choices...Why couldn't you just have herpes or something?...No, wait...I'm pretty sure I'd still pick lycanthropy over that."

Daniel lowered his head and then shook it.

"This is my fault," he said.

"Damn right, it is," I scowled. "Look, you owe me, Danny boy."

Daniel raised his head and gave me a truly flustered look.

"I...I can't do anything for you...What can I do?" he asked. "There's nothing I can do, Saoirse. I didn't know that I could unlock doors, and I didn't know this would happen. I thought the system my parents put in place was working..."

"Wait..." I said unhappily. "What about your dad? Is he still going to kill me when he finds out?... This is such bullshit...You know what? Fuck it. I'll fucking tell him myself."

"Saoirse..." began Daniel, his handsome face twisting in a panic.

Oh, I was going to get under his skin. He needed to squirm. In fact...Oh, yeah. I knew what to do.

"I think that's exactly what needs to happen," I said angrily.

I reached forward and held his head in both hands, and he stared into my eyes with open surprise.

"You owe me big time," I growled. "From now on...From this moment on...you are mine, Danny boy...Every part of you..."

I reached down, grabbed his big balls with my right hand, and watched in satisfaction as he winced when I gave them a light squeeze. I took this time to do a little thinking, because I had an idea, and I just needed to voice it in order to make it come together.

"He can't kill me if you and I are mates," I said, my lips pursed in thought.

"Wh...What?" stammered Daniel.

"You heard me," I said forcefully. "From now on, you're mine. You're my boyfriend...No...You're my mate...Hell, you've already pumped enough sperm in me to get me pregnant...I'm not saying I am, mind you, but..."

"Are you?" asked Daniel, his blue eyes widening yet again.

I gave his balls a firm squeeze this time. He squeezed his eyes shut in return as he grimaced, and this gave me a moment of temporary satisfaction.

"You don't ask that question!" I said a little angrier than I had intended.

"Saoirse..." he squeaked.

I realized that I was accidentally squeezing his balls a little too hard...Men...They're supposed to be the great protectors, yet they have their balls on the outsides of their bodies...Jesus...Even evolution thinks they're lacking common sense.

"You're mine now," I declared, and this time I eased up on his balls.

"Saoirse, I don't..." he started to say.

I squeezed his balls again and watched with smug satisfaction as his face twisted in pain...Hey...He shouldn't have let me grab them. His problem, not mine.

"You don't get a say," I huffed. "You're mine now, and I'm in control. You'll just have to live with it, just like you learned to live with this curse...Hey...Hey, wait a minute! You don't have any scars on your body! I know, because I've inspected every part of you up close. How in the hell are you a werewolf at all?"

"It...happened when I was...a little kid..." winced Daniel. "Saoirse, please..."

I eased up on him once more and nodded my head in response. I wanted to hear this story. "Okay, Danny boy," I said smugly. "Explain."

"My dad went on a hunt and came back with a book," grimaced Daniel. "It was an old book written in Latin. It was written in the Middle Ages...I was ten. I could read, obviously, but my dad made the mistake of leaving the book where I could find it. He was going to send it off somewhere, which he did, but I never did find out where...Wherever the headquarters of the other hunters are...He won't tell me because of...you know...Anyway, I got into the book and read from it because I thought the words looked funny. I couldn't read Latin...still can't..."

"And?" I asked.

"It cursed me," he said unhappily. "The book was cursed. I later found out it was bound in human skin."

"Eww," I said.

I can't even imagine that...So there's shit like that in the world? I wonder what else is real?... Are other types of shit real?... Mummies and vampires and shit?... Wait, wait...Doesn't matter. I'm getting off-topic.

"So you got cursed, and now you're a werewolf," I frowned. "So you're parents just...just locked you up every month? Is that what you're telling me?" "Yeah," nodded Daniel. "Thing is, we worked out a system three months ago where I could just go to the lodge myself and let myself out...We honestly thought that was working..."

"Three months?" I asked. "That's right before we got here...Oh, shit...Have you bitten anyone else?"

Daniel's face sparked up in alarm.

"I...I don't know..." he said, and this time I could tell that he was genuinely upset.

"Well...now you know," I frowned. "Here's the thing...We...not you...We, together, are going to tell your parents what's going on. I don't want to wake up to find your father murdering me in my bed..."

"Saoirse..." began Daniel in obvious protest.

I squeezed his balls hard, and he shut up pretty quickly. I eased off the pressure after that and shook my head no.

"You don't get to speak," I said firmly.

He frowned and gave me an unhappy look.

"Don't give me that look," I frowned in return. "You were stupid enough to let me grab your balls, so now you're fucked. It only takes two pounds of pressure for me to rip them off, you know. At least, that's what I've read on the Net...In fact, I should just geld you right now to keep you from doing this to anyone else...Yeah, I'd like to see you grow those back. Regenerate that shit, Danny boy...Now shut up and listen. Nod your head if you understand."

He frowned and nodded his head twice. Oh, yeah, I was in control now.

"Okay," I said firmly. "We're going to tell your parents, and then every month I'll be joining you at the lodge. We'll have to fix the lock. We can't be roaming around the countryside, as you've already proven."

Daniel's muscular shoulders sank as his expression collapsed into guilt, but it serves him right. He's fucked me, and in more ways than one, so he deserves a little guilt.

"I'm still pissed at you," I said unhappily, "but I...I'm willing to be with you...Yeah, I don't know you, clearly, but I'm willing to be with you. My dad will probably like you, mainly because you're the type of guy that's...well, at least, looks responsible and not, like, a stoner or anything. Anyway...Anyway, we'll be together, and that should keep your dad off of me, especially if I'm willing to work with him and keep this lycanthropy thing under wraps. Plus, I don't know yet if you got me pregnant while you were pumping me full of werewolf semen. We'll just have to play that by ear."

"So...you're not making that up then?" he asked in slight confusion. "I did come in and...I..."

"Oh, yeah," I nodded vigorously. "Yeah...Apparently, ten inches of thick cock is not something most girls should wish for."

I watched in slight amusement as Daniel's eyes wandered to the side in thought, but there was a satisfying upturn of his lips as he processed that statement.

"Yeah, yeah," I frowned. "Don't get a big head...The big head you did get really tore me up inside. You're lucky I didn't have to head to the E.R. for urgent care or anything."

"I'm sorry," he said unhappily.

"Good," I said firmly. "You should be...That comes to part two of this plan."

Part two?" he asked.

"Yep," I smirked. "Up you go, Danny boy!"

I stood up but didn't let go of his balls. He cried out in pain as he stood, but I made sure to keep a tight grip on him. I wasn't letting go of him just yet.

"We're both going to get dressed," I said firmly. "It's about Goddamned time I wore some actual clothes...Walking around in the buff is fun, mind you, but I don't have the urge to do it right now...probably on account of there being no full moon tonight...It doesn't matter. What matters is...now that I have some common sense back in my head...you know...no urge to just fuck and fight all of the time...you and I are taking a little trip."

"What?" asked Daniel in surprise. "Where?"

I finally let go of his balls, put my hands on my hips, and gave him the staredown.

"We're going to your family's lodge," I frowned.

"What?" asked Daniel once more. "Why? There won't be another full moon until..."

"Uh, uh," I said as I shook my head. "No arguments. We are going to that Goddamned lodge, and then you...yes, you...are going to call your mom from there. She needs to know about all of this...this fucked up mess."

His handsome face flushed red as he blinked at me in what had to be total comprehension of what I had just said.

"I'd rather my parents not know about my sex life..." he began to say, but I cut him off.

"Tough," I said firmly. "Your mom needs to know what happened because that should keep your dad from going psycho on me." 'You don't know my father," winced Daniel.

"I don't have to," I replied in a flat tone. "All we have to do is make me look like a little angel, a straight-up 'victim' of their plan...You know what I'm talking about? They designed the 'safety latch' that was supposed to keep you in. We just guilt trip them into taking all of the blame, and then I'm safe. Not only that, but I'll have access to the information I need to know about how to keep this curse under control...I won't say a thing about this to my dad, though. I'll find a work-around on that end. Even so, this is the best plan I've got, but I think it will work, because...because it has to."

Daniel sighed as his broad, muscular shoulders slumped in what was obvious defeat.

"Okay," he said after a quiet moment of visible thought. "We'll try it your way...but...Saoirse...it's going to be really, really tough to convince them."

"Convince them of what?" I asked.

I mean, it sounded pretty solid to me. I could wheel and deal with this. There was no reason off the top of my head that I could think of as to why it wouldn't work. Of course, his reply to my little question still managed to piss me off.

"To convince them that you're a little angel," chuckled Daniel.

"Mother...fucker..." I hissed.

I grabbed his right shoulder with my left hand, spun him around, and gave him a rather harsh and a rather loud smack to his bare left butt cheek. He jumped and rubbed his bare ass with both hands.

*****

CHAPTER 4

I walked out of the Bolten's local supermarket with my paper bag full of groceries, and that's when I spotted them. There they were, easily talking to each other, a close and confidential manner, like they had known each other forever like they knew each other in a closer than just 'friends' manner.

It made my breath seize up in my throat, and I felt a terrible wrenching in my chest, that feeling you get when your heart is being squeezed, your metaphorical heart, the one that's just as valuable as the beating organ within your ribcage.

It was Daniel. It was my old flame, my one true love, but he was with someone else. This new girl was taller than me, and she was gorgeous. I was gorgeous, of course, but that's not the point. The point was that he was with someone else, a beautiful someone else, and that...that did not sit well with me.

This new girl had a good body, not too skinny, not too fat, with long, curly brown hair, brown eyes, and a model-worthy face. She was a heartbreaker, but she was with Daniel, and that made the shades go down inside my head. I didn't know who she was, but I needed to find out. It wasn't fair that Daniel was with someone else...someone who was not...me.

The weather was a little warmer today, so this girl was dressed in blue jeans, a red flannel shirt, black hiking boots, and a blue jean jacket, something very rustic in look and style...something very much to Daniel's tastes.

Daniel, of course, was dressed as he always was. He had on his dark blue jeans, tanned hiking boots, white undershirt, and blue work shirt over that. He was wearing his old tanned jacket, and this look, the look I fell in love with, made me long for him once more, but that longing was crippled, crippled by this...other girl.

My name is Megan, Megan Holly. I'm five-foot-two, Caucasian, German and French descent, actually, with short, dyed-blonde hair, an hourglass body, and C-cup breasts. I have beautiful green eyes, eyes I'm very proud of, but those eyes were green now for another reason. They were green with envy because this young woman standing next to and talking with MY former boyfriend had thoroughly pissed me off.

Today I was dressed in a white cotton print dress with little roses all over it, something old-fashioned but cute, and I had on my good white heels and my white bell-shaped cloth hat, the completed look of a very prim and proper young woman, a facade I put on when dealing with the yokels.

Still, this new girl...I was going to tear her apart for being anywhere near Daniel.

Nevertheless, if I'm anything, I'm judicious. Indeed, I hadn't seen Daniel for months now, not since we'd said our goodbyes for the last time, or rather, he did. He'd broken it off with me so abruptly back then, but that was before I found out about my...the little problem I now had. Even so, I had plans to get back with him, but those plans would have to be put on hold. This little bitch in front of me had to be dealt with first.

"I told you my dad would like you," said this young lady, this interloper.

This young woman shut the passenger-side door of Daniel's old red truck, and just that action, that action of stepping out of his vehicle, really burned inside me. Their current conversation did not help, either, not in the slightest.

"I'm just glad things worked out as they did," said Daniel, "but we've already gone over this a hundred times. Everything's good for now, so...let's just get something to eat...Besides, you'll like this place. It's a diner I've been going to since I was a kid."

"Well, it's got to be better than fast food," said the girl. "I cook most of the time, but I'd rather eat out on occasion, and if I'm going to eat out, I want it to be good."

This burned inside me. They were talking like...like...Never mind. I was fuming inside. Nevertheless, I was careful not to show it.

"Daniel?" I asked in mock surprise.

He looked over when he heard the sound of his name, but the look on his face when he saw me...He turned red with a cornered look, like a wild animal with nowhere left to run.

"Oh, shi..." he began, but he was cut off.

"Who is this?" asked the stranger, the interloper.

I ignored her. She was not worthy of my attention. Plus, I was going to kill her later, anyway.

"M...Megan," stammered Daniel. "I didn't think...It's just...What are you doing here?"

"I live here, silly," I smiled. "You know that. I was just picking up groceries for the house...Who's your little friend?"

This tall tart sized me up in one look. I could tell she was offended, but this only pleased me. She appeared to be the kind of girl that blew her top quite often...Good...I was going to enjoy torturing her before I killed her. Listening to her screams would be most entertaining.

"Little?" asked the stranger.

Daniel politely shook his head no at her and then stepped up to talk to me...Ugh...Finally. It was not right to leave me standing here with groceries in hand.

Megan, this is...uhhh...this is Saoirse," he replied.

Saoirse?" I replied. "That's an unusual name.

"It's Irish," frowned this girl.

"I see," I smiled. "Well...Are you visiting from somewhere? How is it that you know my Daniel?"

"Your Daniel...What?" asked this interloper in an offended tone.

"Megan..." said Daniel, and I could tell that he was embarrassed. "Saoirse is my...my girlfriend."

"Oh..." I said, but I had already figured this out.

It was clear that he had gone and gotten a little fuck toy to soothe his baser urges. Of course, that still didn't change the fact that I was boiling inside. Even so, I knew how to play this game.

"I...I didn't know you had...but you never said anything about..." I stammered.

I put on my best 'wilting' face...You know? The kind where your face just slowly melts into visible disappointment? It was necessary for the guilt I needed to inflict upon him.

You see, I know Daniel quite well. I've known him since we were kids. I'd always thought we were going to be together forever, to be joined at the hip until we died, but...he never told me about his little secret, a secret that he should have revealed when we had first started dating. That, unfortunately, I discovered on my own...but that's beside the point. I knew all of his buttons to push, so I was going to push them one...after...the...other.

Megan..." sighed Daniel. "I...This isn't how I wanted to...Dammit...

"It's fine," I said as I wiped a tear from my right eye. "It's...just...This was unexpected." "Megan...we'll...we'll talk about this later," said Daniel. "I'll...I'll call you."

"Of course," I sniffed. "I have to get home, anyway. I don't want my ice cream to melt." "Yeah..." said Daniel in uncomfortable pause.

"We'll talk later," I choked out. "I have to...go...now..."

I held my face in my right hand, sobbed once, turned, and quickly walked away, knowing full well that Daniel was feeling that guilty knife twist in his heart. He was going to regret that little whore he was with, that was a promise. He'd probably grieve for her once she was gone, but...she looked like trailer trash, anyway.

I walked to my little blue car, my high heels clicking on the pavement, but walking away now was what needed to happen, because this left things unresolved, exactly how I wanted them to be.

I drove home, not a far distance from town, drove to my little house, and pulled into my little driveway. I took a moment to wipe away the smudges in my eyeliner with a tissue, smudges made by tears, some of them actually genuine, and then I reapplied my makeup for the task at hand. I had a hungry boy to feed, but...first things first. I needed to relieve my stress.

My little house was a gift of sorts...I couldn't possibly afford my own home on my meager income, but my Aunt Renee had given me the place when she had moved onward to the city, a gift I would probably never be able to repay, but I was her only niece, alone in the big world, not even a...sniff...man to call my own...That was untrue, but she didn't need to know that. It was a nice gesture by her, though, but in truth, I think she just didn't want to give up the old family residence. She still owned the place, after all.

But enough of that. I had a task to perform, so I walked to the front door and opened it. It was unlocked, but that was due to the two people I had waiting inside. It may seem stupid to leave two strangers in your home while you shop, but I had a reason for this insanity. Thanks to my little 'problem', I could see a person's aura, and that colorful ring told me all kinds of things about the people I came across daily. I knew my 'guests' wouldn't cause me any trouble.

"I'm baaaaack!" I called out as I shut the door behind me. "Let me just put these groceries away, and then we'll have a little meet and greet, get to know each other better."

The first of the two drifters stood up and grinned at me from within his red beard. His name was Darren, a tall white man in his early thirties, someone on a road trip to where- the-fuck-ever, someone with a good bit of natural muscle, tats on his arms, blue jeans, blue jean vest, black undershirt...He was a little ugly in the face, but still fuckable. His aura wavered between red, purple, gold, pink, and pearl, the colors of wrath, pride, greed, love, and fidelity, so he was shifty in attitude and bearing, but he was also malleable to the point where he was kept in line by his significant other.

His girlfriend was a little younger than he, a young white woman in her mid-twenties, with jet-black hair, blue eyes, a thin figure...beautiful face...small breasts, good hips...Very, very fuckable. She wore dark blue jeans, a white T-shirt that she somehow kept clean, little black booties...Oh, her look was simple, but she had made it her own. Her name was Sam, and I have to admit a little guilty pleasure...She was the one I wanted. Her aura wavered between red, pink, pearl, light-blue, and teal, the colors of wrath, love, fidelity, compassion, and mercy, so she was a prize I was going to keep. Why she was with Darren confounded me, however. The guy was a quick, disposable fuck as far as I was concerned...Ah, well. I'd sort her out.

I'd lured these two in from the bus stop. I had no idea where they thought they were going or what they thought they were doing with their lives, but they wouldn't have to worry about that for much longer. They reminded me of hippies, but without all of the 'peace and love' pot-smoking crap...No matter. I had plans for them.

"It's awful nice that you let us stay for a bit," grinned Darren. "I didn't think there were hospitable folks anymore, especially with the terrible year we've had."

"Nonsense," I giggled. "There are plenty of good people in the world. You just haven't met any."

I quickly put my groceries away and walked into my tiny living room, and my 'guests' sat back down upon my rose print couch, so I took to my dark-green comfort chair. I liked the colors of a garden, so my little house was decked out as such, whatever I could afford as a teller for the local bank.

"It is nice of you to take us in," said Sam. "It's kind of dangerous, though, to just pick up strangers, especially for...well...you living all alone, you know.

We're not that way, but...it bothers me a little that you would just...well..."

It was indeed dangerous to pick up strangers...Sam had some working brain cells...not many, but...you know...But anyway, I needed to get this show on the road. It was time to heat things.

"Oh, you're welcome," I smiled. "I know it's dangerous to pick up strangers, but I'm an excellent judge of character, and I knew by looking at the both of you that you were all right...However, I think you have the wrong idea about me. I may look it, but I'm not some little angel. The truth is...I was being entirely selfish for inviting you over."

Oh..." said Sam uncertainly. "How so?

"Oh, I haven't had a good fuck in a while," I shrugged. "I was wondering if you wouldn't mind if I fucked your boyfriend."

This young woman's blue eyes widened as she stared at me in disbelief. I think she was trying to work out what I had just said.

"Wh...What?" she asked in confusion.

"I'm horny," I shrugged again. "I was thinking to pick up someone down at the bar, but I know everyone in town, and word gets around. I saw you two, and I thought...why not?"

This young lady, Sam, stood up and shook her head no, rage building upon her pretty face. I could tell that I had royally pissed her off, but that was understandable. I did just ask to fuck her boyfriend.

"You can't...You can't ask something like that!" she said angrily.

"Oh, dear," I frowned. "I think you've misunderstood me...It's not just him I wanted to fuck."

"What?" asked Sam. "What are you...?"

"I think you're beautiful, Sam," I said as I shrugged yet again. "I saw you, and I thought...Oh my God. I so want to kiss that gorgeous face. He's so lucky to have her...I got to thinking...What if I let them stay for a while, and then maybe, just maybe, we could all...all three of us...have some fun together."

"I...I uhhh...Oh..." stammered Sam as her face turned red.

"It's not like I want to steal either one of you from each other," I said nonchalantly. "I just thought we could have a little fun before you leave town...I mean, both of you are very attractive, and...Oh...Oh, dear...You don't think I'm ugly, do you?"

Not at all," said Darren.

I looked over at Darren's grinning face...Oh, he was already on board. He was definitely ready to leave the dock, but I already expected that reaction from him. It was Sam I was going to have to convince.

"Darren!" objected Sam.

"What?" he replied as he grinned up at her.

"I can see that you're reticent, Sam," I said, "but I meant it when I said that you were beautiful...Is this a lesbian-hating thing? I'm not a lesbian if you wanted to know. I'm just bi-curious. I've never been with a woman before, but you...do something to me...Do you have something against the bi-curious? Are you reluctant because I'm a girl? Is that it?"

She looked at me with the oddest look, something I really couldn't decipher. I don't know if she was confused, horrified, or what. I think I broke her brain.

"No, it's just..." began Sam, but this time I cut her short.

I stood up and walked over to her, and she backed away a little, probably in anxious apprehension. I took her hands into mine and stared up into her blue eyes, my expression one of longing and hope.

"Please?" I asked so demurely. "Do it for me? I just need a little love to keep going..."

I reached up, gently cradled her head in my right hand, and brought her lips down to mine. We kissed lightly at first, and then my tongue slid over hers, and then we were making out right in front of her boyfriend, both of us making out in loud smacking noises.

It's in the pheromones. One taste of my saliva does it. I don't know exactly how it works, but it does. Like my ability to see and read auras, I consider it one of the little 'perks' of my equally little 'problem'.

We unlocked lips, and I stared longingly up into her wide blue eyes.

"Won't you join me for some fun?" I asked softly.

She didn't say anything. No, she merely nodded rapidly several times in reply. I could smell her, too. Her pussy was already wet. It's the lust I carry around like a disease. It goes straight to the brain and then to the loins.

I looked over toward Darren, that troll of a man still sitting on my white print couch. He had the biggest grin on his face, and looking at the throbbing bulge in his jeans, he was already willing to partake in some of my 'fun'. He didn't even need any of my special 'help' to convince him.

"Let's get comfortable," I said.

I grabbed the hem of Sam's white T and pulled it upward, but she removed it for me, throwing it to my light-brown carpet. She reached behind herself, undid her bra, and tossed it to the floor after that.

She had beautiful little B-cup breasts. Her tits were a dark-brown color, with small areolas and pert little nipples. I took her right nipple into my mouth and gently suckled it, and she arched her back and moaned in return.

I felt Darren's hands on my shoulders a moment later. He reached down and pulled up my dress from behind, and I popped off of Sam's nipple long enough for him to pull my article of clothing up and off me. My dress joined Sam's shirt on the floor, and then he undid my bra. I happily took off my bra in return, allowing my ample C-cups to jiggle free.

Sam bent and took my own left, dark-pink nipple into her mouth. It was my turn to moan, and I closed my eyes and raised my head toward the ceiling as she sucked on me, even as Darren pulled my white panties down around my ankles.

My own, heady, delicious scent flooded the room. I was wet, of course, my hairless, thoroughly bald, pink twat dripping and ready for pleasure. Sam sunk her left index and ring fingers into my soaking cunt, and then she pulled off of my nipple, pulling her fingers from my creamy snatch at the same time. She sucked hungrily on those fingers, tasting more of the strange magic I was infecting her with, her face a beacon of wanton lust, exactly what I expected of her.

"Let's go to the bedroom and make a sandwich," I said in a husky breath. "We'll make the bread, and Darren will supply the meat."

I stepped out of my panties and led them to my small bedroom, sauntering to show off my nude body, especially my beautiful, swaggering, heart-shaped butt. True, I was short, but I was built like a sex toy, so why not show it off when the opportunity arose?... Just saying.

My room had a double bed, something I bought just for situations like these, though, I must admit, such a thing would have never occurred to me before my little 'problem'. This 'problem' of mine had forced me to make many adjustments, expensive adjustments, adjustments that had wiped out my savings...Fucking Daniel...I'll deal with him later...Anyway, those adjustments included soundproofing the basement, installing an old-fashioned furnace, finding someone sketchy to supply me with manacles...but that was something I'd show them later. Right now, it was time to have fun in a different way than what was awaiting them down in the dark recesses of my little house.

I led Sam to the bed and urged her to lay down on my olive-green bedspread. She laid her head down between my two white pillows, her dark hair spilling all around her head, and

I pulled off her booties and little white ankle socks. I unbuttoned her dark blue jeans and pulled them off, and her light-blue panties came off after that. I quickly took off my high heels, and I was now completely nude, as were both Sam and her troll of a boyfriend.

Darren had practically ripped off his clothes as I was undressing Sam. His cock distracted me for a second, or rather the length of it, because though it wasn't thick, it was eight inches long and uncut. I hadn't known a man with a penis that long, and men his age that were uncut were fairly rare in the States...Hmm...Sam had lucked out with this guy, fucking troll that he happened to be.

The world average for a penis was five-and-a-half inches, and I'd fucked a couple of guys with average dicks, but Daniel's was the one I wanted to get back into my tight little tunnel. Even this Darren guy's cock didn't appeal to me as much as my Daniel's did. Lance had once told me all of the guys he knew had nine, ten-inch-long dicks, and also that he'd seen a man's fourteen-inch-long dick, but Lance was also full of shit, and he couldn't judge cock length for shit, and that was despite his bisexuality...Eh...I'm wandering again. I have some strangers to fuck, anyway.

I turned my attention back to Sam, and I had to admit, as lithe as she was, she had a gorgeous body. However, she was not shaved like me, so she had a large swath of black pubes around her chocolate brown pussy lips, those brown inner lips creamy white from her juices.

"Let's make a sandwich," I breathed as I laid down on top of her.

Our body heat mingled as we briefly rubbed nipples together, and then our wet snatches touched, and that's when the magic began. I tongued into her waiting mouth, slurping over her tongue with mine as her big, brown, leafy clit rubbed against my small, dark-pink one. We ground like this for a moment, moaning into each other's mouths, but I had to briefly detach from her to look up and back over my left shoulder.

Darren was standing there with eager, ecstatic eyes, that enormous grin still on his bearded face, his right hand stroking his long, skinny, uncut cock, his breath ragged and excited.

"Well?" I asked. "You have two slices of bread...Where's the salami? Get over here and start fucking between our pussies. You've got four wet buns for that hot dog."

"Oh, right," said Darren.

He practically jumped on the bed as he grabbed my curvy, heart-shaped butt from behind. His long meat slid between the folds of my bald, soaking vulva, slid between the folds of Sam's hairy wet twat, and then he was pounding into us a second after that. Sam and I had our legs spread in a V, my feet locked around her ankles, as Darren held up Sam's butt and moved us back and forth with his happy humping, the uncut head of his cock sliding between our pulsing clits as all three of us moaned in electric ecstasy.

Sam pulled away from my mouth and cried out in pure pleasure, her lips wide, her eyes squeezed tightly shut.

"Oh, God!" she squealed. "What the fuck!"

I could tell she was confused about how good this felt, but that 'telling' was more of a 'fact' as I felt a spurt of wetness upon my hairless lower lips, knowing full well Sam had already cum. That was good though because it further lubricated Darren's cock, and that meant more fun was on the way. That stiff organ was already poisoned with my juices, and that infection would keep his erection up, though he did not need to know that.

I lifted my ass and backed toward Darren, who backed up in return. I greedily slurped into Sam's hairy, cum-soaked snatch, slurping up her rich juices and reveling in that delicious taste. Sam's blue eyes widened as she gripped my head and cried out, openmouthed, surprised at the supreme pleasure I was inflicting upon her. Meanwhile, Darren did exactly as I expected him to. He gripped my big butt and slid his long uncut cock into my waiting, wet hole.

"Oh, fuck!" cried Sam. "Oh, oh, oh...It shouldn't feel this good! Why does it feel so good!"

I suckled her large clit while caressing it with my tongue. She had a big clit for a woman, like a tiny little penis, a little dick-shaped pink head surrounded by folds of the dark-brown hood, and this turned me on even more, and this was although Darren was already hammering my cervix with the glans of his long penis.

I huffed into Sam's hairy cunt as Darren continued to pound into me from behind. I gripped Sam's beautiful butt as I tongued deep into her creamy twat, rimming her hole for juices before sliding my taste organ in as deep as it would go.

"Oh, Oh, Oh God, Oh, Megan!" cried Sam. "What is this!"

I lifted my head from her twat and gave her a clever smile, my chin dripping with her white juices. She could see her boyfriend fucking me from behind, his eyes closed, his long cock pounding into my hairless pussy, and I think the surreal quality of that image got to her because there was a glimmer in her blue eyes that something was very wrong with all of this.

"It's called having great sex," I grinned. "Embrace it, Sam. Enjoy life."

I plunged the slender fingers of my right hand into her wet hole, then forced in all five of my slender digits, and she jerked and spasmed as I rammed my entire hand, small as it was, up her muscled love tunnel, right up to my slender wrist, my fingers clutching in a fist, I moving that fist in a slow circle inside her.

OH, FUCK!" screeched Sam. "NO!

She protested this action, but she did nothing to stop me, and Darren was too busy blissfully fucking my hot little twat to do anything, either.

I fisted her, slowly at first, and then faster and faster, right in rhythm with the red-bearded troll fucking my own bald, cum-soaked snatch. Sam got up on her hands as her legs spread wide and shook, her mouth widening in shock, her blue eyes wide around, that look of astonished ecstasy, pure, uncut ecstasy, just as uncut as the long cock of her boyfriend.

"AaaaaaaaAAAAAAAAAAAAAHHHHH!"   she screamed.

Her hairy wet twat squirted a sharp, clear line of liquid from her pee hole, that line spraying over my head to mix in with my short, dyed-blonde hair. Her pussy squeezed my narrow wrist over and over again as she was rocked by multiple orgasms, her body jerking in uncontrollable spasms as she did.

Darren grunted at that moment, his low-hanging balls slapping against my bald, dark-pink clit, and I knew he was going to cum as well.

"Oh, oh, oh, oh, oh, OH, OH, OH, OH FUCK!" he shouted.

His hot semen filled me, splooshing around his cock while filling my fucked tunnel full of that ivory ball sauce. It felt warm and soothing, so soothing that it occurred to me that Darren was good for something after all.

He pulled out of my pussy, collapsing that open space, causing me to moan along with all eight inches of that shaft coming out of me. I immediately popped my hand from Sam's spread cunt, causing her to let forth a short and sharp shriek, and then I pushed her back down upon my bed, mounted her chest, and lowered my dripping wet pussy lips to her facial ones, lowering them so that she could drown in her boyfriend's semen.

I bore down on my muscles, squirting out Darren's hot sperm from my yawning hole into Sam's open mouth. To her credit, she gulped it down without struggling or straining to getaway.

I pulled her up before she could say anything and slid beneath her, spreading my legs, our positions reversed.

"Eat me out," I commanded. "Slurp out the rest of Darren's cum."

I pushed her dark-haired head down toward my bald cunt and moaned as her tongue licked up into my fucked hole. I stared past her to look toward Darren, ready to command him as well.

"Fuck her," I said quickly. "Fuck her before your cock goes down. If you fuck her now and keep fucking her, you won't go limp."

Actually, the real reason it wouldn't go down was because of my little poison running through his veins, but he didn't need to know that.

He grabbed his girlfriend's beautiful ass and plunged that long, uncut dick into her, something, I imagined, he had done many times before. He pumped into her, and this motion rocked her back and forth, moving her tongue up and down my pussy, especially over the folds of my hood and my small, dark-pink clit.

"Oh, oh fuck, yes," I breathed out. "Give it to me, Sam. Give me your love. Eat me out. Show me what you can do to another woman. We're both women, Sam. Both hot, beautiful, incredibly-fuckable women. Show me what you can do...This is your interview, Sam. Show me you can be my slave, my hot, gorgeous love slave."

I squeezed her head in my hands as I choked out a gasp of growing pleasure. She hungrily sucked my little clit and caused me to jerk and spasm without control, just like she had done earlier when I had been servicing her.

"Oh, YES!" I cried out. "Give it to me, Sam! You're amazing! Keep doing it like that! Show me all of your inner lust! Show me all of your inner love for your master! Let me writhe in it! Yes! YES! Oh, FUCK! Now plunge your fingers in my ass! Make me squirt! Make this little fallen angel squirt like a fucking fountain!"

Darren continued to fuck her hard as my asshole spread upon her right index and ring fingers. She worked her fingers back and forth inside my beautiful heart-shaped butt as she sucked my clit, but this was not enough, not for me.

"Suck harder!" I demanded. "Suck me harder, Sam! Make me fucking feel it! This is your interview! This is for the job, Sam! You want to be my slave, don't you! Don't fucking pull back! Give me everything inside of you, everything you've got!...OH, FUCK! OH, FUCKING SHIT, YES!... Now take your fingers out of my ass, so I can suck them! I want to taste my ass! I want to taste my ass!...OH, FUCKING MOTHER FUCK!...Do it, Sam! Do it now!"

She pulled her fingers out and felt upwards with her right hand until she reached my mouth. I sucked hard on those two digits, tasting that wonderfully pungent taste of my asshole on them. She sucked equally as hard on my tiny little sex organ, and this did it for me, causing me to build up to an explosion.

I pulled her fingers from my mouth as my own green eyes widened just like hers had.

"Oh fuck, oh fuck, oh fuck, oh fuck, Sam, oh fuck..." I choked out. "No, no, no, no, no, no, NO, NO, NO, NO! Oh, Sammy, Sam, Sam...Ooooooh, FUCK! Oh, that does it! Oh, suck me, Sam! Oh, suck...ungh...ungh...no...engh...engh...oh shit..."

Oh, this one was going to be a doozy.

"Ung...ehn...enh...EHN...EHN!" I cried out.

"OH...EHNG...EHNG...EHNG...EEEEEEEEEEEEEEEEEENG!"

My pussy contracted as I squirted out a large glob of white cream directly onto her chin, spraying her face from my pee hole at the same time. The explosive orgasms caused me to clutch her head in mad spasms as I screamed, that sexual power rocking me as my legs shook around her lithe body, my toes curling in midair, my slender fingers digging into her soft scalp. I had not had orgasms like this before my little 'problem', had not squirted or had the electric, volcanic explosions I was having now, but now that I was having them, I was not about to give them up.

I picked her up and pulled her off of Darren's cock with ease, and this startled her, spooking her that I had such strength in my little body. I licked across her face in a wide swath of wet tongue, licking up my own delicious, dripping juices, and then I spun her around to face her boyfriend's creamy-wet cock, creamy-wet from her own delicious, dripping juices. Both Sam and I then moved forward, our heads pressed together, cheek to cheek, ready to suck Darren off to finish.

I grabbed Darren's long, uncut cock and slurped up and down it, then guided it to Sam's mouth, making sure to rub it across her face beforehand, rubbing it across mine as well. I then pulled his hairy, low-hanging balls forward, rubbed those all over my face, pulled his cock from Sam's sucking lips, and then rubbed those balls across Sam's gorgeous face, so that both of us could breathe in and absorb that human musk.

"Let's suck this long cock," I breathed out. "Let's suck this long cock and take a shower in his cum. Let's bathe in that semen. I want to take a shower with you, Sam. See your beautiful face sprayed with cum. Let's shower in the cum made from these two tasty balls. Oh, yes, they look so delicious. I could just eat them up...Mmmm...so delicious."

Darren happily, eagerly switched his cock from mouth to mouth, and Sam and I both slurped up and down that hard shaft with greedy, tongue-licking strokes, licking into his foreskin as well. Both of us grabbed one of his low-hanging balls and massaged the little organs as we sucked in his dong up to the backs of our throats, gurgling as we did.

"Oh, oh, oh, oh, oh, oh...fuuuuuUUUUUUUUCK!" screamed Darren.

Darren cried out as he came, a white fountain of sperm to spurt, spurt, spurt upon our faces, once across Sam's face and twice across mine. Sam and I then took turns licking the alabaster juice from the tip of his spent dong, and then I licked the dripping sperm from Sam's face and had her do the same to mine.

I jumped up off my bed after that, energized, ready for the next part of the day's fun. I was ready to go, though I could tell that Sam was not quite as enthused as I. It looked like she needed a breather, but...you know. I had things to do and shit that needed to get done.

"Come on," I grinned. "There's no time to waste. Let's head down to the basement for the next surprise."

"Wh...What?" asked Sam in breathless wonder. "B...Basement? Why? Aren't you tired? Can't we just relax for a..."

"This will be relaxing!" I said with wide, ecstatic eyes. "Trust me, it's great! You'll love it...but...I can't do that up here. I can't have...you know...police showing up at my door."

"Ooooooh, I get you," said Darren with a grin and a nod. "What are we talking about? Weed? Some meth? What?"

"You'll see," I grinned. "I have a nice little surprise down there...Come on!"

W...Wait!" stammered Sam. "I need to get dressed...

I bent down, gave her a quick peck on the lips, and pulled her up off my bed.

"No, you don't," I said quickly. "Let's go!"

"B...but..." stammered Sam, but I silenced that protest with sheer action.

I pulled her up off the bed by her right arm, pulled her through the bedroom doorway, and then dragged her into the kitchen, Darren eagerly following us from behind. Sam was a good deal taller than me, at least six-foot, tall for a woman, but she let herself be dragged by me, by this little, five-foot-two blonde with short hair.

I pulled her to the basement door, opened it, and flipped on the light over the stairs.

"Come on," I said in a hushed tone. "I want to show you a whole other world...You'll love it. It's quite...magical."

"Shrooms..." chuckled Darren. "Yeah, yeah...I love it. Let's go, hon."

"Darren..." replied Sam unhappily. "You know I've never done anything like that be..." "It's fine, it's fine," I said quickly. "You'll love this. Trust me."

I closed the basement door, and it automatically locked. They did not know it could only be unlocked without a key from the kitchen, because you had to have a key from this side, and only I knew where that key was down here. I had put in this little addition after...certain events...had occurred in my life.

All three of us walked down the wooden steps leading into the darkness of the basement below, all three of us completely nude, all three of us smelling and dripping of sex...Well, they do say three is a magic number.

Let's go," I said quietly. "This is the best part.

I stepped into a small circle of light at the bottom of the steps, the concrete floor cold against my bare feet.

"The magic is over there," I whispered. "The light will turn on once you're over there. You'll see. Then we can start the fun...I'll show you a whole other side to this universe, one you never knew existed before...I didn't. It changed my life."

"Awesome," breathed Darren. "This is, like, the happiest day of my life. I feel like I've won the lottery."

"You did win a lottery, Darren," I whispered with a smirk. "A Shirley Jackson one."

We walked forward a bit, and Darren walked past us, but as he did, I turned and held Sam's arms in place with my own two hands, preventing her from moving. She struggled against me, but when she realized she couldn't budge me an inch, her blue eyes widened as her mouth dropped open.

"What the fuck!" she cried out. "How are you...! Stop it! Let go of me!"

Darren had stepped into the dark, but he turned his gaze toward his girlfriend's distress just as the light snapped on above him. Sam looked over my left shoulder to see my current lover, Lance, there in the dark, right in front of Darren's naked form. She screamed in pure terror at the sight of him, and Darren turned to see what the matter was.

Lance's huge maw opened to bite down upon Darren's bare, right shoulder, and Darren screamed long and loud and high-shrilled as his blood sprayed in a scarlet fountain all over the basement. My monstrous lover, Lance, his shape a huge, brown-furred wolf- beast cloaked in partial darkness, gripped Darren's naked waist as he bit down into Darren's throat, then Lance's maw tore up and out, ripping off the man's head as easily as pulling a cap from a beer bottle, a fitting analogy for such a worthless chunk of human meat.

I easily pulled Sam and myself forward into the shower of red, salty spray, and both of us were coated with Darren's hot blood, but I could tell that she did not enjoy that shower nearly as much as I did. No, she continued to scream and struggle against me, and that was kind of disheartening, but she'd fall in line. I had faith in her.

Lance bit down and pulled off the right arm of Darren's corpse, and then he sank his jaws into the abdomen to tear out large, gory chunks from the body. He crunched down on that as Sam continued to shriek in, what had to be, mind-numbing terror, but I ignored her protests and held her firmly in place. She needed to see this.

"Isn't this incredible!" I said in gleeful excitement. "I told you you'd love it!...Oh, you've got the job, by the way, and I can't wait to work with you, Sam! You've made me so happy!"

I focused my attention back on the gory scene before us, taking my time to study Lance's powerful figure. He turned me on just by looking at him, but I'd fuck him later. I'd make time for Lance's...err...lance.

Lance's head was that of a great brown wolf with yellow eyes, that head atop a muscular man's brown-furred body, that brown-furred body soaked red in the blood and gore of the late Darren...uhhh...Darren...whatever. I had no idea what his last name had been, not that I gave a fuck. It was that bloody fur and rippling muscle that charged my little magic button...Oooh, I stroked myself a little just from looking at him.

As long as Darren's uncut cock had been, it was nothing compared to the long, fat, circumcised rope swinging between Lance's angled legs. That thick shlong was a cunt spreader and a belly bulger, something I had firsthand experience in, something Sam would have experience in soon, as well.

Sam continued to scream and cry, great drops of tears rolling down her blood-splattered face as I firmly held her in place. Her noises of distress attracted Lance's attention, and he tossed Darren's body aside to get at her, but I already knew he would, so I put a stop to that rather quickly.

"No," I said firmly. "No, Lance. This one's not for eating...Don't give me that look. I said no."

I turned to look up at Sam to give her an encouraging smile, but her face was...It was an expression of pure horror. She fainted after that, collapsing into my little arms, but she wasn't heavy, not for me, anyway.

"She goes in the chain," I said firmly.

He growled, but I looked Lance square in the eyes so that he knew I wasn't fooling around.

"She goes in the chain," I said once more. "You finish your dinner and then clean up. Throw the bones in the furnace. I don't want you to forget this time."

He whined at my tone, but I knew he'd forgive me. He always did. Besides, he loved pumping my little hole full of beast cum. He wasn't about to jeopardize that.

I dragged Sam's unconscious body over to the east wall, laid her down in a pile of straw, and then snapped the iron manacle around her neck, that manacle chained and deadbolted to the concrete wall. She wasn't going anywhere anytime soon. She had to be conditioned over the next few months, her will broken, or she wouldn't fall in line. I needed a willing slave, not a rabble-rouser.

I walked back to my bestial lover and stared up into his golden eyes. He was beautiful, far more beautiful than he had ever been when he was a man. If anything, this change in him had made him so much more compelling. Nevertheless, I, myself, felt compelled to confess to him. He was my current lover, regardless of what he looked like now.

"I saw Daniel today," I said.

He growled down at me, a low rumbling sound that came from deep within his muscled belly. I reached up to stroke the left side of his muzzle with my right hand, but he had to bend down for me to reach him. He was seven feet tall, after all.

"It's okay," I said gently as I stroked the blood-soaked fur of his maw. "You know I still love you. That's why I bring you these gifts. Who else is going to feed you? Besides, you know no one can find out about you, or they'll take you away from me...That's why I brought Sam down here. She's going to stay with us from now on. She's going to take care of you when I'm not here."

He whined and turned to sniff the air in her direction, but I gently guided his huge brown head back toward mine, so that my forehead touched his wet, black, sniffing nose.

"She's for the both of us, my love," I said quietly. "I like her...She gives a good head...Don't look all sad now...I'm not replacing you with a woman..."

He growled again, but I quickly shushed him. Lance, unfortunately, had a jealous streak in him, but I was sure he'd grow fond of Sam. I know I had...He'd change his mind once his dick was in her mouth. Most men had an epiphany at that moment, anyway.

"Hush, hush," I said firmly. "She's for you just as much as for me...You like the things I do to you, right? She can do the same things...and don't you worry about mean ol' Daniel...I'll deal with him."

Daniel was my real love, my one true love, but Lance didn't need to know that. It was true that I loved Lance, just...not the same as I loved Daniel. It just wasn't the same.

I was, of course, going to have to deal with Daniel's 'girlfriend' first, but that would not be difficult. She would make a nice little snack.

I walked down the wooden steps of my basement stairs, careful to make as little noise as possible, so as not to wake Lance. He was cranky when he didn't get enough sleep, and a cranky Lance was not something I wanted to deal with right now. It was best he stayed in dreamland until I was ready to wake him.

I always undressed before coming down here, making sure that I was in nothing but my birthday suit before interacting with my monstrous lover, because Lance could get a little rough during sex, or just in general, and I didn't want to have to replace any more of my dresses. I was on a limited budget.

My name is Megan Holly. I'm a twenty-four-year-old, five-foot-two white girl of average weight, with an hourglass body, a beautiful, heart-shaped butt, and C-cup breasts with gorgeous dark-pink nipples. I don't mean to be vain, but I'm quite beautiful in the face, that face ringed by short, dyed-blonde hair, that face accented by my emerald-green eyes, which, I consider my best feature. I have a stunning little bald pussy, with a triangular, dark-pink hood covering my little dark-pink clit, and ever since Daniel freed me of my human inhibitions months ago, I've been putting my hot little twat to good use, but I'll explain that later on.

You see, Daniel Christianson's my one true love, my one and only...Well, he's not my only, it's just...he's the one I was meant to be with. He broke up with me ten months ago, just before I discovered his little secret, that secret being his...uhhh...' wolfiness'.

Daniel's a werewolf, and throughout our dating, he...did something to me, and it probably had to do with all of the times we made love. Whatever he infected me with, it...isn't the same as what's wrong with him. I know he changes into a werewolf during the full moon, but that's not my little problem. No, that I could properly handle. What's wrong with me is...well...it's complicated.

It started with strange sexual urges, leaving me sweaty in the middle of the night, having to masturbate a lot more than I normally do. Then came the bloodthirstiness, the awful cravings to dismember people, to destroy things. You have no idea how much money I have spent replacing my vases, my paintings, and my pewter figurines, having to replaster the walls to fill in holes, having to buy new clocks, toasters, and phones...that sort of thing. That rage just gets to you, you know?

Anyway, I started seeing strange lights around people, like a colorful ring around them, so I looked that up on the Net, and that's when I learned about 'auras'. Apparently, I can see people's auras now and can see their true selves via the colors they shine. It's weird, but it's also awesome, because I can really manipulate people now, and that's useful.

The other thing I can do is equally awesome, but it has to do with attraction and sex. Strangely enough, my bodily fluids...saliva, blood, urine...pussy juice...that kind of thing...act as a poison that causes normal people to go into sexual overdrive. It has a different effect depending upon whether you're a man or a woman, but it always makes them horny as fuck and hungry to jump my bones. I've found this ability to be quite useful as well if only to satisfy my more primal urges...and to feed Lance. Of course, it also spreads whatever infection this thing is that I have, but...Lance eats what I don't want. I'm pretty sure that's how Daniel spread it to me, like an STD. A lycanthropy STD.

Anyway, I've made a lot of adjustments to my little house in the town of Lonesome Moon, adjustments that wiped out my savings, but they were necessary. I really had no choice. Thinking back, this is all Daniel's fault, and he fucking owes me for all of the money I've had to spend dealing with this problem, but...I just can't stay mad at him. I love him so mu...That...That doesn't matter. I'm on a tangent again...Anyway, I put in these adjustments after my first...uhhh...encounter...with a suitor after Daniel broke up with me.

I went to the Silver Cup, a little bar here in town, one with a silver trophy and a golf ball on the sign, a place I would have never thought of going to in the past, but I was just...I was burning up inside with lust, and I needed a quick fuck, okay?

The guy I met there, Lance, Lance Denning?... He was your typical college graduate in his late twenties, one with a degree but no decent job to pay it off. I can only assume that's why he was still stuck in Lonesome Moon...Jesus Christ did he not want my attention, but he was the best-looking guy there. He was six-foot, thin, wavy brown hair, grey eyes, average muscle, not fat, really good looking...You get the picture. I wanted him, so fucking badly, and trust me, I could have picked up anyone else, because I got hit on by eight guys that night. That should say something.

Well, turns out that Lance had a boyfriend. Lance was bi, but he preferred guys most of the time, which I find weird, but whatever. It's a modern world. Anyway, he denied my repeated advances until I just reached up and kissed him, and what do you know? His aura changed, and we started sucking faces right in front of his boyfriend, Greg. Greg got pissed, but I got Lance to walk out with me, and...I'll get back to Greg later. Greg was a problem in himself, a messy problem, but that's not important right now.

Anyway, Lance and I went back to my house and fucked that first time, and it was fucking awesome, and it satisfied all of my urges, and yada, yada, yada. Lance broke up with Greg and moved in with me, and we were a happy couple for about three weeks.

Then the full moon hit. It shone right through the basement windows, windows I have since removed.

Lance and I were indeed down in the basement when it happened. He had been helping me with the laundry when...well...that light hit him, and he changed. He just kept staring at the full moon, and...he changed. Apparently, I had infected him with lycanthropy just like Daniel had infected me, but...not in the same way. Not...at...all.

Lance went full beast and never changed back. He's, like, a monster all of the time now, a seven-foot-tall, brown-furred werewolf with a massive ten-inch-long dick. Why did I mention his dick? Because that dick is what's satisfied my urges for some time now...But anyway, I screamed my little head off when it happened, when he changed, but he didn't hurt me. No, he tore off my dress, ripped that little article of clothing to shreds, and then he had his way with me. Well, after that horrifyingly fun little belly-bulging spearing, he then proceeded to destroy my basement...my fucking basement. Jesus.

Well, right after Lance fucked me in his new form, something awesome happened to me, something awesome and terrifying, but it didn't last long. What happened, you ask? I'll fill you in on that later. Needless to say, it freaked me the fuck out, so once I rode that out, I knew I needed help. It was another reason besides Lance destroying the basement that I needed help.

Okay, so what did I do? I got dressed again, and I called up Greg. Greg was furious with me...on account of stealing his boyfriend, obviously...but I told him something was really, really wrong with Lance...an understatement...and I needed his help. I was too scared and freaked out to handle it myself. I knew Greg would see this as an opportunity to 'steal' back his ex, so he rushed right on over, but that was fine because I knew Lance wasn't going to get back with him...But anyway, Lance hadn't hurt me, so I didn't think he'd hurt Greg, either...but Greg hadn't been infected with lycanthropy. I didn't know at the time that this was a condition of Lance's...uhhh...control. I led Greg down to the basement, and...can you guess what happened next?

Lance tore him apart. Just ripped him into little itty, bitty pieces...and then he ate those pieces. Here's the thing, though. That little meal that Lance had...calmed him down. In fact, he stayed calm for a couple of months after that. Really, it's usually a buildup inside him, something wild and uncontrollable, and then he starts getting edgy, and then I have to...uhh...' locate' some more food for him. I can usually keep him quelled with stray animals and such, but they don't keep down his bloodlust as well as a real live human does.

But I digress. Lance tore apart Greg, showering me in blood, gore, and guts, and...that really did something to me. It did something in my brain that...changed me. I liked it...I liked it a lot. It satisfied my urges as well. That rage and anger I had? That went away for a while, just like Lance's had.

Well, I'm not stupid, and I knew I was in deep shit after that. I went and rented a moving van, coaxed Lance out of the house in the middle of the night, and spent a whole month renovating my basement while Lance stayed in a storage shed outside of town. It's funny, too, because some thief broke into that shed one night looking to steal anything of value, probably some meth addict...we have a lot of those in Lonesome Moon...and Lance promptly ate her. I know it was a woman because I found one of her shoes along with her foot in it the next morning. Her toenails had been painted a shiny gold color. I also found part of her face. She had brown eyes with green eyeliner.

I had to clean out the interior of that storage shed. It was not fun.

So, now I've got a soundproof basement, reinforced concrete walls, manacles and chains on the walls, and an old-fashioned furnace for the disposal of evidence. I've even got a grated sewer system down there. All of that wiped out my savings, but it was worth it. It's been tough living this new life, but now that I know what to do and how to live this new life, everything's fine. Better than fine, even. I've got awesome new powers, I have Lance to satisfy my baser urges, and I'm going to get Daniel back. It's perfect.

Of course, I can't tell Daniel that I know about his secret. How did I learn about his secret, you may ask? You see, I had a dream one night after that fateful full moon when Lance changed.

I dreamed of the moon, and the woman within it. She had silver eyes with no pupils, and long silver hair and the moon was her chariot, driven by a long train of silver wolves. She was huge, so big that I cowered in her presence. I was naked and prostrated on the ground before her, bowing before her in worship, and she pointed out behind me, so I turned, and that's when I saw them. I looked upon hundreds of naked men and women, all there in the wilderness, all bowing like me, and one of them was Daniel. I called out his name for help, but he ignored me, and he changed into the Beast right in front of me…They all did.

I turned around to ask the Lady in the Moon why, why this was happening, but she pointed away into the darkness, into the thick night of the woods. I was terrified, so I got up and ran, ran away from the Lady in the Moon and her army of beasts, ran and ran until I was all alone in the dark. I heard her call my name, the Lady in the Moon, heard her call my name and tell me to stop, but as I said, I was terrified of her. I wasn't going back.

So there I was, all alone, in the thick of night, in the middle of the woods, a place without moonlight, not even enough to reflect off of the snow underneath me. I shivered, naked and afraid, in the dark, but then someone else came to me, the Lady Cloaked in Night.

This lady wore a sheet of cloth so dark that it was darker than night itself, and it was in stark contrast to her pale, pale skin. She was huge like the Lady in the Moon, and her long hair and deep eyes were as dark as the cloak she wore, those eyes just black, bottomless pits. She picked me up and held me close to her giant, bare right breast, and then she carried me towards a small group of others like me, but I was terrified of her, but for a different reason, different than why I was afraid of the Lady in the Moon.

This woman whispered terrible secrets to me, secrets I didn't want to hear, yet secrets I still wanted to know. She confirmed what I had already suspected about my new abilities, and she confirmed what the

Lady in the Moon had shown me, that Daniel was a werewolf.

Now I don't remember anything she said to me, and that dream was completely psychotic and fucked up if you want to know, but it did teach me one thing...Daniel had done this to me. Daniel had spread this disease to me, and now I had it in me, like some kind of fucked up STD, and I'm pretty sure there's no cure for it, so I've learned to live with it. Besides, my new powers are pretty darned cool.

This comes to my last ability, my hidden one. You see, I have one more power I haven't mentioned, but I'm saving that one as a surprise. It's pretty fucking awesome, though, at least, I think so. I'm going to use this last power to have my way with Daniel again...You'll see.

I stepped off the bottom of the stairs and into the soft circle of light above me. Sam lifted her head up from her reclined position in order to eyeball me, her breathing quickening at the sight of me. I knew she was afraid that I was going to order Lance to tear her apart, just like he had Sam's boyfriend, Darren, but I had no such plans. Still, I could understand her fears. She was new to this life.

Sam was a young white woman in her mid-twenties, twenty-six, I think, and she was tall for a woman, six-feet-tall, a good ten inches taller than me. She had a beautiful face with gorgeous blue eyes, a lithe, athletic body, B-cup breasts with hot little dark-brown nipples, and long, long, silky, straight black hair on her head. I wanted to eat out that hairy, dark-brown snatch of hers, but that would have to wait. I had some training and conditioning to do with her first.

Sam was naked, of course, though Darren's blood and gore had long been washed off her, and though she was nude...mainly because I wouldn't let her wear clothes...all part of the brainwashing process, you know...she was thoroughly bound by the large iron manacle around her neck, that manacle chained and deadbolted to the reinforced concrete wall behind her.

I sauntered up to her, swaying my delicious big butt as I did, but she scooted away from me as I approached, huddling up into a little ball next to Lance's giant sleeping form. My monstrous lover had taken a likening to her over the past week, so it appeared he had switched sleeping spots. Normally, he slept over by the furnace, next to the south wall.

I sat down next to Sam, sat in her pile of hay that I had spread out for her, reached over, and softly touched the fingers of her right hand with my left, but she pulled her hand away from me to huddle up with her knees pulled up to her chest.

Hey," I whispered. "I came down to see how you were doing.

"Please..." begged my captive. "Please, let me go. I...I...I won't tell anyone. I won't. I'll just leave town. I won't tell anyone. Nobody has to know...I...I won't tell anyone. I promise...I won't tell..."

"Sweetheart," I said with a click of my tongue, "that's what everyone says. Haven't you seen the same thing on movies and TV shows before? Now you tell me...When has asking that ever worked?"

She quietly choked out a sob into her bare knees, but I didn't have time for her self-pity. I had a schedule to maintain.

"Now, now," I said in a soothing tone. "That's enough of that. I did come down here to see how you were doing, but I also came down here to start instructing you. I'm going to teach you all of the things I've learned, and that way, you don't have to learn the hard way...like I did."

"Wh...What?" choked Sam.

I put my right index finger to my lips in careful thought. Sam had been down here for a week now, and I'd taken care of her...cleaned her up, fed her, brushed her hair, made sure she brushed her teeth, shown her where to take a shit, that sort of thing...but I hadn't done anything but hold her hostage. She had needed to be broken before I could mold her into something different, something better. It was clear that she was improving, starting the bartering phase with me rather than just sitting around in a catatonic stupor, so...it was time to start molding her now.

"I'm going to begin the lessons," I said softly, "and when I think you've done a good job, you'll get a reward. Today's reward is a pair of panties. I'll give you a pair of your panties to wear once the lesson's up. You can have some pads or some tampons, too...I don't know when your period starts, but you can't be bleeding all over the floor down here; you'll drive Lance into a frenzy...Not good."

Sam quietly turned her head toward the sleeping monstrosity next to her. Lance's great brown wolf head was currently lying next to her, his eyes closed, his breathing steady through his huge, moist black nose. I could see the look of absolute fear upon Sam's beautiful face, but it would not be long before I expunged that fear. She would learn to control him, just like I had.

She turned her head back toward mine and choked out a response.

"Wh...What do you want me to do?" she stammered.

"First, I want you to answer my questions with all honesty," I said firmly. "That means honestly, now...Okay. These questions are simple, and this is the first one...Are you feeling angry? Hostile?"

Her face scrunched up in fear as she swallowed hard. I didn't need to look at her aura to see that she was going to straight-up lie to me. It was all over her pretty face.

"N...No," she stumbled. "I...I'm not mad...I'm not...Really..."

"Don't lie to me," I said flatly as I shook my head no. "You're feeling rage, and you want to hit and smash things, don't you? You won't, and you haven't, because you're afraid of Lance. Am I right?"

This time her face wilted in defeat as her bare shoulders sank in return.

"Y...Yes," said Sam in audible anxiety.

"Good," I smiled. "That's what you're supposed to be feeling...Now...tell me about your sex drive." 'What?" asked Sam.

"Your sex drive," I repeated. "Your libido? How horny have you been?"

"That's...I...I haven't...I don't understand..." stammered Sam.

What a fucking liar. She was struggling hard against me...Oh, well. Doesn't matter. I'll get her in line. She has to learn, or she's just going to suffer more than she already has.

"You've been masturbating, hon," I said matter-of-factly. "I know you have because you were doing it right before I stepped into the light."

"What?" asked Sam in obvious shock. "How did you...Uhh...No. No, I wasn't..."

"Uh huh," I said as I gave her a tight-lipped frown. "You can't lie to me, you know. Without taking out your frustrations in anger, the only option you have down here is to play with yourself, and you've been doing that...a lot. It smells like Lance down here, but I also smell pussy, because this sleeping area is flooded with that aroma, and you'll find that I have an ex-cell-ent sense of smell."

"I...uhhh..." she tried to say, but then she hid her face behind her bare knees.

"It's nothing to be ashamed of," I smirked. "It's what I'd do if I were trapped down here for a week, but I digress. You see, what you're feeling is normal for one of our kind."

Sam poked her face up from behind her knees and stared at me in both wide-eyed confusion and alarm.

"One of our kind?" she asked in a shaky voice. "What do you mean 'one of our kind'?"

"I mean, you're either like me or Lance," I shrugged. "Maybe you're like Daniel, I don't know. That's irrelevant, however, because I'm going to give you a little test just to see." "What did you mean by that, Megan?" repeated Sam, and I could hear the anxiety in her voice. "What did you mean by 'one of our kind'?"

"I meant that your either like me," I said as I brushed my own right-hand fingers against my bare chest, "or you're like Lance."

I took my right hand and gently scratched underneath Lance's left, pointed ear. He snuffed a little in his sleep, and Sam scooted away from him a bit in response to that action.

"You'll either have my abilities...," I continued, "ooooor you'll turn into a raging beast on the next full moon. It's one or the other."

Sam turned her head toward Lance yet again, but even in the shadow of our surroundings, I could see the blood drain from her face. She turned her head back toward me, took an audible gulp, and waited for what I was going to say next...Good. She was learning.

"The next question I have is very important," I said with a slow nod. "It's also a little strange, so bear with me...I need to know...when you look at me...what do you see? Do you see a ring of light around me?"

Sam gave me the strangest look but said nothing for a few seconds. After that few seconds was up, however, she slowly nodded her head yes.

"What does it look like?" I asked. "Do you see colors?"

She quickly nodded her head again. Of course, I needed to see if she was being honest, or if she was full of shit again. Even if she wasn't lying to me, she could be lying to herself. I needed to find out which.

What colors are they?" I asked.

Sam studied me again, swallowed hard, and then gave her reply.

"I...I see...red...and purple...blue, green, a...a strange off-white..." she stammered. "S...Sometimes there's a little bit of pink in it."

Well, that answered my question. She was like me, and that was a huge weight lifted off of my little bare shoulders. I didn't want to have to feed two Lances...Jesus. Could you imagine the body count on that?

"Do you know what those colors mean?" I asked.

Sam shook her head no.

"You will," I said confidently. "You'll just know...What you're seeing is my aura. It tells you what people are like, what they're really like, on the inside. It's how I know when you're lying to me, so don't lie anymore, okay?... At any rate, you're like me, not like Lance. That means you won't change during the next full moon."

I smiled as I watched her sink into herself in what was obvious, total relief. She did not want to be a bloodthirsty beast. Of course, I was going to have to break it to her that she was still going to be bloodthirsty, but that could wait.

"Can I have my reward now?" asked Sam in a meek voice. "Can I have my clothes back? I don't want to be naked anymore. I answered your questions."

"No," I said as I shook my head in reply. "You'll get your clothes back when you've earned them. I'm going to let you out of the chain soon, but you have to behave. Besides, we're not done yet." 'What?" she asked. "Wh...Why not?

Because I haven't shown you your real power," I said.

I reached forward, gripped her bare right leg, and pulled it toward me. She struggled a bit, and I could tell that she was getting stronger, but she was still nowhere near as strong as I was. I could bench press up to five hundred pounds...I know. I tried it out at the gym a few months ago. It was one of the perks of...whatever the hell it was that I was now. I wasn't a werewolf, I knew that, but...well...not a full one, anyway. Not like Lance or even Daniel. No, Sam and I were something else.

I pushed the key I had been hiding in my left hand into the keyhole on her manacle, turned that key, and popped open her constricting neck brace. I tossed that prisoner's lament aside into the hay as Sam reached up out of instinct and massaged the now free skin of her neck, but I did not give her the chance to relax.

I pulled her into my embrace and then kissed her deeply on the lips. She was reticent, very uncooperative, but she gave in as I forced my tongue in over hers. It was time for the next lesson, but this one involved all three of us, including Lance.

We made out as I ran my small hands up and down the smooth skin of her back, our bare breasts rubbing together, our lips smacking, with her hands around my waist. Her scent mixed with mine to flood her sleeping area, our pussies wet and dripping, those happy lower lips ready for additional stimulation.

I pulled my lips away from her and hugged her close to me.

"I love you, Sam," I whispered into her ear. "You and I are the same now. We'll be together from now on...all three of us. I'll teach you everything there is to know about this gift we've been given, and then you'll live here with me, and we'll take care of Lance together."

I stroked the back of her long, silky black hair, and she breathed out a loud, husky breath in return. I nibbled on the soft lobe of her left ear, and her bare chest moved up and down, up and down, as she felt that pleasure sink into her.

"You don't have to be naked," I whispered. "You don't have to be chained up in the dark. You can be with me from now on...Haven't you seen all of those vampire movies? We're not vampires, but we do live in another world, a world far apart from normal people...You can't go back to the world you used to live in...They'll call you a witch, they'll hunt you down, torture you, kill you...All we have is each other now...but that's okay. I'm here for you...and Lance will protect you...and it's all so simple to understand...All you have to do is love me, give yourself to me, and I'll take care of you...and we'll both take care of Lance together."

In truth, I was grooming her to take care of Lance. I was going to be with Daniel, but I couldn't just leave Lance all by his lonesome...No, that wouldn't be right. Hence, Sam.

I reached over with my right hand and stroked the soft brown fur upon Lance's head. His golden eyes snapped open as he snuffed in the air around him, bringing in our rich, heady scent, that scent going straight to his feral brain, causing that massive brown cock of his to grow firm and erect.

I held Sam tightly to my naked body as Lance rose up next to us. Sam shook in my arms, but I stroked the back of her long black hair and shushed her.

"It's all right," I said softly. "Lance won't hurt you. He won't ever hurt you. It's time for the next lesson, anyway...Are you ready?"

She shivered in my arms for a few seconds before silently nodding her head yes.

"Good," I said. "This lesson should be a familiar one...Come on...I'll show you."

I gripped her right arm in my left hand...I had stashed my key in the hay...and then slowly turned her toward Lance's towering shape, that Wolfen-form wreathed in the semidarkness of the shadowy basement. I took Lance's swollen cock into my right hand, brought that huge circumcised mushroom head to my lips, and greedily took it in.

"Mmmmmmm..." I moaned out as I slathered it with my own saliva.

His massive dong still drove me wild, the primal taste of it, even now, after all this time, when there was no actual surprise from taking it into my mouth.

I licked up the A-spot of that huge cock, tasted a small spurt of salty precum, and then gently angled Lance's giant meat toward Sam's quivering lips.

"Go on," I said gently. "Take it...Take it in...Lick it...That's it...Take it in...Good girl..."

Sam closed her eyes as she took in Lance's huge shlong, slurping in six inches of it before pulling her lips backward over it, her supple tongue gliding along the bottom of that magnificent shaft. Her body shook as she tasted the power within it, the power that I, myself, was addicted to, that power of the full and raging beast, that power channeled into head-on, train colliding, primal lust.

"Yesss..." I hissed. "That's good, isn't it? It surges right through you, doesn't it?"

Sam silently nodded in reply, but her eyes were still closed in what looked like ecstasy, her lips refused to part from the massive cock in her mouth. She held Lance's beast-meat with her left hand, her right hand lowering to stroke herself in a gentle, circular, easy manner.

"You're such a good girl," I softly whispered. "Give it to me now...Give it to me...Give it to...Give it...That's it...We share, now...We share Lance...Good girl..."

I took Lance's huge penis from her mouth, and I could see a look of wanton, lustful disappointment in Sam's blue eyes, but this was a good thing. She was getting hooked, doing exactly what I expected her to do. This power was like a drug, a deep soul-wrenching, life-altering drug.

I slurped up and down half of Lance's incredible cock, holding it with my left hand, stroking myself with my right, just as Sam had done. Doing this was like taking a hit from a bong and then sharing that bong, but different in that there was a connection between us, a strange, ancient, mystical connection between all three of us, not just like sharing drugs between friends.

Lance's huge, clawed hands reached down and rested upon our heads. He rumbled out a low, soft growl, but that sound was not a threat. No, he was thoroughly enjoying this. He now had two bitches at his beck and call, so I knew there would be no more complaints coming from him.

I popped Lance's giant cock from my mouth and then nodded to Sam.

"Kiss his balls," I commanded. "Lick them. You'll taste his musk, and it will drive you wild...Go on...Do it..."

Sam leaned her head forward, gently cupped Lance's huge brown balls in both hands, and slurped up the wrinkly skin of them with her tongue. Her whole body shook and shivered from this, and I smiled as I stared past her beautiful naked bottom to see her toes curl.

I gripped her around the waist and slowly pulled her back, then I guided Lance's cock to her lips once more. She greedily took in that huge phallus, took in what she could all the way to the back of her throat, though she could not even come close to bringing in its full length. She slurped backward up it as her blue eyes rolled up in the whites, and I leaned back on my hands, only to see her bare butt rise up, that gorgeous bottom shaking, a line of white cum dripping down from her hairy wet snatch.

It's time," I said firmly. "You're ready now.

I pulled Sam away from Lance's cock, I was still on my knees, and she struggled a bit, but as I had mentioned before, she was not as strong as I, not yet. Lance growled at this forced removal of his new bitch's lips from his living rod, but he was going to like what was next on the agenda, so I ignored his rumbling protest.

I guided Sam around to where she was facing away from him, guiding her to her hands and knees, and then I placed my right hand on her back and my left on her stomach so that I could raise her bare ass and waiting for pussy into the air. Her hairy lower lips were swollen and puffy with lust, smeared with that delicious white cream that her body made automatically in response to her own mating instinct. Her scent was so strong that it made me dizzy, but I resisted plunging my face into that sacred valley. She was Lance's for the moment.

Sam shook in fear as Lance's huge, clawed hands gripped her beautiful ass.

"I...I...I don't want to do this," she quavered. "I'm scared...Can't I just go back to sucking him?"

"It's okay," I said in gentle encouragement. "It's scary the first time, but it's wonderful. I was scared, too, my first time, but you have nothing to worry about. I've done this many, many times with him before...Trust me. He won't hurt you."

"Oh, oh, OH!" cried Sam as her soaking-wet hole spread wide around upon Lance's massive penis.

She squeezed her eyes shut and then sucked in her breath with a "Ssssfffff" sound as that giant dong slid into her. Her belly pooched out as she raised her head, eyes still closed, and she released a loud "AH!" as Lance pulled back.

My monstrous lover gripped Sam's bare butt as he began to slide in and out, in and out, pumping into her with faster and faster thrusts.

"Oh, oh, oh, oh, oh, oh fuck..." moaned Sam, her eyes still closed.

She moved her head up and down from the sensation of it, moved it around in a circle in reflexive motion, an uncontrollable sensation of body-rocking pleasure I was well familiar with. I had not been exaggerating when I had told Sam that Lance had fucked my happy hole many, many times before. I was well used to that experience.

"That's it..." I whispered.

Watching this gorgeous young woman's pleasure stoked the embers of my lust. I reached down and rubbed my own thoroughly bald, hot little cunt with my whole hand, feeling my ivory gel stick to my fingers and smooth over my bare lower lips. I rubbed my little dark-pink clit and my triangular hood with furious strokes, gritting my teeth as I did.

"Nnnnng...Nnnnng..." I grunted out. "Oh, fuck yeah..."

"Oh, oh fuck, oh Megan, oh fuck..." moaned Sam. "Oh fuck, it hurts, but it feels so good! Why does it feel so good! What is happening to my body!"

I balled my little hand into a fist and dug it into my sacred valley, turning it at the wrist to give it an extra twist of pleasure, then I went back to rubbing my whole pussy, and then pinching, pulling, and stroking my little clit.

"It's the power...of the beast..." I huffed out. "It's like...nothing you've ever felt...before..."

Lance pumped into her harder and faster upon hearing the sounds of her distress. It was a primal thing to capture your prey, to feel the helplessness of her in your grasp, to control your bitch so that she could not struggle against you.

I stroked faster and faster as Lance bent down and took the back of Sam's neck into his massive jaws. He liked to do this for some reason, because I had been on the receiving end of that terrifying vice many times, but that action had locked my spine, preventing me from moving.

It was the same for Sam. Her gorgeous face took on a look of shaking fear as Lance violated her in this unholy union of maw and neck, and she refused to open her eyes, clearly too scared to do anything but whine in return.

"Oh, nnnng, oh, nnnng," she whined. "Oh, oh, oh please, Megan...Please, help me...please don't let it kill me..."

"He's not going to kill you," I said firmly. "This is how he mates. It's the instinct for him...It will become instinct for you, too."

I stopped talking and concentrated on building my pleasure. Unlike Sam, I did not want to close my eyes. I wanted to watch the live show in front of me, instead.

Lance pumped into her faster and faster, his huge, luscious, muscular furred bottom pounding back and forth as he humped over her, driving that huge stake into her stretched pussy, driving it in and out, in and out, bulging her belly until Sam begged for mercy.

"Oh, oh, oh, oh, oh fuck, oh fuck," she pleaded. "Oh, oh, oh fuck, oh please, oh please, Megan! I can't take anymore!...oh please, oh please, oh please, oh please...OH PLEASE! OH PLEASE! OH PLEASE!"

I stopped stroking myself to briefly hold up and snap the fingers of my cum-soaked right hand. Lance's left golden eye looked toward me, so I spun my hand in a circle, the signal for him to finish.

Spike her," I commanded.

Lance released the back of Sam's neck and then picked her up with ease, picking up all six feet of her lithe, naked body, his massive cock still thoroughly spearing her creamy, sopping-wet love tunnel. He bent down to push in his huge meat as far as it would go, and Sam's blue eyes finally snapped open from this new violation.

"AaaaaaaAAAAAAAAAAHHHHHGGGG!" she screamed.

Her bare legs shook as she bowed them out like she was riding a horse, her mouth wide, her blue eyes equally as wide, staring down at her own bulging belly with a look of horror mixed with both extreme pleasure and strange pain. Her arms were out in a downward V, locked and shaking, her fingers straightening to curl upwards at the knuckles, her feet straight out and locked at the ankles, her toes curling, as well.

She pissed out a long stream of clear cum, squirting globs of white gel all over my monstrous lover's enormous, throbbing phallus and huge brown balls. Her spraying cum splattered all over my face and my bare chest, across my breasts and belly, and I shook as I came, my pussy contracting to squirt out my alabaster love liquid upon the cold concrete beneath and between my bare legs.

"Oh, ho, ho, ho, ho, fuuuuuck..." I hissed out as I shivered and shook from my own trembling aftershocks.

Lance shook a bit while still gripping Sam around the waist, and I knew he had cum inside her, pumping his life-giving seed into her thoroughly wrecked love tunnel. He lowered his current bitch to the cum-soaked straw beneath him after that, and then he pulled out his huge dong, pushing against Sam's gorgeous butt as he did in order to pop her off.

"Aaaaaahggh!" cried Sam as she collapsed upon her sleeping area.

Lance ignored his new bitch and laid back down, intent upon sleeping once more. I, however, took this opportunity to steal some power, because I was not about to let Sam take in a full dose of it, not yet. I'd had a full dose the first time Lance had fucked me, fucked me on that fateful night he'd changed, but I did not want to unleash such horror upon Sam. She wasn't ready.

I rolled her over, but she didn't fight me. She was too weak to fight me, too weak from the savage fucking she'd just received. I spread her bare legs, bent down, and slurped into her hairy and open, monster-fucked, cum-flowing hole, slurping up as much of Lance's primal semen as I could get. I licked into that speared tunnel to gulp down Lance's ivory sperm juice, tasting that hot, salty spice mixed with Sam's rich cunt sauce while loving every tongue slurping second of it.

Sam whined as I did this, but I let her go, sat up, straightened my back, and licked my lips clean of any cum. She was not going to like what was going to happen next, so I decided to give her a fair warning.

"Relax yourself," I breathed out with my eyes closed. "Get loose and relaxed. This is going to hurt."

"Wh...What?" choked out Sam.

I opened my eyes to see her staring up at me in alarm, and then she squeezed her own blue eyes shut, her lips grimacing in terrible pain as we both listened to the sounds of her bones cracking.

She jerked and spasmed as her bones lengthened and thickened, her muscles bulging, black fur erupting from her skin along her belly, chest, and back. Her small, B-cup breasts billowed out to the size of C's, her little, dark-brown nipples growing in size, as well. She cried out in both pain and fear as her voice deepened into a growl, her teeth sharpening into pointed fangs, her eyes yellowing from their normal blue.

She was only hit with a partial change, what I surmised was a quarter change. Her fur only went up from her snatch across her belly to go up in between her breasts in a V, looping around her waist like a belt to go up the middle of her back. I, on the other hand, knew what was coming for me. I was going to get a half change because I knew how to draw out more power than Sam did. She was new at this, but I'd already had months of experience with it.

It was my turn to cry out in pain as my body changed. Light-brown fur, light-brown because of my natural hair color, spread like an infection all over my body as I grew in both size and muscle, pushing me up to a height close to six feet tall, puffing my breasts up to double-D's, giving me the fangs and black snout of the she-wolf, and electrifying me with the wild pulse of nature itself in my veins.

"Oooooh, yesss..." I growled.

I flexed my bulging biceps and stared down at my new pupil, and Sam stared back up at me with wide, horrified eyes, but I expected as much.

"Stand up," I commanded in a deep, yet still feminine voice. "Feel Lance's power within you."

I offered one furry, clawed hand to her, and she reached for it out of instinct. I pulled her up to her feet, and though she was still taller than me, I was still stronger than her, so there was no issue of control here. She would not be trouble, even in her new, more powerful form.

"What is this!" growled Sam. "What's happening!"

"It's the power of the beast," I said in a deep voice. "We can take it in, change any time we want, but we're like the Whore of Babylon. We have to earn it the old-fashioned way."

Sam stared down at her partially furred body and then ran her clawed hands over the new muscle in her abs and legs. I watched as she shivered in excitement from the raw fury pulsing through her veins, taking her over, taking over her soul, sending its dark tendrils of the night down into her very spiritual depths...Oh, yes...I finally had her. Her will was broken. She had accepted this darkness...Good.

"You'll learn to absorb it as I do," I growled. "If you take it all in, you'll change like Lance, but the changes are always temporary. They don't last long."

"How long?" asked Sam as she stared down at me.

"A half-hour, maybe, for you," I replied, "but it will last longer the more practiced you get."

Sam looked up toward the concrete ceiling, stretched her muscular arms above her head, and moaned as she cracked the bones in her back. She then looked me straight in the eyes, golden eyes to golden eyes, and demanded something I had been waiting to hear for a week now.

"Teach me," she said.

*****

I dragged Daniel into his father's study, dragging him into that tiny library by the front of his dark-blue T-shirt. It had been an entire week since he'd struck me, and my period was going to begin...hopefully...next week, so it was now or never. I wanted him back where he belonged, or at least, the penis part of him, anyway.

The study was a little room with a few bookshelves lining the dark-wood walls, some nice dark-red carpet with gold fleur-de-lis print upon it lining the floor, and a studious dark-wood desk near a large pane of nook windows, those windows decked round with dark- red curtains, though those curtains were open right now. There was even a big blue globe of the earth on a bronze stand near the desk, and this gave the whole room a classic 'university' feel, so which made it the perfect place to defile.

"Now, while your parents are distracted," I said hungrily, that sexual glimmer in my brown eyes.

Daniel looked at me with wide eyes, those eyes an ocean blue, but if he was comprehending my lustful desire, he certainly wasn't showing it.

"Now...what?" he asked in confusion. "Why are you looking at me like that? What is it you want, Saoirse?"

Really?... Is he being serious, or is he fucking with me?...He...He's being serious...He really doesn't know...God, he is so STUPID sometimes!...Ugh...Never mind.

My name is Saoirse Lennon, a young white girl of Irish descent, and my name is pronounced 'Serr-Shah' if you're wondering. I'm pretty hot in my own right, and I'm not into other girls, but I'd fuck me. I'm a twenty-two-year-old white girl with long, curly brown hair and brown eyes, an attractive face...I think so, anyway...a great butt, and nice C-cup breasts with beautiful pink nipples in the centers of them. I stand five-foot-eight as opposed to my oblivious boyfriend's six-foot-even, and if it weren't for the fact that he's so Goddamned hot, I'd have probably shot him by now.

Today I was wearing my blue jeans, black winter boots, and a white T-shirt with the pink word 'Foxy' on it in cursive letters. My jean jacket was in the foyer closet because the Christianson's kept their house pretty warm. It was a simple but sexy look I put on for Daniel, but not too slutty due to the fact that I still wanted to make a good impression on Daniel's parents.

This brings me back to Daniel. Daniel Christianson is my new boyfriend, and as far as boyfriends go, he's pretty fucking hot. As I previously mentioned, he stands six-feet-tall, broad-shouldered, with all-natural muscle and a...grrrrrowlll...tight, a muscular ass that's to die for. He has the most glorious pecs, like...like a flat board of rippling muscle, not like a weightlifter, but still something I fucking love to run my fingers and hair over. He has a circumcised, six-and-a-half-inch long cock when it's erect, and it's quite thick, and it's also the very thing I wanted right now because my happy hole was feeling somewhat unhappy at the moment, mainly because it was empty...Wait, wait...I forgot to describe his face...Uhhh...Daniel's cute, like, really cute, with ocean-blue eyes and short, kind of stiff black hair, but...his face is very kissable. Very, very kissable.

Today he was in his dark-blue T-shirt, his dark blue jeans, and his signature tanned hiking boots, but this look, this rough, working-man look, really lit my candle. He could turn the ladies' heads, and he did quite often, but they couldn't have him, because I'd rip their fucking heads off and play kickball with those heads if they so much as breathed on him, but that's neither here nor there.

He would be perfect if it weren't for the fact that he can be stupid sometimes. Like really stupid. It's because of him that I'm a werewolf now, you know. Yep, you heard me. Werewolves are real, and I'm one now because of him, because he's a werewolf, and usually it takes one to make another one.

I'm not going to go into the backstory on that, because it's a long story. Let's just say that Daniel bit me when he was wolfed out, I fucked him when he was a human, and he fucked me when he was wolfed out again. All that biting and fucking cursed me with lycanthropy, so a few days a month I have to stay with Daniel at his parent's lodge, locked away during the full moon, so that neither one of us goes on a bloodthirsty rampage across the countryside.

Daniel's parents are pretty cool, and I had known his dad was a veterinarian, but I hadn't known his mom was one, too. Together, they're pretty loaded in the money department, and their home is pretty fucking big. My dad's little house, a cabin he bought from them, looks tiny in comparison.

Anyway, Daniel and I told Daniel's mom, Mrs. Christianson...her name is Laura...what Daniel had done to me while he was wolfed out. You see, Daniel was supposed to be locked up in a holding cell at his family's lodge during the full moon. He would lock himself in with a safety latch, and then unlock the door in the morning once he had changed back into a human. Problem was that neither he nor his parents realized that werewolves can lock, unlock, and open doors. Mindless as they are, werewolves in the beast form at least have a glimmer of human intelligence, and they can ambush and lay traps, too, which makes them pretty fucking dangerous.

Anyway, Daniel got out last month, and he used that opportunity to bite and fuck me and turn me into his little wolf bitch...Men...Even when they're out of their fucking minds, their minds are still on fucking. What the fuck?...Oh, hey, look, it's pussy. Never mind that it's injured and lying in bed whimpering because of a massive fucking injury you gave it when you bit it...Oh, wait, I think it's reluctant. No matter, just stick your dick in it, and it'll wet up, right? It's like getting a hard-on, but for a girl. It just has to get wet. They think with their pussies, don't they?

No...No, we do not...Okay, well that's not entirely true, but that's beside the point. What Daniel did to me is...That's an old grievance. I've let it go.

Anyway, Daniel and I hiked out to his family's lodge, called his mom, and filled her in on what had happened when the full moon was up. Naturally, she was upset, but I put on a show of tears, and she felt so sorry for me, she cussed out Daniel, even though it wasn't his fault. She called in Daniel's dad, Mr. Christianson...his name is Robert, by the way...and he wasn't happy about it, but I put on another show of tears and some genuine fear of him, and he caved right away. It turns out that Daniel was being paranoid the entire time he was warning me about his father because his dad was a total softy for my daytime soap routine...Hey, he doesn't need to know that I'm a horny bitch that seduced his son the moment I saw him, now does he?

Did I forget to mention that Daniel's parents are hunters? Oh, yeah, his parents aren't just veterinarians. They belong to a secret organization that hunts monsters and shit, but it's not like on the TV shows where they go around doing all kinds of illegal shit. No, they just cover things up with the money, something they get for expenses donated by the organization itself, which apparently has some very wealthy, very powerful backers. I know the Queen of England is one of them, as is the CEO of a major tech company, but in truth, I haven't gleaned a lot of information about that mysterious organization. They're called the Seraphim...not to be confused with any other companies or organizations with that particular title...and that's all I know about them. I'm not allowed to know anything else about them, and neither is Daniel because we are both the very type of thing they hunt.

Oh, and that leads me back to me, myself, and I. My own dad knows that Daniel's my boyfriend now; he just doesn't know that Daniel's a werewolf...or that I'm a werewolf...I'm pretty sure he'd be pissed about that second one. Whatever the case, he's met Daniel, and he likes him a lot, but I already knew he would. Daniel looks like the nice, respectable, down-to-earth type of guy that my dad would approve of, and to his credit, my dad does approve of him, so everything's good again. My life is right back on track.

This brings me to my current predicament. Daniel and I haven't had any...uhhh...alone time...for a week now...Oh, fuck it, I'll just put it in plain English. We haven't fucked in a week, and I want his cock in my mouth again, Goddammit. I have needs, too.

So here we are, in the study. Apparently, Daniel is clueless, so I was about to give him a clue. Yep, the slutty seducer was Saoirse, in the study, with her very agitated, very turned on twat...Look at that. I won the game. Fun time.

I walked back to the door of the study, closed it, and flipped the lock latch.

"What are you doing?" asked Daniel.

I didn't answer him. He was still clueless, so I walked over to his dad's study desk, unbuttoned my jeans, and pulled them plus my panties down until both articles of clothing fell around my ankles and black winter boots. I leaned over his dad's desk, hands down on that flat wooden surface, stuck out my bare ass, and stared straight out the large window right behind his dad's wooden study chair. It was in the middle of the day, though there was no one outside right now, they could walk by at any moment. However, that little danger just made it more exciting for me. I was already wet, anyway.

"Here's a hint, Daniel," I said firmly. "I trust you'll figure out what to do."

"Saoirse, are you...are you out of your mind!" he hissed.

Okay, I'm not going to get mad...I'm not going to get mad...Just control that Irish temper of yours, Saoirse...

"Get over here and stick your dick in me," I demanded. "I'm not going to say it again."

"Saoirse!" said Daniel, his voice panicked. "You actually want to do this in...in my dad's study! This is his office!"

"Yeah," I shrugged. "So what? I bet he's fucked your mom in here, too."

"Eww," said Daniel in disgust.

"Look," I said in frustration," you and I haven't had any chance to be alone together...in this way...for a whole week now, and I'm sexually frustrated. Yeah, I can masturbate, and I do, but I want you."

"You masturbate?" asked Daniel in surprise.

I smacked my forehead with my right hand and wiped that hand down my face before placing it back down on the desk I was leaning over.

Every girl masturbates, Daniel," I sighed.

They do?" he asked.

"Shut up and get over here," I growled.

"Saoirse, I don't think this is a good idea..." he began, but I cut him off.

"Get over here!" I hissed. "Get over here now, or I'm going to strip down and walk around naked in your Goddamned house! I'll take a piss on the carpet right in front of your parents and tell them it's the lycanthropy doing it, the lycanthropy that's all your fault!"

"Okay, okay!" he panicked. "Jesus Christ...I'll do it...We just...We have to be quiet."

"Yeah, yeah," I replied. "Come put that big meat in my wet hole. I'm horny, and your big dick is the only thing on my mind right now."

"You think my dick is big?" he asked.

"Daaannnieeel..." I growled.

"Okay, okay," he replied.

I waited patiently as he walked up behind me and ran his hands along the smooth skin of my hips and bare bottom. I let out a long sigh of relief at his touch because I had been waiting for that gentle touch for some time now. I heard him unzip his jeans, there was a slight pause from him, then I heard his jeans drop down around his ankles, and then the bulbous head of that delicious cock of his slid up and into my hairy happy hole.

Oooooh. That's what I needed. I really fucking needed that.

"Ooooh, yeah," I sighed. "You don't know how much I've been looking forward to this. Just give me a quickie, something to satisfy me for the time being, and I'll be happy. It's like having a snack before dinner, you know? You're just really fucking hungry, and you need something to carry you over until you can eat a full meal. Something like that."

"Yeah," breathed Daniel.

He moved his thick cock in and out, back and forth inside me, and it felt so good that I just closed my eyes and breathed out another sigh of relief.

"Yeah," he said again. "Now that I'm doing it, I have to admit that I missed this."

"See?" I shrugged. "It's not so hard to...Wait, it is hard, and that's exactly what I want, but..."

Daniel chuckled but continued to slowly fuck me. I gave a quick laugh and shook my head, but I kept my eyes closed, intent on enjoying that thick piece of meat sliding back and forth inside my happy wet tunnel.

"I meant, I'm really, really happy right now," I purred. "I've finally got my cur to admit that I'm his bitch. That makes me happy. Gives me a happy one."

"That's one way to describe it," breathed Daniel.

I chuckled again, and then I used that opportunity to reach down and stroke myself with my right-hand fingers. I liked to give myself a slow stroke at first, a slow and even, circular stroke to my clit and hood, taking a little bit of time to give myself a quick and jerking stroke, then rub my whole pussy for a moment, sinking my fingers into my wet hole, right between my pussy and his cock. It feels good to get your fingers creamy, then goes back to stroking your clit, that way you can get some more of that gel in the folds of your hood. It also feels good to feel your man's cock and the softness of his balls while he's moving in and out of you. It's warm, it's wet, it's wonderful, and it's just good sex, but that's something I've discovered that most guys don't understand.

Daniel, on the other hand, let me do whatever I wanted because he was my little bitch...even though, technically, I was his little bitch...but he'd made a promise to me, a promise to be mine, and I owned him now, so he was like the best fucking boyfriend I'd ever had...I had control of this boy. Couldn't ask for better than that.

"You're the best boyfriend I've ever had," I breathed out. "You are."

"Really?" asked Daniel in a husky exhale of breath.

"Oh, yeah," I nodded with my eyes closed. "You've done some really stupid things, Daniel Christianson, but I have to admit, I think I'm falling in love with you."

"Whoa, what?" asked Daniel in surprise. "What did you say?"

"You heard me, Danny boy," I grinned. "I think I'm in love with you."

He moved his hands up to my bare waist and ground his crotch into me, thrusting deep inside my quivering, cum-soaked snatch. The smell of my vibrating twat was all over his dad's study, so we were going to have to light a scented candle or something because if I could smell that rich, tangy aroma, his dad was going to have an aneurysm coming in here.

Of course, stupid me should have expected him to say something equally as stupid as my high expectations of him.

"You sound like Megan," he said quietly.

My brown eyes snapped open as my lips turned down into a very noticeable frown. My shoulders tensed as I took in a sharp breath.

"Danieeeeel!" I growled. "Never mention another girl's name in the middle of sex! What the fuck!"

"Sorry! I'm sorry!" he apologized. "This is just...It's all so sudden. I'm having trouble processing it."

Okay, okay. I could understand that. I had taken over his life over the past three weeks. He was just nervous, anxious about this whole new relationship. I get it...Still...what the fuck...

"Just don't mention Megan again," I said unhappily. "That's a sore subject."

He ran his hands up my sides within my shirt and cupped his hands underneath my breasts, right around my bra, squeezing that article of clothing and the soft bulbs within as he continued to slowly fuck me. I rubbed my whole pussy...well, the top half of it, anyway...I can't very well rub the whole thing with Daniel's dick and balls in the way, but...anyway...I rubbed my whole pussy and moaned, and then I took that time to bring my fingers up to my mouth to taste my juices, sucking on those digits to bring in that rich flavor to my taste buds.

"I was with Megan for a long time, Saoirse," said Daniel quietly. "I can't just forget her. I broke it off with her because I was afraid of inflicting her with the curse..."

"I get that, you meathead," I frowned. "It's still bad form to mention another girl's name...Wait...What are you saying?... Hey!...I just confessed that I was in love with you, and I did it in the middle of having sex with you, and...What the fuck are you saying, Daniel?"

He leaned down and kissed the back of my bare neck, right on my right shoulder, and he ground into me again, causing the mushroom head of his thick dong to grind into my cervix. It made me shake and shiver, temporarily sabotaging my ability to think.

"I'm saying that..." breathed Daniel, "I'm saying that I don't know what my feelings are yet. I thought I was in love with Megan, but that was a long time ago. Now, you're saying you're in love with me, but the truth is, you don't know me at all, and I don't know you. Can't we get to know each other first?"

I sighed as my shoulders sank in disappointment. He was really getting under my skin, and not in a good way.

"I know I've been bitchy and kind of mean," I said unhappily, "but that's understandable, considering you inflicted me with a Goddamned lycanthropy curse and raped me in my own bed...though that wasn't your fault. You were possessed by your animal side, so I'm not blaming you for that, but...you have to understand where I'm coming from, okay? I've sunk all of my feelings into you, and I don't want to lose you, and it scares me to think that you might get back with Megan. Can't you see that?"

"Yeah," he whispered.

He ran his hands down my sides and along the smooth skin of my bare ass, kissing into my right shoulder and up, up to my right ear, nibbling on my earlobe for a moment...Goddamn. He could make love when he wanted to, you know?

"I do love you..." he whispered into my ear.

This caused my heart to jump, but what he said next killed that little joy.

"But I still have feelings for Megan," he finished.

"Goddammit," I breathed out. "Goddammit, I knew it...Fine. Resolve that shit, so you can be mine. I want you all to myself."

I...I will," he stammered. "I will. I promise.

Good," I smiled. "Now stop all this negative talk and fuck me properly. I want to cum.

He chuckled and rubbed the left side of his head against my long, curly brown hair.

"You are a little bitch," he said, the distinct sound of mirth in his voice.

"I'm a big bitch, Danny boy," I grinned. "You should know that by now."

I closed my eyes and pushed back with my butt, forcing him back a bit to give us some room.

"Now fuck me, cur," I said forcefully. "Fuck me hard, so I can cum. Fuck me right over Daddy's desk."

He didn't say anything after that. No, he gripped my narrow waist and then pounded into my beautiful butt, and oooooh, it was like drinking from a cool, clear stream after wandering around in the desert for hours. That thick, circumcised cock of his thrust deeply into me, moving in and out, in and out, hitting my cervix over and over again, stroking my wet tunnel, making me feel it right up in my lower belly and bladder.

"Yeah...Yeah," I choked out. "Ooooh, fuck yeah. Gimme, gimme, Danny boy. Fuck me over Daddy's desk. Fuck me, fuck me, fuck me. Fuck me over Daddy's desk."

He grabbed my beautiful ass and squeezed it, and then he fucked me hard and fast, pummeling my hairy wet twat, ramming my long, wet tunnel with his magic love stick.

"Yeah, yeah, yeah," I moaned. "Ooooooh...I'm such a little whore, Danny boy. Gimme, gimme that big dick. Give it to me right over Daddy's work desk...Oh, yeah. I wish I could just strip down and let you take my titties into your mouth...Just take 'em right in...Suck on my titties and my fat little clit...Oh, yeah...Give it to me..."

"Fuck," huffed Daniel. "Fu-huh-huck...This feels...really, really good, Saoirse." "Yeeeeaaaaah," I moaned. "That's it, that's it. Hit me like that...Oh, yeeeaaah. You're a Goddamned beast, Daniel. You're my wolfy-wolf. Oh, oh yeah. Hit me like that."

I reached down and went back to stroking myself. He was really pounding into me now, shaking and rattling the desk I was leaning against, and I could feel that magic circling inside my lower belly, right underneath my clit, sinking in and spreading up and out...

"Oh, fuck..." I choked out. "Oh, ho, ho, fuck...I'm going to cum...It's coming, Daniel...I'm going to pop. Oooooh, fuck."

I stroked my clit and hood hard and fast as he grunted and huffed into me. My fingers were sticky wet with my own congealed gel, but I didn't care. This only increased my pleasure.

"Fucka, fucka, fuck!" I hissed. "Oh, oh, oh...fuck! Keep going! Don't stop! Ooooh, I'm almost there! Daniel, I...Daniel...Daniel, I...Oh, oh, oh..."

He picked up his thrusting, hitting me harder than before, hitting me deeply, banging my cervix like a fucking gong. It hurt a little, but it also felt fucking awesome, and that hit the button, made that bomb go off in a little mini-nuke right inside me.

"Oh my fucking God!" I gasped. "Oh my fucking God! Oh, oh, oh...my...fucking...GAAAWWWD!!"

I came in a nuclear explosion of squeezing pussy and dripping white gel. I didn't squirt like I had during the full moon, but I figured that was due to being 'apart' from my bestial instincts. Even so, it felt fucking amazing, my happy wet tunnel clutching Daniel's thick cock over and over again, my own cream squeezing out of me onto his big balls, my clit pulsing underneath my fingers like it was going to pop off.

I shivered and shook from aftershocks as he groaned and came into me, and I once again felt that wonderful seed of his spread throughout my belly, filling me up and causing me to sigh in contentment. I was probably going to get pregnant like this, but at that moment, that moment when you feel that incredible warmth spread throughout you, you don't really give a shit about pregnancy. It's a problem that every woman has to deal with at some point, and I dealt with it by ignoring it entirely...Yeah, yeah, I know...It's irresponsible, but I was a few French fries short of a runway at that moment, so cut me some slack.

We stood there and breathed in and out, in and out, I with my eyes closed, both of us just giving each other a little break before we had to move again.

The door handle of the study rattled a few seconds later, and then a loud and steady knocking occurred after that.

"Oh, shit!" hissed Daniel.

He quickly popped his dick out of me, and that caused my eyes to widen as I choked out a gasp, but he was panicking, so I didn't call him on it...You gotta pull out slow, guys, gentle like, you get me? Are you sinking that in? It doesn't hurt when you pull it out fast; it's just a rude surprise.

Daniel scrambled to pull up his jeans and underwear while I calmly pulled up my own panties and jeans. I buttoned myself up as Daniel panicked and screwed around with his belt buckle for entirely too long...It was actually kind of funny. He had no experience with walk-ins.

"Daniel?" asked a female voice from behind the study door. "Daniel, is everything all right?"

That was not the sound of his mother. It was the maid...yes, the Christianson's have a maid...but I didn't know her name. I'd seen a glance of her at one point; she was an older white woman with glasses and greying hair. She was in her late fifties, if I had to guess, but she didn't dress like a maid. She was just wearing blue jeans and a light-purple wool sweater when I saw her. I guess the old maid tropes on TV weren't quite accurate when translating over to real life.

"Coming, Donna!" called Daniel.

"Came," I giggled.

He flashed me an ugly look, but I couldn't help but grin back at him...Hey, it was his fucking fault for saying it, not mine.

He finished with his stupid buckle, trotted over to the door, unlatched it, and quickly opened it. This older woman, Donna, walked in and gave Daniel a quick, worried look.

"Is everything all right?" she asked. "I thought I heard a shout..."

"Everything's fine," said Daniel sheepishly. "I just...uhhh...hit my knee on the edge of the desk."

"Oh..." said Donna.

She looked over toward me, but I was leaning backward against 'Daddy's' desk, a wicked smile on my lips. I knew damned well she could smell the heavy scent of sex in this room, small as it was, especially the aroma of my wild, wet, cum-dripping snatch. It didn't take a rocket scientist to figure out what we'd been doing.

Donna's lips turned upwards in a slight smile as she rested her gaze back upon Daniel.

"Well, you should be more careful," she said, a slight chuckle in her voice. "You know how your father feels about this study...You don't want to damage anything with any...' activities'...you might be up to."

"Right," said Daniel meekly.

"Well, I'll get back to cleaning," replied Donna. "You kids have fun...Just not too much fun."

She walked out and shut the door behind her.

Daniel turned to look at me, but his face was a sheet of red, a look of slight horror on that handsome mug of his. He closed his blue eyes, took in a sharp breath, and then held his face in both hands...I just burst out laughing at that little reaction. This was funny as fuck.

My Daniel walked through my front door, his new little whore right behind him. This was fun, though, because this was exactly what I had expected him to do, to bring his little fuck toy as a show of possession and separation, possession of her and separation from me.

My name is Megan Holly. I'm a twenty-four-year-old white woman of German and French descent, and I stand five-foot-two and weigh one hundred and twenty-eight pounds. I'm an adorable, gorgeous little thing with a cherub face, short, dyed-blonde hair, and beautiful green eyes. I look like a hot little sex toy when naked, with squeezable, malleable C-cup breasts and dark-pink nipples, and the prize in my package is a completely eatable, fuckable bald cunt with an amazing dark-pink triangular hood and a tiny little dark-pink clit. I'm what every boy fantasizes about when they stroke their manhoods in the dark of night.

Today I was in a light-green dress that went down just past my knees, little white print flowers all over it, with my comfortable white canvas shoes on, and I had topped that off with my good pearl earrings and matching necklace, a homey, housewife look to make Daniel regret leaving me for this fucking trailer trash he had brought into my home.

CHAPTER 5

My Daniel is Daniel Christianson, my one true love, and he's the one I'm going to marry and be with together forever. Daniel is a twenty-four-year-old white man that stands six- foot-even has broad shoulders and is lined with all-natural muscle on that delicious working man's body. He's gorgeous in the face, with sapphire-blue eyes, rugged yet soft features, and beautiful short black hair that's a little stiff in the front. He is every girl's dream, or at least, he should be.

He was in his signature light-blue long-sleeve button-up with a white undershirt, dark blue jeans, and tanned hiking boots, and...and...Sigh...He looks so dreamy that I could just eat him up.

His little whore was named Saoirse, and apparently that's pronounced 'Ser-Shah' because it's an Irish name, but I really didn't care about that. She was a temporary speed bump in my taking back of Daniel, a little trollop of cow jizz that I was going to feed to Lance at the first opportunity. I wanted to watch, however. I wanted my Lance to take small bites out of her in order to keep her alive for a few minutes before he ate her. I'd have him start with the softer parts, probably the breasts.

She was taller than me, about five-foot-eight, and she was a little slender for her height, not quite an hourglass-like me, but she was still quite beautiful, and this really burned me up inside, made me want to snap her bones one by one, which I could, by the way, but I'll explain my unnatural strength later on. Anyway, she was a white girl, obviously, of Irish descent, with long, curly, brown hair and brown eyes, and she sported C-cup breasts on her chest, the same make and model as my own...Yes, I was probably going to have Lance start with those breasts.

This little bitch was in a pair of stonewashed jeans and a red T-shirt with the white letters 'So Perfect' in cursive. On her feet was a pair of black hiking boots, and this overall look just screamed trailer trash, making me want to slap Daniel and ask him what the fuck he was thinking.

But onto the main gist of my complaint.

You see, Daniel's a werewolf, but I won't get into how I know that. It's too long of a story. Needless to say, I'm positive he broke up with me all of those months ago because he was afraid of infecting me with lycanthropy, but I'm also positive that he infected me just by all of the times we'd made love, kind of like transferring a supernatural STD. My time for my plans was running out because it was only a matter of time before Daniel infected his new fuck toy with lycanthropy, and that would make her much more difficult to kill, and THAT would interfere with me getting back together with him. Nevertheless, I always have a backup plan just in case...No matter. I was setting my plan into motion, and that plan was starting right...now.

"Daniel!" I said gleefully.

I ran up and hugged him at the doorway, but he politely pried me off of his handsome chest. I admit this angered me, but I knew how to play the long game, so I did not show a hint of that anger.

"Megan," breathed Daniel.

"Come in, come in!" I said excitedly. "I've just finished baking some bread. Please...come have a slice...both of you."

It ground into me to offer any hospitality to Daniel's whore, but it was necessary. I had to keep up the charade.

Uhhh...okay," said Daniel nervously.

He gave a quick and anxious glance to his new 'girlfriend', but she only rolled her eyes...What a little cunt. Oh, I was definitely going to enjoy ending her. A snippy-snippy here, a snippy-snippy there...Cutting parts off of her sounded fun. Hmmm...Why should Lance have all the fun? Perhaps I should keep her execution all to myself.

I led the pair into the kitchen and waved a hand toward a couple of small wooden chairs at my little square kitchen table. My kitchen was an immaculate white, with garden print upon the wallpaper, images of green bell peppers, onions, tomatoes, and whatnot decked out all over the kitchen walls, and this give my little cooking area that downhome feel that went straight to a man's heart.

I slipped on an oven mitt, opened my white oven, and pulled out my finished loaf of sweetbread. I'd already made this bread some time ago, but I had the oven on low heat to keep it warm for my guests. I placed that loaf on the table, cut a slice for each of them, and put those slices on my small china plates for that extra special touch.

"Megan..." said Daniel nervously. "This is nice and all, but we really can't stay. I came here to...well...to try to get you to understand..."

"Oh, I know, silly," I said with a warm smile as I waved him off. "It's okay. I know we weren't meant to be. I'm just glad you came by to see me. I'm doing all right if you wanted to know."

"Oh," said Daniel in visible surprise. "Oh, well...I...Okay, then."

"Yes, I had a heartbreaking moment or two," I said with a sad smile, "but sometimes that's life. I cried for a while, but I got over it. I mean, we've been apart for a long time now. I guess it just shocked me to see you with someone else."

"I am... sorry about that," said Daniel sheepishly. "I didn't want to break it to you like that...It just felt...cold."

It's fine," I smiled. "Saoirse is very beautiful, by the way. You couldn't have done better.

"Oh...thank you," said this 'Saoirse' in a polite tone. "I...uhhh...am happy to be your guest for the moment."

"Nonsense," I said as I waved her off. "Any friend of Daniel's is a friend of mine. I'm just hoping we can get along and be good friends. That way I can spill all of my dirty little secrets about Daniel to you. That should keep him under your thumb."

This young lady gave a short guffaw as Daniel turned a slight red. Yes, I had a way with people now that I never had before my little infection. I could tell that this was going to be easier than I had first thought.

I took that moment to study her aura. You see, I have the power to see people's auras, that ring of light around each person that defines their soul. That perk came with the infection that Daniel inflicted upon me. It's a great little power, because it allows me to see people as they truly are, and therefore it allows me to properly pull their strings.

This girl's aura was red, purple, pink, light blue, green, and teal, the colors of wrath, pride, love, compassion, envy, and mercy, a strange mix for an individual to possess. It was like she was a perfect balance between darkness and light, but there was one thing missing...the color of pearl...the color of fidelity. This little whore was not the loyal type, and I could use that. All I had to do was turn Daniel against her, and she would run. Of course, I was still going to kill her even after I parted her from Daniel...I do have principles, you know.

This young woman in my target sight picked up my slice of bread and bit into it, nodding her head in appreciation of my home cooking. She chewed, swallowed, and then gave me an earnest look.

This is really good," she said thoughtfully.

'Thank you," I replied. "Cooking is something I have a bit of talent in.

"Oh, you too?" asked Saoirse. "I cook all the time. Maybe we can swap recipes."

"Maybe," I smiled.

I had a recipe for her. It involved screaming agony followed by slow, drawn-out death.

"I think..." said Daniel anxiously, "I think maybe we should go, Megan. I don't want to be rude, but we have somewhere to be. I just...I had to come by to make sure you were all right."

"Oh, absolutely," I said in mock happiness. "I just want us all to be friends. That means you have to stop by again soon...Next time for at least a couple of hours."

"Oh, that would be great," smiled Saoirse. "We'd be happy to."

Daniel's eyes flitted back and forth in nervous effect over this. This 'Saoirse' was clearly in the dark about how he was currently feeling because he did not want to deal with me anymore...Oh, well. I'd punish him for that later.

"We really have to go," urged Daniel. "I need to use the restroom anyway, and you know how long it takes to get back to my house."

"Nonsense," I chuckled. "Just use my bathroom, silly. You know where it is." "I...uhhh...don't think that's a good idea..." began Daniel.

His little whore had just finished swallowing another piece of my sweetbread when she cut him off.

"What's the big deal,?" asked this 'Saoirse'. "Just go use her bathroom, stupid. Nothing bad is going to happen for the two minutes you'll be gone...Sheesh..."

"Uhhh...I don't think that's..." began Daniel, that nervous tinge in his voice.

"Go take a piss, you mook," frowned Saoirse. "What the hell?"

"You...You don't under...Dammit...Never mind," sighed Daniel.

My Daniel knows better. I don't know how he knew, because he's oblivious most of the time, but he sensed something was up. Even, so, he got up, walked out of my kitchen, and headed right toward my bathroom. We both watched him in silence as he opened up my white-wood bathroom door, walk into the bathroom, and close the door behind him. I waited for him to turn on the vent fan before putting the next part of my plan into action.

"You know, you're really sweet, Meg..." began Saoirse.

I leaned over my square kitchen table and knocked that piece of sweetbread out of her hands, sending it flying across my kitchen to land on the white kitchen tiles near the basement door. She gave me a look of complete surprise, a moment of temporary shock, so I capitalized on it.

"You listen to me, you little whore," I hissed. "You keep your slutty little twat away from my Daniel, or

I'm going to dig out your balls with a spoon and feed them to you. Do you understand me?"

She looked up at me in wide-eyed amazement, a vacuous look, like a deer caught in the headlights, but that astonished expression quickly devolved into a pure liquid rage, exactly what I expected from her.

She kicked back my kitchen chair as she stood, arms at her sides, and the fingers of both her hands balled into fists as her biceps tensed in response to what could only be adrenaline running through her. I needed her furious, and she was off to a good start.

"What the fuck did you just say to me?" she hissed in a low, warning tone.

"Are you stupid, you little cunt?" I hissed back. "You'll break it off with Daniel now, today, or I'm going to cut off your clit with a pair of shears and sew it to your forehead! Do you get me! He's mine, you little slut! If you don't grow some fucking brains and dump him now, I'm going to..."

She swung her right fist, connecting directly with my left cheekbone, right underneath my left eye...Bingo. That was the reaction I wanted all along, which was good because I was running out of gruesome threats to come up with.

She hit with such force that I was spun to my right, slipping in my shoes, and I fell, hitting the corner edge of my table with the right side of my head, just above my right eye. It hurt like fucking hell, but it also split me open, the exact effect I needed for my little game. I fell to the kitchen tiles right after that, sat up on my butt, and then held my bloody wound with my right hand.

There was a lot of blood, more than I could have hoped for. I had an inch-long gash in my head that stung like mad and gave me an instant headache at that very spot. A normal person would need stitches for a wound like that, but all I had to do was fuck Lance, and that little wound would go away. I only needed this wound for the length of time it would take for Daniel to freak out over it, but knowing him, he'd drive me to the E.R. right away, so I'd probably be getting stitches, anyway.

It was time to put on the rest of this show.

'Ah...Ah...AaaaaaaaAAAAAAHHHHH!"   I screamed.

I clutched my head wound with my right hand as I rocked back and forth, blood just seeping through my fingers to spill down the right side of my face. I let the tears come next because the sobbing would give this situation the extra little touch it needed. I had practiced with my reflection in the bathroom mirror earlier in the day, that look of abject horror at being injured, mouth wide open with eyes squeezed shut in pain, very, very dramatic, but I hadn't expected to get a gash like this. I'd just thought I'd have a black eye, maybe a split lip, but this was sooooo much better.

Daniel came running out of the bathroom at the sound of my screeching. He entered the kitchen at lightspeed, only to grind to a halt once he rounded my kitchen table and saw me bleeding on the floor, sobbing, my eyes squeezed shut, my mouth wide open, that look of the horrified victim just down to a T...Ah, sometimes I even impress myself.

"What the fuck!" he cried out.

I opened my green, tear-stricken eyes, and this little whore, Saoirse, held yet another look of shock and surprise upon her pretty face, one that rivaled my initial verbal assault upon her.

"Daniel...I...I didn't..." she stammered out.

He knelt next to me and held me in his strong arms, and I gave an internal sigh at his loving touch. I was bawling now, of course, because there was no point in screaming anymore, but the whole scene in its entirety pushed all of Daniel's buttons at once, kind of the whole point of this little shit show.

He flashed a look of pure rage at his little fuck toy, and I knew right then that I had won. "What happened!" yelled Daniel, clear anger in his voice. "What did you do!"

"I...I didn't mean to..." stammered Saoirse. "She...She fell after I hit her...Oh, shit..." 'You did WHAT!" yelled Daniel. "What the fuck were you thinking!

"Daniel, I didn't mean to..." said this Saoirse girl, obviously a pathetic attempt to cover for herself.

"Go to the truck," ordered Daniel.

"Daniel, it's not my..." began Saoirse.

"GO TO THE TRUCK!" yelled Daniel. "You and I are going to have words, Saoirse! Right now, I have to get her to the E.R...Dammit...Dammit!"

This little whore of Daniel's stormed out of my kitchen, out of my living room, and out my front door, fists clenched, tears in her eyes, her whole body shaking...Good...Yes, I think I was going to kill her myself. Torturing her to death would be more entertaining than just watching Lance take bites out of her.

*****

I was nervous, that kind of nervous that turns your stomach upside down and makes you want to throw up and take a shit at the same time. Daniel and I were out in the forest, and the sun had just gone down, but we were outside his family's home, and there was no full moon tonight, so we were safe. We wouldn't be romping around the countryside eating anyone...uhhh...I'll have to explain that in a bit. Whatever the case, he'd decided to take me on this little hike for a talk, a red electric lantern in his left hand for light, but...I was not looking forward to that talk.

Daniel and I were both bundled up against the cold, he in his tanned winter coat and I in my new grey parka. The cold wasn't so bad for me anymore anyway, but that was likely due to my 'condition', or the fact that I was growing more and more into that 'condition' every single day.

My name is Saoirse Lennon. Daniel is my new boyfriend, but...I fucked up today. I blew my top and decked his ex, a psycho little squirrel named Megan. She fell, hit her head on her kitchen table, and then Daniel and I spent the rest of the day in the Lonesome Moon St. Francis of Assisi's hospital E.R. She had to have ten stitches, and each one of those stitches left me looking like a fucking idiot.

Daniel's pissed; I know he is because he hasn't said a word to me all day long. Now we're out on this hike because hiking 'helps him think'. Honestly, I was kind of scared, because Daniel's parents are 'hunters', the kind of people that hunt monsters, not animals. Daniel and I are both werewolves...long story...but I was scared because I didn't know whether or not Daniel was going to 'put me down out here. Yeah, I know, I'm paranoid, but I was genuinely afraid for my life at that moment. I was afraid he was going to lead me out to some back pasture, pull out a gun, and shoot me in the head with a silver bullet or something.

"Daniel..." I gulped. "Please, talk to me."

He sighed and shook his head.

"Why did you hit her?" he asked.

"You know why," I said unhappily. "I told you why, like, forty times."

"Yeah, I know," replied Daniel.

"A...And?" I asked, my voice wavering from that nervousness I was currently suffering from.

"That's why I'd wanted to leave," he said grimly.

I don't understand," I said unhappily.

I didn't. He wouldn't tell me anything. He had barely spoken to me all day.

"My fear of spreading the curse to Megan was not the only reason I broke up with her," he said unhappily.

"Oooookay..." I replied.

I had no idea where this train of thought was going, but it was better than him not talking.

"Megan is..." said Daniel with an exhale of breath. "Megan is sweet ninety percent of the time, but...Look, I've known her since we were little. She's always been attracted to me, and she's obsessed with me, and I've known that for a long time."

"Uh huh," I said. "So what's going on?"

Our boots crunched through the snow and frozen scrub grass of the forest floor. This area of the woods was all snow-covered, coniferous pines, and it all looked the same, so my complete trust was in Daniel to lead me out of here if I got lost, because he knew this area like the back of his hand. I...I would be lost as fuck out here, another reason I was nervous as hell. It was a good thing I could still see the lights of Daniel's house because I was still scared. True, the conversation was taking a turn for the better, but that paranoia of mine refused to just get up and leave. I was still worried he was taking me somewhere to kill me.

"Megan has some issues," frowned Daniel. "As I said, she's sweet ninety percent of the time, but that other ten percent...She has explosive tantrums. I suspected something like that was going to happen. She's good at hiding her emotions, but I knew...I just knew if I left you two alone together that this would happen. Megan can't control herself, because she bottles up all of her emotions until they erupt, like...like Mount Vesuvius. I didn't think that she'd just let it slide that I had a new girlfriend."

Goddamn. As stupid as this boy is at times, he's pretty fucking astute at other times. Seriously, though...what the fuck? Why doesn't he explain any of this shit beforehand?

"Daniel..." I sighed. "You could have saved us all a lot of heartbreak if you had just said something about it before we walked through that door. You do realize that every single time you've kept information from me, it's blown up in our faces, right?"

"Yeah, I know," he sighed in return. "I have trouble talking about things. It's probably because my parents are hunters, and they like to keep secrets...for obvious reasons."

He held up his lantern with his left hand, reached over, and took my own left hand into his right. This lifted a huge weight off my shoulders and made me sigh in relief.

"I was afraid you were taking me out to some backwoods area to shoot me or something," I said. "Are you...Are you still mad at me?"

"Oh, I'm furious," he said unhappily. "Megan may have tantrums, but she's harmless. She is not physically capable of hurting anyone. I know damn well she blew up at you and said those things, and trust me, I believe every word you say, because I know her, but you should not have hit her. It's like kicking a puppy or like...like punching a child...I want you to understand this because it's very, very important...I need you to understand this because I don't know what I might do if something like this happens again...You are to never lay a finger on her again...Do you understand me?"

I knew what that meant. That wasn't just a warning...It was a threat. I didn't like the sound of that.

"Daniel..." I winced, "I know we haven't known each other for that long..."

"I know you have a fiery temper," he frowned. "I've been on the receiving end of it several times, and that's why I didn't want you around Megan...It's like carrying a lit torch around gunpowder...That's a pretty accurate simile, now that I think about it...That fact is...you could easily kill her, Saoirse. I know you might find that offensive, but with you being cursed and all...you don't know your own strength or how to control your rage. I've had years and years of practice at it, but you're a newborn at this. You're lucky you didn't hit her hard enough to fracture her skull and give her brain damage...or...or even break her neck...Just...Just don't ever hit her again...Don't do that again."

I hadn't thought of that...I guess I could have killed her...Goddamn, he can make me feel like shit. Even so, this wasn't entirely my fault, and I knew it, and I knew he knew it.

"I'm sorry," I winced, "but now that I know, it won't happen again. Still...you have got to start talking to me and filling me in on things, Daniel. You can't leave me hanging in the dark about all of this shit. This wouldn't have happened if you'd just said something."

"I know, I know," breathed Daniel. "Honestly, though, you're lucky she didn't press charges. You can go to prison for something like that, you know. Thankfully, Megan may have her explosions, but she's also obsessed with me, so sending you to jail would have really pissed me off, and she knows that...Still, Megan's little explosions are why I absolutely could not spread the curse to her. Can you imagine her as a werewolf? I'm afraid she'd rip through a bus full of school children or something. She has no control over her tantrums...I know...Trust me."

"I know you know," I frowned. "That's what I'm talking about...I'm the one that doesn't know. You need to share this info with me before something really serious hap..."

A loud and ringing metallic howl erupted out of the night, cutting off my spoken sentence. I'd heard that howl before, but that was impossible because there was no full moon in the night sky.

"I know that howl," I said in a fearful whisper.

"So do I," said Daniel, his voice trembling in sudden fear. "But that's impossible! There's no full moon for another two..."

That howl rang out again, this time closer, this time from behind us. We both turned as Daniel held up his lantern in obvious apprehension. Another beast, one not us, came pawing forward out of the darkness, its massive hands and feet crunching through the snow and scrubbing all around us, right into the edge of the lantern light. It stood up on two angled legs and sniffed the air, and I got a good look at this new werewolf for the first time.

This beast was about six-and-half-feet-tall, covered in light-brown fur, with the hips and triple-D-sized breasts of a woman. It had the head of a great wolf upon that fur-covered woman's body, with bright yellow eyes that gazed directly upon the both of us. She growled at us, a low and terrifying rumbling sound from deep within her chest, revealing her giant, razor-sharp fangs, and she spread out both huge, muscular arms, her hands lined with those deadly black claws...Oooooooh, shit.

Daniel pushed me back behind him as he waved his lantern slowly from left to right, probably in an attempt to distract this new she-wolf.

"Run, Saoirse!" he hissed. "Get back to the house! I'll lead it off!"

"Daniel!" I choked out.

"Run!" he commanded. "Head toward the house lights!"

He rushed forward a few feet toward this thing while waving his lantern through the air. "Hey!" he shouted. "Come on, you big bitch! Come and get me!"

"Fuck!" I hissed as I started running.

*****

I crouched as I gave out a low and terrible growl, my hands in the snow, ready to chase him down. Daniel was going to regret all of the shit he'd put little ol' Megan through; that was a promise.

I launched forward a second later, and I was distinctly aware of his little whore running in the opposite direction, but that didn't concern me. Lance had explicit orders to chase her down, capture her, and drag her slutty ass back to the moving van. I'd decided to torture her to death myself rather than have Lance eat her. I was going to make a blanket out of her skin. Lance could eat what was left.

Of course, whether that happened or not depended upon Lance. Yeah, he had explicit orders to bring her back alive, but he was...pretty...fucking...pissed...at the sight of my headwound. No, he was not happy at all about that. Not only did I have to calm him down with a blow job, but I had to convince him not to just shred Daniel's whore on sight. I let him know that if he couldn't control his urge to kill her, then he was to abandon his mission and head back to the van. I'd deal with the little bitch later. Besides, I wanted that Saoirse-skin blanket. It was going to keep me warm at night. I'd keep her long, curly, brown hair attached to her scalp and use that as a wall decoration. I was also thinking of fashioning her skull into a drinking cup...maybe for wine, something like that. A goblet for wine sounded good.

But I had a more pressing urge to deal with at the moment, something I had been waiting a long time to do, something that I fantasized about when I was cumming during masturbation.

I bolted through the woods after my one true love. Daniel could run when he wanted to, but he couldn't hide, not from my canine nose, not from my Wolfen sight. Everything around me was coated in a soft sheen of silver as if my new eyes could see just as well at night as during the day. Plus, he had that stupid lantern. All I had to do was follow the moving light.

I sprang through the air to pounce on his back, and he cried out as he stumbled and fell from my heavyweight. He dropped his lantern as he rolled over in a desperate attempt to get up and escape, but I grabbed him by the throat with my right hand and picked him up with ease. He gripped my thick, fur-covered wrist as he futilely struggled against me, but I simply laughed in his face, a deep, growling laugh that caused his sapphire-blue eyes to widen in surprise.

I threw him down after that, and he landed on his back with a loud "Oof!". It was time to connect with him once more, connect in that way that only mating partners could connect, that magical union of flesh and unfettered desire, but this time I was going to do it in the body of this great she-wolf, and it was going to be amazing.

"You're mine, handsome," I growled out.

It's actually pretty difficult to speak when you have a wolf snout instead of a human mouth, but I managed it. I'm pretty sure he understood me, too, because his eyes were so wide that I could have just plucked them right out with ease...Sigh...Sometimes I do just want to eat him.

"You can talk!" choked out Daniel.

"I can also fuck," I rumbled. "It's time for some fun, luscious!"

I laughed as I sliced his black leather belt in two, and then I popped off the button of his dark blue jeans, tearing down those restrictive pants a second after that.

"Hey!" he yelled up at me.

"Shut up," I growled.

I gave him a light backhand across his right cheek, but even that light blow turned his head, smashing his left cheek into the snow, almost knocking him out.

Oh, fuck!" he hissed in pain.

"Time to unpackage my new toy!" I said in a guttural chuckle.

I ripped into his coat and shirts, shredding them while leaving fine red scratches along his bare skin. Oh, to see that hot, muscular, nude body again...I could barely contain myself.

"Stop!" he cried out. "Stop it!"

He tried to push me off him, tried to hit me with his open hands and balled fists, but this only further excited me, making my monstrous, fur-covered pussy wet and ready to fuck. I completely unwrapped my little present, pulling off his boots and shredding his clothes until he was nude, and then I held him up in front of me by his muscular waist, inspecting his luscious male body once more. It had been almost a year since we'd last made love, so I was burning inside with a terrible lust for him, an affliction of madness that only he could cure.

There was just one little problem I had to solve first, but I knew how to fix that. His thick penis was only a shriveled little winky right now because of the cold air around us, but I'd solve that with a simple lick of saliva.

"Give us a kiss, cutie," I growled.

I opened my maw and clamped my jaws down around his head, angling my own head so that my lower jaw was across his right cheek and my upper jaw was across his left. He opened his mouth for a second to scream or gasp or say something, and I used that opportunity to lick in my long wolf's tongue, so long that it went to the back of his throat for a second. I pulled out my tongue, released his head, and watched as he coughed and sputtered from that oral violation.

'You fucking bitch!" he spat out. "Let me go!

"I'll let go, all right," I rumbled, "but not until we mate, sexy. I won't hurt you, and I won't even hunt down that little bitch you were with, either, but you're going to comply, or I'm going to rip the both of you in half...Got it?"

He trembled in my grasp as he stopped struggling against me, and I could tell that he had given in. Daniel was stupid sometimes, but he wasn't stupid to the point of getting himself killed.

"I...I'll do it..." he said weakly. "Just don't hurt Sa...the...the girl I was with. I'll do it...I don't care what happens to me; just keep your word and don't hurt her."

I had no intention of keeping my word, but he didn't need to know that.

"You're such a good boy," I chuckled. "I'm going to enjoy this."

I mashed him up in-between my huge furry tits and trotted over to a line of nearby pine trees. His thick cock was already hard, but I had already known it would be. He was immune to the control effects of my lustful power, the infection I carried around like some succubae's curse, but he was not immune to the cock-swelling effect it had. No, his swollen member was throbbing against the fur of my inhuman, angled left leg.

I rushed him forward as he shivered in my thick, muscular, fur-covered arms.

"I'll warm you up, sweetie," I said with a happy growl.

I pushed him down into the grass and snow as I slid my huge, pulsing cunt over his luscious cock. I pushed his head forward toward my big left breast, forcing him to take in the large brown nipple that was poking out from my fur like a tiny penis.

'Yeah, suck it," I commanded. "That's it...Good boy.

Daniel's eyes rolled up in the whites, and then he closed his eyes as he suckled upon my large left tit. I eased up and down his swollen cock with my own swollen, soaking-wet cunt, my monster gel thick and white around his little soldier, my arms wrapped around his back to hold him tightly to me. This was what I had waited for and fantasized about for so long now, and now I was finally living that dream.

"Yessss..." I rumbled out. "That's a good boy. Suck on my big bitch tits. Suck them, little man...Good boy.

Make my pussy wet. Fuck my bitch pussy with that man-cock."

Okay, that's a little weird, but I just went with it. It was a little odd to dirty talk while fully wolfed out, but it turned me on anyway, driving up my lust and desire to a new level.

"Give me that cock, little man," I growled. "Make my pussy squirt. Make it squirt my bitch cum all over your little body. I'll mark you as my territory with it."

I ground myself into him, forcing him further into the snow and grass, and then I rolled over so that he was on top of me, splayed out, arms around my chest, his lips locked around my left nipple, his cock buried in my pulsing wet cunt. My body heat was keeping him warm, so I wasn't worried about his hairless ape body freezing to death out here...Besides, he wasn't that far from his house. He could make it there after I'd had my way with him.

"Fuck me, little man," I rumbled. "Fuck me and prove to me that you can please me."

Daniel moved his muscular butt up and down as he pumped into me, rubbing my now much bigger clit against his pubic bone, stroking that little lady dick for all he was worth. It caused me to scratch my warped, paw-shaped feet across the snow underneath us, my toes pulling down in reflexive motion, my breath exhaling in ragged puffs of steam from my open maw. I squirted a little, peeing out a line of clear cum all over his hairless crotch...He had shaved, probably to please his little bitch, but that detail just drove me into a sexual frenzy.

Oh, yeah, little man!" I growled. "Fuck me for all your worth! Pump me full of man-cum!

I forced him from my tit with my massive left hand, and then I took his head into my maw again, my lower jaw on his right cheek with my upper jaw on his left. I slurped into his mouth with my long, canine tongue, but this time he sucked on that tongue out of reflex, feeling the power of the beast sink into him against his will.

I slithered my long tongue down the back of his throat, making it extend until he gagged on it, then I whipped it back into my mouth before he could bite down. I let him go once more, raised my great head, and huffed out a loud snort of steam into the cold air of the night around us.

He picked up his thrusts, making me feel it in my belly, causing my muscular, angled legs to shake in pure pleasure. It felt different in this form than it did as a human woman, but I liked it, loved it even, as it was so wild and decadent that it defied description.

"Fuck me harder!" I demanded in a deep rumble. "Fuck me harder, little man! Make me feel it!"

He pumped even harder than before, as hard and fast as his little body could go. It was fun being bigger and stronger than him, being in complete control of his little human body, knowing full well he was feeling that humiliation and would be feeling it for a long time to come. He would think back on the bitch werewolf that took him for a ride, forced him into a wild fuck in the woods, and he would feel that shame deep, deep down within his soul...That made me extremely happy just thinking about it.

Uh...uh...uh...uh..." he huffed out. "Oh...oh fuck...oh fuck...

Daniel squeezed his blue eyes shut and grimaced as he thrust into me over and over again, pushing his own little human body to its limits. I knew he was going to cum, because that was his 'straining to squirt' face, and I was quite familiar with it.

"Yeah, little man," I growled. "Cum in your big bitch, little man. Cum in your big, ferocious bitch. Give me some pups, little man. I'll squeeze out a litter for you..."

"Oh, oh, oh, oh, oh fuck, oh fuck, oh fuck!" grunted Daniel. "Oh, mother of mercy! Fuck, fuck, fuck, fuck, fuck, FUUUUUUUUUUUUCK!"

He came inside my furry, swollen, throbbing wet cunt with a gush of white-hot semen, his sperm squirting throughout my monstrous, living tunnel, filling me with his incredible speed, giving me exactly what I wanted at that moment. This was my fertile time, and with my deliberate lack of birth control, I wanted him to inseminate my wild pussy so that I could bear a pup for him and attach myself back to his hip once he had figured out he was a new daddy.

I pushed him up and off me with ease, forcing him down my furry body until his head rested right above my dripping wet snatch. Normally, I would have my man eat me out after that, slurp up his own cum, because that always turned me on, but I wanted that semen to stay exactly where it was, so I ordered him to do something else, something equally as fun to get me off.

"Suck my big clit, little man," I demanded. "Suck my big brown clit until I squirt. You're not getting away until I cum, so you'll suck my big wolf clit until I spray, got it?"

He didn't answer, no. His answer was in the form of something else, deeds not words, and that something else was exactly what I wanted.

"You bite down, and I'll tear off your fucking head," I warned him. "You'll suck me off, or I'll rip the arms and legs off of that little bitch of yours. I'll pike her on a sharp branch and let gravity do the rest."

Daniel took in a short breath, closed his blue eyes, lowered his head, and wrapped his sweet lips around my big brown clit. He sucked on that magic little lady dick, causing me to squeeze my own golden eyes shut and let out loud, quick huffs of steam-filled pleasure.

"Ooooooh, yessss..." I growled.

I gripped his head with my huge clawed hands as my toes curled and I scratched the snow-covered ground beneath us, pawing that wintry terrain, and I set forth a deep growling moan as that unbearable pulse of pleasure shocked straight through me. Directly sucking my clit was the only way I could cum without masturbation, though Lance's huge cock could do it to me with enough pounding.

"Urrg...Urgg...Huff...Urgg..." I grunted as Daniel sucked my clit while running his soft tongue over it in light flicks.

That pleasure shot through my little organ down into me, like a railroad spike right through Phineas Gage's head, shooting up in a V into my lower belly while subsequently blasting through the big, brown, hot, wet lips of my furry, swollen vulva. It was that pulse that got to me, that continual surge of electric sex running through my whole body up from my burning snatch.

"Ung...agh...Urrgg...Fuck..." I huffed out.

"Urgg...Grrr...GRRRGARR...AARRRROOOOOO OOW!"

I moved my great, furry head back into the snow as I howled from the incredible spasms lancing throughout me. I squirted out globs of white cream from my open hole, pissing out a stream of clear cum at the same time, blasting Daniel in the chin and chest with my wild, passion-filled juices. My muscles all tensed at once, and I had to concentrate to keep from crushing Daniel's head like a squeezed melon. I shook uncontrollably after that as I came twice more, a quick squirt, squirt of my cum mixed with his semen. It was true that I'd lost some of his life-giving sperm, but there was still enough in there to do the job; I was sure of it.

I breathed in and out after that, my huge tits moving up and down along with the sucking in of the frigid night air above me. I pushed him off me after that, pushing him to roll his naked form into the snow, scrub grass, and pine needles around us.

"Go, little man," I growled. "Go now, before I change my mind and have myself an evening snack."

I stood back up as I watched Daniel run, pick up his lantern, and take off in the direction of his house, his tight little bare ass moving in time with those sexy, rugged legs of his...Grrrrrrowwwl.

I stood up to pad away on all fours, heading back to the van. As much time as I took having my way with Daniel, Lance was probably already back there waiting for me, waiting there with the necessary materials I needed to make a new blanket and goblet.

*****

I ran. I didn't know what Daniel thought he was going to do, but I was hoping, really hoping and praying that he would be all right. I know it sounds cold, but if that bitch werewolf had come around looking to fuck, I would rather it do that to him than tear him apart. We could find out who she was later and hunt her down, but Daniel had to be alive to do that. I was in love with him, and I didn't want to lose him, so either he had to get away now or...or he had to engage in some other activity with it, preferably one that didn't involve him getting eaten. I know that's what I would do if I were in his posi...

My thoughts were cut short as a massive shape slammed into me from out of my left peripheral. It hurt and knocked the wind out of me, and I didn't even have any breath in my lungs to scream as I was rolled through the snow and scrubbed beneath me.

I sat up, terrified, terrified that this she-wolf bitch had decided to come after me, but that little theory was flung out the window when this new werewolf hopped over me, because its big swinging dick smacked me right in the face, thwapping me hard right across my left eye, the impact knocking me onto my back.

"Oh, ho, fuck!" I finally cried out as my breath returned to me.

It growled, a terrifying rumbling of primal rage, and then it picked me up with two massive brown-furred, clawed hands, picking me up around the waist to squeeze me hard like some kind of stress toy. I pissed myself because of it, an automatic response to being both terrified and squeezed, my urine soaking my white panties to run down my right leg in a trail into my boot.

"Aaagh!" I screeched from that nasty surprise.

It brought me up to its great head, and this beast, this huge, seven-foot-tall, brown-furred wolf-thing, was male...the big, swinging, ten-inch-long circumcised cock between its legs gave that away...and it was not Daniel. This thing growled at me, its yellow eyes staring me down, and there was something about it that lacked description, something even more primal and more feral than Daniel had been when he had been wolfed out.

It held me up like its own personal play toy, bent its huge head down, and took in a pull of chill air from right around the piss-stained crotch of my jeans...Goddammit. You can certainly call 'em, Saoirse. It looked like my own principles were going to be put to the test. I was just going to have to hand over my pussy, or it was going to rip it off with its fangs. It sank into me that I was going to have to do this, and I felt like a real slut at that moment, but Goddammit, I was terrified, and I couldn't think of anything else to do.

H...Hey, there, big guy..." I said nervously.

It raised its head and roared right in my face, and I had to close my eyes from the animal odor of death wafting from its open maw as its hot breath blasted back my long, curly brown hair.

"Oh, sh...shit...It's okay..." I stammered. "You don't have to h...hurt me. I...I'll be good. You set me down right now, and I'll give you what you want."

God, I felt like shit for doing this, but...it's better than being turned into a werewolf scat. Daniel was just going to have to forgive me again.

It bent its great brown wolf's head down again and took in another smell of my crotch.

"Yeah," I breathed. "Y...You like that? You can have that...Just let me down, and I'll strip for you..."

It raised its head and gave me a low growl, that rumble piercing straight through me.

"I'll be your bitch," I said meekly. "Just set me down, and I'll be your bitch...Come on...I'm not going to run..."

It, or he, rather, growled again at me, and I could tell he was suspicious.

"Look, look," I said quickly. "I'll take off my pants for you...That's what you want, isn't it?"

I slowly reached down around his thick, muscular arms and undid the button on my jeans, unzipped them, and then moved my arms up and around to reach through his grasp to pull down my jeans and piss-soaked panties. They came down to fall around my ankles

and black winter boots, and I just hung there in his grasp, bare-assed, waiting for him to take the bait.

He sniffed into my hairy twat, took in a long pull of that wild aroma, and then he slowly raised his head to stare me down again.

"S...See?" I stammered. "I...I...I can't run like this, not with my pants around my ankles. Just put me down, and I'll be submissive. I won't struggle. You can have it, big guy. I know what you want, and you can have it."

I looked down to see that huge ten-inch cock of his grow firm and erect, almost like a wooden spike ready to impale me and impale me it did. He spun me around and rammed that huge cock into my unprepared hole, not even waiting for me to get wet. His gigantic dong slid in over halfway, spearing me on the end of it like I was some kind of dick ornament for him, a living pocket twat for him to wear and show off to the other werewolves in the area.

"AAAAHHHHGG!" I cried.

He held me firmly in his grasp as he walked forward a bit, that walking motion bouncing me up and down on his huge meat, spearing me over and over again as my own cream slid and gelled around that giant living rod.

"Oh, oh, oh, oh..." I whined out as I was bobbed up and down, up and down, my pants still hanging down around my ankles and boots.

He stopped, spread his angled legs, bowed them out wide, bent down, and pushed me down hard upon his enormous Wolfen cock. The huge mushroom head of that dong, that head as wide around as a golf ball, touched against my cervix, and then something incredibly fucking painful happened...My cervix was thoroughly rammed. Most of his cock slid into me after that, pushing that massive head and rod right against that tiny little opening of the mine, elongating my wet tunnel, instantly bulging my belly. This caused me to piss out the rest of whatever urine was left in my bladder.

"No, wait, stop, stop, stop, stop, STAAAAAHHHP!" I screamed as it happened.

My screeching only excited him. It was like a switch being flipped for this new beast, and he became even wilder than before. He gripped my waist through my parka and pulled me up, my pussy sliding upwards along that huge dick, then back down, up, down, up, down, up, and down again...I really was like a pocket twat for him, something you would buy online or at a sex shop, a little silicone vagina to jerk off your dick with.

"Fuck...fuck...fuck...fuck...fuck!" I cried out with each stroke of his huge shlong.

Needless to say, this was incredibly humiliating. This proud, strong, Irish girl was being used like a pocket pussy...by a monster. Out of all of the bad situations in my life that I'd suffered through...this had to be the weirdest, and the most humiliating.

He slid me up and down faster and faster, effortlessly gliding me up and down his huge cock, my poor pussy stretched and flowed like a fucking pastry full of white cream, and unfortunately for me, it started to feel good, which shut off the working, protesting part of my brain.

"Oh, oh, oh, oh fuck, oh..." I moaned out. "Oh, my fucking God..."

Of course, he didn't care about my needs. No, this new beast in my life used me to stroke his cock to completion, shaking and grunting and growling as his lava-hot semen spurted up and into me, bulging my belly further while causing my eyes to flutter from the sheer liquid heat of it.

Oooooooh!" I moaned out as he let go.

I was shot off his cock like a spent condom to land face first in the snow, my bare ass in the air, a rain of monster semen splattering down upon my quivering butt cheeks, and my big pink butthole. I laid there for a moment in dizzy wondering, wondering what the fuck had just happened, but this big bastard wasn't done with me yet, not by a long shot.

His claws raked down and ripped into my brand-new grey parka. I heard and felt the fabric pull and tear, and this sent me into a panic because I was afraid he was going to kill me.

"N...No, no, wait! I'll be your bitch! I'll be your bitch!" I cried out, but I soon found out his intent was not to kill me.

My bra snapped as it twanged apart, and I was forcibly pulled out of my coat, shirt, and bra a second later, leaving those shredded articles of clothing on the ground. Yeah, he just pulled me out of my clothes like a piece of candy from a wrapper. He lifted me into the cold night air, and my big pink nipples went as hard as diamonds because I was now naked right down to the jeans around my boots. He held me up for a second, spun me around to face him, and then set me down upon my bare knees right in front of his huge monster shlong.

I was still dizzy from all of this as he held his massive, slightly limp cock in his huge right hand, and at first, my brain registered that he wanted me to suck it, but he had other plans for it. He smacked that huge wet dong right across my right cheek, turning my head, leaving a trail of his semen mixed with my cum across the soft skin of my face.

"Mother fu...!" I started to say, but he cut me off before I could swear out that expletive.

He thwapped me across my left cheek with his giant cock, turning my head in the other direction...Okay, this bullshit was getting out of ha...

He growled as he grabbed my left shoulder and spun me to my right, right back down to the snow-covered ground. I grimaced as my left cheek slid along the snow and scrub grass, but that was nothing compared to the shriek I let out as he lifted my bare ass up, only for me to feel the touch of his monster meat on my quivering, sperm-lubed asshole, that monster meat nice and firm and erect again, probably from smacking me in the face with it.

"Oh, fucking God, NOOOOO!" I screeched.

My asshole spread wide, wide around on that massive dong, my poor anus stretching as wide around as a golf ball, and all ten inches of werewolf cock plunged into my ass, bulging out my belly once more. I shrieked over and over again as he grabbed my ass with both giant hands and pounded into me, humping over my bare back to hammer my poor bottom with a viciousness I had never expected.

"Oh, oh, oh, oh fuck, my guts..." I choked out. "My fucking guts..."

Ass fucking was not something I was used to. I'd tried anal before, but it wasn't my thing. Don't get me wrong, I loved it when I guy ate out my ass, but usually, I'd had nothing more than a couple of fingers in it, and certainly not a huge werewolf dick to spreading it.

My face slid across cold snow and frozen grass as I was mercilessly fucked in the ass from behind. As insane and painful as this was, this savaging of my bottom built a steady drumbeat toward a powerful orgasm building from deep within my belly. It felt like he was fucking me all the way up to my liver, but that thump, thump, thump of his huge cock up in my guts caused my whole body to shake and spasm without any volition on my part.

"Oh my God, oh my God, oh my God..." I choked out. "OH, OH, OH, OH, OH, FUCKING SHIIIIIIT!"

My feet turned in my boots as my ankles moved side to side, my fingers raking the snow and dirt beneath me. My pussy squirted out a hot glob of both semen and cream as I pissed out a short burst of spray from my pee hole, my hairy, savaged cunt contracting along with my ruined asshole, my big pink anus squeezing that massive monster dong over and over again. I went into convulsions as I temporarily lost consciousness, but the squirt, squirt, squirt of two giant balls worth of werewolf cum filling my ass immediately brought me back around.

He pulled out all ten inches after that, and I shrieked as that huge living rod left a giant vacuum in my guts, pulling part of my anus out of my body. Blazing hot splurts of his ivory ball-sap came shooting out of my savaged asshole, dripping down over my already soaked, monster-fucked twat, only to spill between my bare knees and onto the top part of my jeans, the only article of clothing besides my socks and boots that were still intact.

"Oh...Oh my God..." I choked out. "My ass...My fucking ass..."

Oh, my asshole was burning, just on fire, and I knew that damage was going to haunt me for a while.

I watched in helpless immobility as he trudged around to my front, and then I shrieked yet again as he pulled me up by my long brown hair with his huge clawed right hand. He held his huge meat in his left hand and thrust the tip of his giant dong into my open mouth, causing me to sputter in the ass cum it was coated in. He rammed it to the back of my throat to where I choked and gagged on it, and then he pulled it out quickly before my teeth could sink into that giant sausage. He then dropped me back to the snow, my right cheek landing in that uncomfortable position this time, and his huge right foot stepped onto my head to push my face further down into that frigid, packed landscape.

Goddamn, this guy had something against me. I don't know what, but holy shit was he pissed at me for some reason. What the fuck did I do to him?

He took a brief moment to push my head further down, and that hurt like fuck, but all I could do was give out a muffled cry for help. He then let up the pressure, removing his huge clawed foot, and I thought that was the end of this torture, but he still wasn't done.

He rolled me over with his right foot, reached down, pinched both of my big pink nipples with his giant fingers, and pulled up. My breasts pulled out like traffic cones, and the son of a bitch lifted me off of the ground that way.

I screamed bloody murder for a couple of seconds I was in the air, but he let go rather quickly. He dropped me back to the ground after that new pain, rolled me over again, this time with his left foot, grabbed me by my cum-soaked twat, and pulled me up to my knees by my own pussy, so that my ass was back in the air. It hurt like fucking hell as he squeezed my hairy lower lips together, squelching cream out of them like he was squeezing a Twinkie, pinching them together so that they were pulled up like a handle, pulling them out slightly as he did.

This new pain broke something in my brain, and I did something that I'd sworn in the past that I would never, ever do.

"Mercy, mercy, mercy!" I babbled. "Oh, God, please, have mercy!"

I couldn't believe I was begging. It was not like me to beg like this, because that was beneath my Irish blood, but the worst humiliation was yet to come.

Hot liquid splattered down upon my face, hair, and bareback as his steaming piss rained all over me. That pretty much snapped it for me, broke even my strong will, and I started crying, which is actually pretty rare for me. I had never, ever been this humiliated before in my life, and...it was not cool. It was not cool at all.

He walked around to my front, bent down, lifted my head by my piss-soaked hair, and roared in my face in pure rage for a few terrifying seconds. After he was finished with that, he dropped my face back into the snow, took his huge right hand, and smacked my ass hard on my right butt cheek, instantly bruising it, knocking my butt down, and causing me to lay flat upon the cold ground from the sheer force. He then padded off into the night, leaving me there to cry in the snow.

I laid there for a bit, my bare, savaged, cum-dripping, piss-coated body exposed to the open, frosty air, just wondering what in the hell I had done to deserve the absolute trashing I had just received. I know it wasn't my fault...I hadn't done anything to that beast. I had no idea who in the hell that was, anyway. I had just stupidly thought if I gave in, he would have his way with me and runoff because that's what Daniel did when he'd been wolfed out. I certainly wasn't expecting that absolute ass-kicking I'd just taken...What the fuck?

"Saoirse!" called a familiar voice.

I weakly pushed up on my hands and looked up to see a very naked and very scratched-up Daniel running toward me, his red electric lantern lighting the way for him. It was a safe bet that something similar had happened to him that had just happened to me, only from that big she-wolf bitch that we'd first encountered.

"D...Daniel!" I sputtered out.

He ran up to me, picked me up in his strong arms, and held my shivering, naked body close to his bare, muscled chest, warming me just from the gentleness of his touch alone.

"Are you all right?" he asked in deep and audible concern.

"No," I choked out as I wiped at my own tears. "No, I'm not all right. Another werewolf just...a male...it just...it fucked the shit out of me...It beat me up and fucked the shit out of me...It beat the shit out of me!... Why did it do that! What the fuck just happened, Daniel? Who were those people? I thought werewolves couldn't change outside of the full moon! What the fuck is happening!" "I don't know," frowned Daniel, anger brimming in his voice, "but I'm going to find out. I'm going to find them, and when I do...I'm going to kill them."

Outside of when I hit Megan...that was the angriest I had ever heard him.

*****

Sir Patrick Bijou

CHAPTER 6

I laid in Daniel's naked embrace as he pulled me closer to him, pulling the sheets up around us both. My dad had gone into town again to see his girlfriend, so I was in charge of the house, but...there was no reason for my dad to know that I wasn't there right now. No, I was in Daniel's bed, his big king-sized bed with carved wooden poles and a tester canopy and everything, soft red velvet sheets, scented candles burning in their sconces...It was just what I needed after what I'd just been through.

"Are you all right, Saoirse?" he asked softly. "And don't lie to me. I need to know if..."

"Yeah," I sighed as I held him close. "I am now."

I brushed my long hair up against his muscled chest, purring as I did.

"What happened to me was traumatic, yeah," I said unhappily, "but I'm built a little tougher than most girls. That son of a bitch made the mistake of leaving me alive, so he's in for a world of hurt when I catch him."

"Not before I do," frowned Daniel. "I'll have him stuffed and mounted."

I gave him a quick guffaw as I shook my head. Still, there was something seriously fucked up about all of this, especially after what little information Daniel had told me about his encounter.

"I know you told me earlier, but I was kind of out of it," I said quietly. "So explain this to me one more time, will you? You're saying that she-bitch that fucked you could talk?"

"Yeah," frowned Daniel.

"How is that possible?" I asked.

I didn't know a whole lot about werewolves, but my experience with Daniel had taught me that they were mindless, or rather, they did not have the complete intelligence of a human being. They mostly ran on instinct. Of course, I could still think and remember stuff when I had changed, so maybe only the females could speak and think like a person. I had no idea, though, because all of this shit was new to me. I had no clue as to what was going on.

"I don't know," replied Daniel. "I'm going to have to research it, though. Whatever the case, I'm not telling my parents, because I don't want to attract the attention of other hunters. They'll be drawn here if my dad reports to them on this. Trust me, they won't be as forgiving toward you or me as my parents are. I know my dad wouldn't turn us in, but I'm afraid they might find out about us somehow."

"I hear you," I sighed. "It's just...that werewolf that attacked me...it acted like... as it hated me. Why? That's what I don't understand. It didn't want to kill me, no, it wanted to make me feel like...like trash like

I was nothing. That's a human thing, isn't it? Why would a mindless creature do that?"

"I honestly do not know," shrugged Daniel.

"What did yours do to you?" I asked.

I was curious. I'd told him exactly what had happened to me, but so far...he hadn't said a damned thing to me about his experience.

I...I don't want to talk about it," he winced.

"Oh, for the love of..." I said in frustration. "Listen, Danny boy, I told you that you needed to start telling me things, okay?... Talk to me...Come on...You know what happened to me."

"It...She..." began Daniel.

"Take your time," I coaxed.

"She forced me to mate with her," he grimaced.

"And?" I asked. "That's it?"

"She said she'd kill us both if I didn't," frowned Daniel. "I'm sorry, Saoirse. I don't care what happens to me, but I couldn't stand the thought of you dying. I didn't want to do it, but..."

"Hey, that's okay," I said in understanding.

"Really?" he asked in surprise. "But I gave in...I gave into her...I thought you'd be mad..."

"You did what you had to do," I nodded. "At least you didn't get the shit smacked out of you in the process. I got hit in the face with a giant dick...multiple times...I got picked up by my nipples and my privates...I've even got a huge clawed handprint on my ass for my trouble...not to mention my asshole still hurts. At least you didn't have to go through that. She could have flung you around by your dick and balls or something..."

"That would have sucked," frowned Daniel. "I can't imagine what you must have felt, and...I'm really sorry all of that happened to you. I am. That's why it makes me feel even worse that I betrayed you like that." "I'm not mad at you for wanting to save my life, Daniel," I replied, a soft smile on my lips. "It makes me happy that you...you were only thinking about me. You didn't even think to defend yourself. That's about as selfless as you get."

"Wow," he said as he stared at me in wonder. "You are...just...You are special, Saoirse. I don't know what I was thinking when I...It doesn't matter...All that matters is...I...I think I am in love with you...Yeah...Yeah, I do love you. I do."

Now that made everything better. Yeah, I wasn't happy about the ass-kicking I had received, but hearing those words leave Daniel's lips...that made my day...Besides, he doesn't need to know that I gave into my beast, too, now does he?

My name is Megan Holly. I'm a short, twenty-four-year-old white girl, five-foot-two, one hundred and twenty-eight pounds, short, dyed-blonde hair, beautiful cherub face, lovely green eyes, hourglass body with a beautiful heart-shaped ass, C-cup breasts, dark-pink nipples, bald, gorgeous little dark-pink twat...basically a hot little sex toy for any guy or girl out there looking for a great time, but...I was currently terrified out of my mind.

Sam was with me, and Sam was also a beautiful young white woman like me, though in a different way. Sam was twenty-six and tall for a woman, six-foot, lithe athletic body, beautiful, beautiful face with stunning blue eyes, long, long, silky, black hair, great ass, little B-cup breasts with pert little brown nipples, a hairy snatch with a big clit, twice as big as mine, a pink little penis-shaped head surrounded by brown folds of the leafy hood...She was thoroughly fuckable, which was why I had converted her in the first place, but I digress.

Both of us were together, both of us thoroughly nude, huddling together in the pitch black, staring up in terror at the Lady Cloaked in Night. The Lady Cloaked in Night was huge, a giantess, wrapped in a dark tunic that was so dark it stood out in the darkness around us, and she had long ebony hair, raven feathers in that hair, and deep, deep pits of darkness for eyes that were in stark contrast to her pale, pale skin. She had her pale right breast bare and free from her cloak, its large round presence something to focus upon rather than the terrifying visage that held her stern, empty gaze.

She spoke to us, spoke directly to our souls, and the secrets she told me sank into the very depths of my being. They were terrible, horrifying secrets, and I didn't want to listen, but I did anyway. I clutched Sam close to me, our bare-naked bodies quivering together in fear, both of us in agreement for once, that agreement being that we did not want to be, be here in this temple of Night.

I woke up shaking in my bed in the middle of the night. My naked body was underneath my olive-green bedspread, my right hand between my legs, my fingers sticky and wet with my moist juices. I took a couple of minutes to breathe in and out, in and out to calm myself down. That was the second fucked up dream I'd had about the Lady Cloaked in Night, and I was not looking forward to another one any time soon.

Even so, I remembered some things the Lady had told me, and these things were very, very important. They taught me new things, things I needed to know because the Lady could see through time, and she knew things that were going to be. If that was the case, then I needed to get prepared, and that preparation had to start now.

I got up out of bed, left my bedroom, walked into the kitchen, and opened my basement door. I shut the door behind me, and it automatically locked, but that was no trouble. It could only be unlocked without a key from the other side, but I knew where that key was down here, so that didn't matter. No, what mattered was getting together with Sam, and quickly.

I didn't bother to flip on the overhead light. I could see in the dark due to the powers I now had, so there was a soft silver sheen coating everything around me, including the wooden steps beneath my bare feet.

I quietly walked down the steps so as not to wake Lance, but Sam was already up on her hands, staring at me from her sleeping space over near the east wall.

Lance was next to her, but he was sound asleep, hibernating for the time being...He'd had a rough night the night before...It had taken everything he'd had not to kill that little whore bitch of Daniel's, or so I'd gathered. It was difficult to understand him, he is a giant, seven-foot-tall werewolf and all, a beast that spoke in snuffs and growls. Whatever the case, he slept next to Sam now, his new bitch, one he'd been exercising his penis in over the last couple of days. He'd found her hairy pussy and lip service just as enjoyable as he'd found my bald cunt and supple tongue.

Sam stared at me with keen blue eyes as I approached her. She could see in the dark, just like me, and her hearing was supernatural in its perception, just like mine. Right now, she was nude save for a pair of light-blue panties...She had taken off the bra I'd given back to her to sleep. She was chained to the concrete wall behind her by a large iron manacle around her neck, but I was going to remove that in a second, this time for good. It's what the Lady wanted.

"M...Megan..." she stammered in a whisper. "I had a dream..."

"I know," I whispered back. "I was there. It wasn't a dream...at least, not a normal dream." "Wh...What?" asked Sam in fearful reply.

I unlocked her manacle with the key I held in my right hand, and then I gently set that restrictive metal collar down in the hay next to her. Sam reached up and massaged the skin of her neck, breathing out a little in relief as she did.

"You're free," I said.

'What?" she asked again.

'You're no longer my slave," I whispered. "That's what she wants.

"What who wants?" asked Sam in a hushed voice. "What's going on? Is this a trick?"

I reached down, grabbed her right arm, and pulled her to her feet. I pulled her close, wrapping my small, slender arms around her narrow waist, and hugged her tightly. She hugged me and held onto me out of reflex, though I knew her feelings for me were mixed. I had fed her late boyfriend to Lance and enslaved her, so there was still a lot of animosity in her aura toward me, but that was going to have to change, and quickly. We had a lot to do, a new life to lead, something so special and important that it was almost too much for me to accept, but I had to accept it. I had no choice.

"This isn't a trick," I replied. "We were both there. The Lady Cloaked in Night has plans for us."

"The...The Lady Cloaked in Night..." said Sam in a quiet, terrified voice. "That was real, then?"

"Yes," I whispered. "She has plans for us, and that means you're going to have to throw away all of your hatred for me and love me instead. I know you hate me, but...you saw what I saw. You heard what I heard. You know I don't have any choice in this."

Sam shook in my arms as she nodded and choked out a quiet sob. She held me closely, my head between her small breasts, and we both quivered in each other's arms.

"I didn't want this," I said as I sniffed, my eyes brimming with tears. "I didn't...but...I just want you to know that...I really do love you. You're a beacon of hope for me, someone I should emulate, my role model. It's because of you that...I think we can win."

You do?" asked Sam in a choked voice.

"Yes," I nodded into her bare chest. "You're free now, but you're not free. Neither am I. That's why we're going to build a new life for you here...here in Lonesome Moon with me. You're now my new girlfriend, and I'll get you a job as a teller at the bank. I'll make an opening for you; don't worry about that. We'll come up with a story as to how we met. Do you understand?"

"Y...Yes," stammered Sam. "I...I did hate you, but...now I know. Now I know why you've been doing all of this...I don't think I hate you anymore...or Lance. I understand, Megan. It's not your fault. None of this was."

"Good, because that makes me happy," I said, and I meant it. "Let's get out of this basement, then. Lance will be fine by himself for now...I was thinking...anyway...that you needed a shower...and so do I. Then we can go back to sleep...in my bed...together."

"Yes," sighed Sam. "That sounds wonderful."

I led her by her right hand in my own left, took the basement key from underneath an old, overturned coffee can, and led her up the stairs, unlocking the door so that we could leave. We stepped into the darkness of my kitchen, and I led her to my small bathroom so that we could get to know each other better, this time in a more sensual, loving way.

We both covered our eyes for a moment as I flipped on the bathroom light, and we stepped into my small white bathroom for some much-needed relief after our shared, harrowing dream. Sam slipped out of her panties and set them aside as we both stepped into the tub, and I closed my garden-print shower curtain after that, fully intending for both of us to enjoy this much-needed time together.

I turned on the hot water for the shower and coaxed Sam in next to me. She sighed in contentment as those heated droplets hit her skin, and this made me happy because I did not have to abuse her anymore.

I've so needed this," she sighed.

"I know," I breathed out. "Now that I have some sense back in my head, I've realized what a fool I've been toward you. It's difficult for me...to see other people as anything more than tools. I didn't use to be that way, but ever since this change in me, this change in us, I've...struggled...to empathize. That's probably why I wanted you when I saw you, because you were something I desperately needed, someone who understood compassion and mercy."

Sam ran her long black hair under the water, running her fingers through that wet hair, and I reached down, grabbed my bottles of shampoo and conditioner, and handed them over to her. She stepped out of the running water to use a liberal amount of my hair products, lathering her hair up as she did.

"I've had trouble, too," replied Sam. "I keep wanting to feel grief for Darren, but...sometimes there's nothing there. It's like a pit that opens up inside you and swallows all of your feelings. I was with Darren for a year and a half, and he wasn't always the best boyfriend, but he was still there for me. Now, it's...It's just...Yesterday, I was brushing Lance's fur as you told me, and I asked him if my Darren tasted good when he ate him. I called him a 'good boy' and scratched him under his ears. I didn't even catch how wrong that was until after I'd already said it."

"Yeah," I breathed out. "I know. I know what it's like...That's why...That's why I want to enjoy this time with you now, right now, before I forget what this feels like. I'm afraid the next time I forget, I won't ever remember again."

I got behind Sam and placed my wet hands upon her equally wet hips, and she turned her soapy head, looked down at me, and smiled. This warmed my heart, a feeling I'd been missing for quite some time now.

"You are gorgeous, Sam," I said wistfully. "I've only ever been in love with my Daniel. I've never been attracted to another girl before. It's so weird..."

"You're beautiful, too, Megan," replied Sam, and I could hear the smile in her voice. "I'd kissed a girl before, but I'd certainly never...uhhh...I hadn't ever done anything like what we've done before."

"I know," I sighed. "I knew that the moment I met you."

I dutifully waited as Sam rinsed out her hair, and after she was finished with that, she turned toward me to give me her full attention. I took in a choked breath, because the feeling I had inside was...different. I felt really weird, nervous and excited and yearning all at the same time, and I hadn't felt that since the first time Daniel and I had made love. I was feeling that all over again, but with another woman. It was hard for me to process.

I nervously ran my right-hand fingers over the wet skin of Sam's bare belly, over her belly button, and then down into the dark V of her curly brown pubes. She shivered a little as she ran her wet hands down my shoulders, holding the tops of my arms as she smiled down at me. God, she was gorgeous.

"I'm so nervous," I said, my voice shaky. "It's like I'm losing my virginity all over again, like when I lost it with Daniel...Why is that?...I've fucked the crap out of you before...I don't understand this at all."

"It's love, Megan," said Sam in a shaky voice that rivaled my own nervousness. "I feel it, too. Strangely, I wouldn't hate you anymore, but I feel a connection with you, something I can't resist. It's like we were always meant to be together, since the beginning of time, since before we were born...Do you feel that? Do you feel it like I do?"

"Yes," I said quietly. "This must be why the Lady put us together. A final gift to us."

I sank to my knees as I stared at her gorgeous, hairy, wet snatch. Her big pink clit was poking out from the brown leafy folds of her hood, and I couldn't help but run my hands up her long wet legs to grip her beautiful ass from behind. I wanted to suck that tiny little lady dick, that penis-shaped little head that was her magic button, take it into my mouth and make it my own.

"Here's my gift to you," I said softly.

I leaned forward and licked across the soft, giving head of her big clit. She moaned as I did, arching her back a little to push out her small breasts, those little brown nipples hard from sudden arousal. She gripped my head between her hands, running her fingers through my wet hair, clutching my scalp as I buried my face into her pulsing snatch, my sweet lips around her even sweeter cherry.

"Ooooh, Megan," moaned Sam. "Let's be together...forever..."

I loved her at that moment, that moment of sweet suckling upon her little sex organ, loved her as much as I loved Daniel...Yes...I'd have my Daniel, and Sam would have Lance, and Sam and I would have each other whenever we wanted...Yes...That sounded perfect.

I pulled my lips away from her magnificent honeybee, stood up, and held her in my little arms, grasping her around the waist while running my small hands over her beautiful wet bottom.

"Let's go to my bed," I said quietly. "I'll be your slave tonight. You can be my master for once...I have a strap-on in my closet. You can punish me with it, take my sweet pussy and make it your own."

She took my head in her hands, leaned down, and kissed me, our tongues running together, the ambrosia of her taste in my mouth transferring over to her. She parted from me, stared down into my green eyes with her sparkling blue orbs, and said the very thing I needed to hear.

"That sounds amazing, my love," whispered Sam.

There was nothing else left to say. I turned off the shower, we stepped out of the tub and quickly dried off, and then it was off to my bedroom, my bed the target of our short quest. We both shivered in the chill air of the night after stepping out of our hot shower, our nipples hard, our lower lips wet and hungry for excitement.

Once in the bedroom, I fished through my closet for my purple strap-on and handed the black leather strap to her, which she eagerly snatched from my grasp. Sam buckled on the eight-inch-long dildo, pushed me down upon my olive-green bedspread, and gave me a wicked smile, an equally wicked gleam in her blue eyes.

"You're mine, my little doll," she said firmly. "That's what you are, Megan. A little fuck doll that I'm going to teach a lesson to. My little slave that needs to be punished."

"It's what I deserve," I said shakily. "P...Please, punish me, Master."

"Oh, I will," grinned Sam, and then she took to it.

She grabbed my left arm and spun me over onto my stomach with such force that I knew right then she had come into her full strength. There was no way I could control her now. As of that moment, we were equals in partnership, so if I wanted to control her, it was going to have to be through means other than brute force.

I hit the sheets face first as my mattress bounced up and down from that sudden, savage turning. WHAM! went her right hand against my ass, smacking my right butt cheek hard, creating a sonic echo that reverberated throughout my bedroom. I shrieked into my bedsheet from the sharp pain it caused, but that was fine because this was what I deserved.

"Scream for me, little doll," said Sam, a grin in her voice. "Scream, little puppet!"

SMACK! went her right hand onto my left butt cheek, striking with such force that the mattress bounced again and the bed rocked a little. I shrieked once more, and she used that opportunity to grab a handful of flesh on my beautiful, heart-shaped butt. She pulled up on the skin and muscle of my right butt cheek, twisting as she did. I raised my head from my bedsheet and squealed at this new pain, but doing this not only excited my temporary master but excited me as well.

"Ooooh, FUCK!" I screeched. "Oh, punish me more, Master!"

She shoved the index and ring fingers of her right hand into my asshole, parting the dark-pink ring of muscle with her digits, shoving those digits in up to her knuckles. This didn't hurt so much as surprising me, so only a low moan escaped my lips over the action, but her demeanor changed all at once, taking on an angrier tone, her voice growing in a sudden rage.

"You put me through hell!" hissed Sam.

She grabbed a handful of flesh from my left butt cheek with her left hand, pulled, and twisted, and she used that knob of flesh to balance as she plunged all five fingers of her right hand into my quivering ass.

"AH! AH! AHHHHHGH!" I screamed out in three loud bursts.

'You little bitch!" screeched Sam.

She let go of the chunk of flesh from my left butt cheek, reached up, and grabbed a handful of my short, dyed-blonde hair with her left hand. She pulled back hard on that wet hair, arching my back, bending my spine backwards to the point where my ample breasts left the bedspread. She pushed in with her right hand at the same time, something gave, and then her entire right hand was up my ass.

This, of course, caused me to scream my little head off. This was a little more pain than I'd been expecting. Of course, this had to be the rage affecting her, but she didn't know that. Even so, I was still loving it. It was the darkness inside us taking over because we were connected by that eternal night, two strangers of the same sex strung together by cosmic forces beyond our understanding.

I sank into my soul, feeling that envy and hate and lust flow throughout me like a black venom in my veins. I was losing myself again, but this time...I knew it would be for good. There was no coming back this time.

"You fucking puppet!" cried Sam.

She lifted me off the bed by simultaneously lifting my head by my hair and pushing up my big ass with her clenched fist inside me, and I have to tell you...this was a new experience...Don't ever try this at home. Being infected with lycanthropy has some strange benefits you never see on TV or read in a book.

"OH, FUCK!" I screamed, but she cut off that shouting with a sibilant hiss in my ear.

"Shut the fuck up!" hissed Sam. "You've had this coming, you little cunt! You fed my boyfriend to that monster in the basement, locked me up naked down there with it, had me doggie-fucked by it! You've destroyed my life, you little shit! So, now it's time for you to fucking pay!... I should kill you right now, but I want you to suffer!... You're going to dance, little puppet, and I'm going to pull the strings!"

I could tell she had completely lost it. She was in it now, into the rage, and I was just going to have to ride it out. Even so...I was still loving it. Sam was coming into her own. This was exactly what I wanted, and exactly what I had expected of her.

She picked me up off the bed this way, carrying me like the very puppet she had mentioned, her left hand pulling my hair so that my neck was straight, my neck straining with my eyes squeezed shut, her fist and half her arm up to my ass, my belly pooched out from that internal torture.

"Dance, little puppet, dance!" laughed Sam. "Dance for your marionette!"

She cackled in pure insanity as she whipped me around while holding me this way a good two feet off the floor. With her new great strength coupled with my paltry weight, she shook me around for a moment, making my legs twitch and kick like a wooden doll, my arms flailing behind me to stop her, her fist and arm up my beautiful butt, causing an intense internal pain that burned up through me. I screeched over and over again from this torment, but this did not last very long.

"DANCE!" she yelled, but then her voice died down to a mere whisper, a shaky rendition of its former self. "D...Dance...Dance..."

She held me in the air for a second, her beautiful, nude, lithe, athletic body trembling from some inner turmoil, and then it was over. Her rage was spent.

She laid me face down upon my bed, pulled her arm and hand from my ass...that fucking hurt...and then let go of my hair. She sat down next to my feet after that, both her and I huffing out heavy breaths to recover from that little episode of fitful, repressed rage.

"Are you done?" I asked with a muffled voice from within my olive-green bedspread.

"Yeah," breathed Sam. "Yeah...I just needed to get that out. I don't know what came over me. I just needed to get that out."

"I figured," I said. "It's a good thing my ass was clean."

I pushed off the bed, turned around, and gave her an evil smile. She returned a look of slight fear, probably fearing that I was going to retaliate. She didn't need to know that we were on equal terms now. I needed to show that I was unaffected, however, to maintain the illusion of control.

"It was still fun," I said lazily. "However, I'm tired of this game. Let's do something gentler now."

She cocked her head to her right, her long, wet, black hair spilling down her right shoulder, and she gave me a slightly horrified, slightly confused look.

"You're not mad?" asked Sam in no small wonder. "But I just tried to kill you...I just...What?...I don't understand..."

"You won't kill me," I said as I rolled my green eyes. "You can't kill me, silly. The Lady connected us...Oh, we can hurt each other, but we can't go all the way...Besides, it's the rage, and I understand the rage. It's something you have to control, but you'll learn...But enough talking...Let's wind down a little with some pleasant fucking, shall we?"

I could tell that she was still agitated from her momentary fit of insanity, but she would calm down after we started into a more pleasant routine. She just needed some incentive.

I walked toward her on my knees, placed my hands on her bare shoulders, spread my legs, and angled up onto her lap. I reached down and held up my purple dildo currently strapped around her waist, lowered myself, and let it slide into my sopping-wet hole. I rested upon it, all eight inches inside me, and brought my lips to hers.

We kissed in a passionate embrace as I slid up and down the strap-on, and then I released our kiss in order to bend a little to take her hard, little, brown nipple into my mouth. I greedily suckled it as she moaned and arched her back, and then I popped off the dildo in order to have my full way with her, backing up on the bed as I did.

"It's my turn," I said in a husky breath.

I gripped her shoulders in gentle persuasion, guiding her down and around to her back, laying her down so that her long black hair spilled all around my two white pillows. I mounted her again, this time with the full intent of fucking to completion.

I moaned out and laughed a little as I slid down upon the strap-on, thoroughly enjoying that silicone penis in my long wet tunnel. I slid up, down, up, down, up, down, thumping into Sam's crotch as I did so, watching her beautiful face breathe in and out in concentration, the concentration of simply holding me up, feeling what it was like to be in the position of a man.

"Let's...Let's find someone to...to torture and kill..." I huffed out with a smile as I closed my eyes in peaceful bliss. "We have to...to feed Lance, anyway."

"Oh, yeah," replied Sam, and even with my eyes closed, I could sense the happiness radiating off of her. "That sounds fun, plus Lance deserves a good meal...I know you want to catch that Saoirse girl, though. Let's just use her."

"Yeah, but that...that's complicated," I puffed.

I pumped up and down on the strap-on, feeling that faux-penis thrust up inside me with each drop of my wide bottom. I thumped into Sam's wide hips, but she took it in stride, getting into the rhythm of pushing up as I dropped down. The bed rocked with our steady fucking, the mattress bouncing up and down in steady motion.

How so?" asked Sam.

"This Saoirse bitch has attached herself...to my Daniel," I huffed. "Killing her...requires some skill...I'm going to have to...extract her from where she lives...but I don't know where that is. That's where...where you come in."

"Oh?" asked Sam.

"Yeah..." I grunted. "Plus, I want to make a...a blanket out of her skin. We're going to skin her first...before we feed her to Lance. I was also thinking...of keeping her skull to use as a goblet, and maybe keep her hair. She does have nice hair."

"That's a great idea," grinned Sam. "That does sound like fun...but what about this plan you have?"

"I'll tell you...the plan...after we fuck," I huffed. "I want to cum first, and then...then I want you to cum."

"Saucy," giggled Sam. "Let's do it, then."

Our current conversation would have to wait. I concentrated on fucking my new gorgeous girlfriend instead.

Getting fucked like this was giving me a steady pulse toward orgasm, which was unusual because I normally didn't cum without oral stimulation, specifically the suckling of my gorgeous, little, dark-pink clit. It was probably just the very presence of Sam that was doing it to me, working her magic into my bones, probably the fact that she was a woman and a hot one at that.

"Oh...oh...oh...oh fuck me...ooooh..." I moaned. "Oh, I want to...to cum, but I can't quite...do it. I need some additional stimulation...Grab my ear and pull. Pull it hard...I want it to hurt."

I opened my eyes just as Sam reached up and grabbed my left ear with her right hand. She didn't even hesitate in inflicting my pain...Good...She need to embrace the darkness connecting us.

I shrieked as she pulled hard, threatening to rip off my small ear, but I kept up my steady pumping, and she kept up her rhythm with me, convincing me further that she had indeed been an excellent choice as my second life partner.

"Oooooh...GODDAMMIT!" I shrieked. "Oh, fuck, that hurts!... Oh, oh, oh, oh, oh, oh..."

I could feel it down around my bladder, pulsing up from my cunt, threatening to blow, an explosion of hot juices waiting to be released. It was the pain that was moving my lesbian ride toward completion, a masochistic pleasure I usually only received from the over-stimulation of the magic little button parked between my bald, lower lips.

"Oh fuck, oh fuck, oh fuck, oooooh..." I puffed out. "Oh, oh, oh, ooooh...Ung, ung, ung, ung, ung..."

It hit me in a wonderful little burst of spray and cum as my pussy clenched my purple strap-on over and over again, causing my toes to curl and the lips on my face to wince.

"Ung, ung, een, een, een, EEEEEENNNNG!" I cried.

I arched my back so that my pussy lifted, lifting it on purpose so that my pee hole was properly lined up. A line of my clear cum shot straight and true over the smooth skin of Sam's belly, chest, and across her face, like a quick spray of water from a garden hose.

'You little bitch!" grinned Sam. "You did that on purpose!

We both laughed as I popped off the strap-on, creaming all over it as I did. I reached down to her belly and unbuckled my strap-on, whipping it from her a moment later. I threw that little device to the floor, spread her legs, and lowered my face toward her hairy wet snatch, those leafy, brown, pussy lips ready for my loving attention. I took a moment, however, to explain what I had meant in the previous conversation.

"I was talking about some rando earlier," I said matter-of-factly. "Not Saoirse. We need to pick up someone like how I picked up you. Not a townie but a transient. Someone who won't be missed...I'll leave the choice up to you. Man or woman. Your pick."

"I'm thinking a woman," breathed out Sam as she closed her blue eyes in preparation for my attention. "Someone young and attractive...Someone we can have fun with befoooooooh..."

I cut off her sentence as I slurped into her hot, cream-filled twat. Sam had a rich taste, something akin to tuna, but with a strong hint of lemon added in with a little bit of sugar. I took my time swirling my tongue around her open hole, and then I pulled up lightly upon one of her leafy inner lips with my teeth, giving myself a star of satisfaction for the hiss of slight pain she gave in response to my light torture.

I popped my head up as I stared down at her oversized clit. She did have a big clit for a woman, so I had to marvel over it for a bit.

"You have a big clit," I smirked. "It's like a little lady penis I can suck on."

"I do not," giggled Sam. "You just have a really small one."

"Mine's a perfect size," I said in false umbrage. "You're the one with the jumbo. If that thing was any bigger, I wouldn't need this strap-on." "You're just jealous," grinned Sam. "Yours is so small, that if you were a guy, you'd have a three-inch dick. Now shut up and make me cum."

"Oh, you are getting uppity, now that you're free!" I laughed. "Well, then, I'll have to punish you for this insolence. I'll shut you up...Make you beg for mercy."

"I'd like to see you try, you little bi..." she began.

And I did. I wrapped my lips around her little lady dick and sucked hard, that little pink head slurping across my tongue and the roof of my mouth. Sam bolted straight up and gripped my head with both hands, sucking in her breath as she did.

"Oh, I'm sorry, I'm sorry, I'm sorry!" she spat out in rapid speech.

Too late. She was going to cum like I usually did, and she was going to beg me to stop before I was finished with her. I suckled hard on her female electric switch, making her little cherry vibrate along my tongue, causing her to drop to the bed, sit back up, and drop back down again.

"Oooooh, FUCK!" she screeched. "Megan, Megan, Megan! STOP!"

That's the begging I wanted to hear. Of course, I wasn't going to stop. She needed to learn.

I pulled up slightly with my lips as I dug my fingers into the soft skin of her ass, sucking her little organ for all I was worth. Sam had a very sensitive clit, big as it was, so this was fun in a way I hadn't expected.

"Megan, Megan, MEGAAAN!" she screeched. "Oh please, oh please, oh please...Ah...Ah...Ah...AH...AH!"

I gave one more pull with my sucking action, bringing my cheeks in and turning my head for that extra torque. Sam sat up and down in convulsive motions, violently rocking the bed, causing my little body to bounce along with it, but I wouldn't let go. I was like a fish on a hook with her little wormy in my hungry jaws.

"AH...AH...AH, AH, AH, AAAAAAAAHHHHH!" screamed Sam.

Her pussy was a fountain in my face. She pissed a hot spray of cum all over my chin and neck, her hairy wet hole contracting to squirt and spurt her white-hot gel upon my bare chest and my olive-green bedspread.

I popped off her clit after that, my chin dripping with her juices, and I gave a satisfied smirk at the result of my suckling because her little demon had to be raging, exactly the result I was going for.

Sam collapsed onto my bed in heavy breaths after that, nothing more to say...Good. I still had firm control over her, but through manipulation rather than force. She would follow my plan to the letter now, and she would do it the way I wanted. Deceit was a tricky game, and for my plan to work, she was going to have to sell that deceit believably.

*****

"What the fuck is taking him so long?" I asked no one in particular.

I was sitting in the passenger seat of Daniel's old red truck, and I had been waiting patiently for him to come out of the gas station, but now I was waiting impatiently because Daniel had apparently stopped to read War and Peace or something. After all, it had been at least ten minutes since he'd gone in.

My name is Saoirse Lennon. I'm a twenty-two-year-old white girl of Irish descent, and my name is

Irish, which is why it's pronounced 'Serr-shah' but has a fucked-up spelling. I'm five-foot-eight, weigh one hundred and thirty-seven pounds most of the time, and I have a good-looking body and an attractive face. I have long, curly, brown hair and brown eyes, and I have a nice butt and C-cup breasts, so I've always gotten my fair share of boys, which was one of the reasons I had Daniel.

Today I was wearing a dark-blue long-sleeved shirt, a simple V-neck with no lettering or picture, and this was completed by my blue jeans and black winter boots. It was that time of year when the mornings were cold but the days warmed up a bit, so this outfit kept me warm or cool when I needed it.

Now Daniel? Daniel Christianson is my boyfriend, and he is a looker. He's a twenty-four-year-old white boy that stands six-foot-seven, with broad shoulders, a great ass, and all-natural muscle on that working-man frame. He's always been cleanshaven with that handsome mug of his, and he has the most beautiful ocean-blue eyes, something I fell in love with right away. He has short black hair that he keeps a little stiff in the front, and this just tops off that hot guy look I can't get enough of.

Today he was wearing his white undershirt and long-sleeved, light-blue button-up, along with his dark blue jeans and tanned hiking boots, and I cannot underscore enough how hot this makes him look. God, he does it for me. When I masturbate anymore, it's always Daniel I fantasize about, even when I'm watching porn.

Now, Daniel and I happen to share a dark secret...We're both werewolves. Yep, werewolves are real, and I'm not making that up. Trust me when I say...it was a surprise to me, too. Daniel bit me when he was wolfed out, and I was lucky enough to survive, so now I'm a werewolf, too, but I've already forgiven him for that terrible atrocity. He has no control over his actions when he changes during the full moon, but I've discovered that I do...but that's another story.

Right now, I was waiting for his sorry ass to come out of the gas station because my patience had worn thin seven minutes ago. He has that effect on me sometimes.

"Goddammit..." I said unhappily. "What the fuck? Where are you?"

Well, that was enough of that. Time to go get him.

I got out of the truck and made my way across the pumps and to the gas station. Daniel is quite stupid sometimes, so it occurred to me that maybe he'd just gotten a call and was talking on his phone or something, not realizing that he could do that out here with me...I don't know. I know that checking on him seems kind of smothering, but I get kind of paranoid when it comes to being apart from...

That...That mother...fucker.

I pushed open the gas station doors and saw...Daniel talking to another woman. They were over in the snack aisle, and Daniel had the pack of mustard pretzels I'd asked for in his left hand, so at least he'd gotten that right, but still...I'm gonna kill him.

The woman he was talking to was gorgeous. She looked to be in her mid-twenties, and she was tall, the same height as Daniel. She had a thin, athletic body, long legs, little boobs, a beautiful face with blue eyes almost the same color as Daniel's, and long black hair underneath her white Stetson that went down to the middle of her back. She wore bellbottom jeans held up by a thin black leather belt and a spotless white T underneath her light-blue jean jacket. She wore a pair of black booties that, when put with the rest of her outfit, made her look like she'd walked right out of a modern western romance. Goddamn, was she good-looking? She made me jealous in an instant, and underneath that jealousy was rage at Daniel, and underneath that rage was that paranoia of losing him.

Daniel," I said calmly, but I wasn't calm.

I was a vibrating little ball of fury at that moment. The truth was and had always been that I didn't know Daniel very well. For some reason, it had never occurred to me that he might be the cheating type. I don't know why, it's probably that handsome good-boy face of his, but I just never even thought about it.

"Who's your friend?" I asked as I gripped Daniel's left arm with both hands.

I pulled up next to him, close like a hug but not quite a hug, as a show of possession. Guys don't seem to understand that women often protect their territory with little nuances such as these...A hand on his thigh, an arm around his waist, a calm glance that actually said "Get the fuck away from my man, bitch!"...It's something we learn in grade school.

"Oh, Saoirse," said Daniel as he nodded toward me.

Clueless motherfucker. Can he not feel me shaking in my skin?

"This is Samantha," continued Daniel, clearly oblivious to my little nuances. "She's new in town."

"Samantha Cotton," said this woman, and she offered me her hand.

Okay, this is bullshit. No woman who's new in town just walks up to a piece of candy like Daniel and starts talking to him for no reason. This is fucking bullshit...Nevertheless, I knew how to play this game.

I shook her hand and gave her a wary glance.

"Saoirse Lennon," I said politely.

She let go of my hand, put both hands on her hips, and nodded toward the doors.

"I was just asking Daniel what there is to do in this burg," she said in a friendly voice. "I don't really know anyone yet, and I was looking for someone to show me around."

I knew it. I fucking knew it. Why in the hell is Daniel talking to...

"Saoirse's my girlfriend," said Daniel matter-of-factly.

Good for him. Just throw it out there. I was proud of him at that moment, and trust me when I say...there weren't a lot of moments like that. Daniel's kind of fucked up my life...a lot...but that's a long story, and I've forgiven him for all that, and yeah, that shit bothers me sometimes, but that didn't mean I wanted to lose him. If anything, it just made me hold onto him tighter.

This young woman laughed and shook her head no. I didn't know what that was supposed to mean, but it kind of pissed me off. I wanted to take her head off right then, just rip it off and throw it through the glass of the gas station windows.

"I think you have the wrong idea," she said in amusement. "I wasn't trying to hit on you. Besides, we both have that in common. I also have a girlfriend."

"Oh," said both Daniel and I at the same time.

Well, then. That solved that problem. My anger disappeared in a puff of smoke, just a magic 'poof' with that accompanying cartoon noise in the background.

"Yeah, I just moved here to be with her," continued this 'Samantha'. "We met online a few months ago. She had a pretty bad breakup with her old boyfriend, and she's had some trouble with him recently, and that threw a hitch in our relationship, but I think things are better now that I'm here by her side and not halfway across the country. I drove up here from Texas."

I'm sorry," I said without thinking. "That's a long drive.

"Yeah, it's a killer," shrugged Samantha. "It's also tough living down there and then coming up here. Everything's so different up north."

"Tell me about it," I said as I rolled my eyes. "I just moved here about four months ago." "Do you live in town?" asked Samantha.

"No," I said unhappily. "My dad and I live out near Daniel's place. It's out in the middle of nowhere."

"It's a cabin my folks used to own," said Daniel nonchalantly. "It used to be their old office once upon a time."

"Oh," nodded Samantha. "Well, I just moved in with my girlfriend, and she lives here in town."

"Oh, really?" asked Daniel. "Maybe I know her. Who is she?"

Daniel had a cup of coffee in his right hand, and he'd already paid for it because the receipt was in his left hand with my bag of pretzels. He had brought his cup of coffee up to his lips when Samantha gave her reply, and trust me, my reaction would have been similar had I been drinking something.

"Her name is Megan Holly," said Samantha. "She works at the bank down the street."

Daniel sputtered and spat as he desperately tried not to spill his coffee. I, on the other hand, had my brown eyes widen as I gripped Daniel's arm like a vice. This was not something either one of us had expected, like...ever.

Well, Samantha picked up on our distress and immediately questioned us over it.

"What?" she asked in slight confusion. "Is there something wrong? Do you know Megan?... Wait a minute...Daniel...and Saoirse...Oh no..."

This woman let out a hiss of audible frustration as she closed her blue eyes, moved her head up toward the ceiling, back down again, opened her eyes, and then shook her head.

"Goddammit..." I heard her say under her breath.

She gave Daniel a sheepish stare and a tight smile and then shook her head once.

"I probably shouldn't be talking to you," she said in an apologetic tone.

"It's okay," said Daniel quickly. "It's fine. Considering that Megan and I still bump into each other...somehow...I'll be seeing you around, anyway."

"And I don't hate her," I blurted out.

I don't know why I said that, but I felt that I needed to. I just started talking like an idiot, because I knew as well as Daniel that Megan had probably been talkative about us.

"Megan may think that I do, but I don't," I rattled off. "What happened was an accident...kind of...and I feel really bad about it, and I just feel like she hates me, but I hadn't even done anything to her before that, and I wish we could be friends, but I think she reaaally hates me now, and..."

What the fuck are you saying? Have you lost your mind, Saoirse?

"There's no need to explain," smiled Samantha as she shook her head. "I'm sure things will work out between all of us."

Daniel took in a sharp breath and released it because I think the actual gravity of what this woman had said was just now sinking in.

"But...But Megan?" asked Daniel in rightfully-earned disbelief. "She's your girlfriend?... Megan Holly?... I just...I'm having a hard time processing that..."

"It's a modern world," shrugged Samantha. "You never know. If something broke up between you and Saoirse, you might end up with a guy...I could see you with a boyfriend."

Okay, that offended me, but it also had the strange effect of turning me on. I mean, on the one hand, it offended me that she would suggest that Daniel would break up with me, but on the other hand, I had a quick flash of Daniel kissing another hot guy, and this...kind of turned a key for me...This day was getting weird, weirder than usual, and considering the way my life had been lately, that was saying something.

"Daniel and I aren't going anywhere," I said firmly.

I pulled him closer to me, practically burying myself in his side. He held onto his coffee for dear life, because if I had been anymore smothering, it would have spilled all over his shirt.

"Just tell Megan that I don't want to be enemies," I blurted out. "I really don't."

"That's something I think you should discuss with her," replied Samantha. "Megan is...if she wants something and can't have it...she's the kind of person that doesn't want anyone else to have it, either."

"Don't I know it," breathed Daniel.

Samantha gave a quick guffaw and shook her head once, flashing us a keen smile...Goddamn, was she good-looking. I knew she wasn't interested in Daniel...obviously...but I was still kind of jealous...It's a girl thing. Every other woman is a potential rival, regardless of who they're with or what they look like. Unfortunately, though, the better looking they are, the worse that feeling of possession toward your significant other gets. It's kind of on a scale.

"Well, I'll be seeing you around," nodded Samantha. "I guess I should get back to looking for work. Can't exist without money, you know."

"Y...Yeah," I said sheepishly.

She doesn't know that you don't have a job or any life prospects right now, Saoirse. That wasn't aimed at you...Ugh...I need to figure out what to do with my life.

She walked past us to take her to leave, but as she did, she looked me up and down for a second.

"You know," said Samantha, "you are really pretty, Saoirse. No wonder Megan was jealous. Oh, she won't admit it, but I could tell when she went off...Never mind that. Anyway, it was nice to meet you both...Oh, by the way, Saoirse. You have nice skin. Very lovely."

"Oh...thank you," I said in a polite reply.

That was a weird comment. Even so, I was glad that Megan had hooked up with her. Samantha was really nice, so maybe she could keep a cap on that psycho little squirrel. She seemed really kind, and that was even though I was still kind of jealous of her.

*****

I got up out of my bathtub, dripping wet, but that didn't matter. I toweled off and took a brief moment to inspect myself in the mirror because I had shaved recently, but my hair hadn't grown back in as it had during that fateful week when I had slowly been transforming into a werewolf. I couldn't control that growth when my time neared the full moon, but that was two weeks away.

"No pit hair, no leg hair," I said to myself. "You are finally looking like your old self, Saoirse, and not like some Sasquatch."

Yeah, I still had my pubes, but...I don't like shaving those. I like rubbing that hairy pussy in Daniel's face, anyway. Serves him right. He needs to be humiliated for all of the shit he's put me through.

Tonight, my dad was in town to see his girlfriend, but that was okay. Whatever he wanted in that department was fine with me. I hadn't met the woman yet, but as long as she wasn't a total fucking bitch, I didn't care if he shacked up with her.

I was here all alone...Daniel was off with his parents renovating the lodge. His parents owned a lodge north of this little cabin, and it was that lodge that was going to keep me safe each month when I was wolfed out...and it would keep everyone else safe, too, so there was that.

Now, his parents know Daniel's a werewolf, and they've known since he was a little kid, ever since he read from a cursed book and was...uhhh...cursed with lycanthropy from it. It sucks that he's cursed, but at least he didn't get a chunk taken out of his right shoulder like I did. That had sucked, like, royally. His parents now know I'm a werewolf, too, because we told them, and they know my 'wolfiness' was because of Daniel's nightly escapades when he was escaping his holding cell in the lodge, but as I said, they're renovating the place so that both Daniel and I will be thoroughly contained. I figure it will be boring there, but we'll probably fuck a lot locked up together in a confined room, so that will certainly pass the time.

I had the lights on in the cabin....My attack from the other night had made me paranoid. Daniel and I had a run-in with a pair of werewolves, a male and a female, and these two could somehow change outside of the full moon. Now, don't ask me how that's possible, because I don't fucking know. Whatever the case, Daniel's werewolf threatened to kill us both if he didn't fuck her, and mine just straight up fucked the shit out of me, but it also beat me up, and that's why I was on edge. Daniel wasn't here right now, so I was paranoid to the point where only some weed, whiskey, and masturbation to internet porn was going to calm me down.

I didn't bother putting on any clothes before I left the bathroom. I'd walked in there naked, anyway.

I made my way down the hall past my dad's bedroom to the kitchen. I was going to make a sandwich before engaging in my little fun fest, because smoking pot always made me hungry.

I walked into the kitchen, but my breath caught in my throat. The kitchen door was open, slightly ajar, and I knew I'd closed it before I'd taken my bath. Maybe Daniel had come back, or maybe my dad had come back, but that second option wasn't a pleasant one. I didn't want my dad to catch me walking around naked in the house, plus I'd have to hide the booze and weed without him noticing.

"Daniel?" I asked. "Are you here?"

The hairs stood up on the back of my neck. I sensed a presence behind me, in the living room, in that dark area where I had the lights off. I had the kitchen lights on, but...I liked to keep the lights off in the living room whenever I was having a little 'me time' on my dad's easy chair. Nevertheless, I was creeped out now...I was afraid to turn around, and being that scared wasn't something normal for me. The other night's attack had fucked me up in the head worse than I'd thought.

D...Daniel?" I stammered.

There came a low rumbling sound, a terrible growl I was already familiar with. I slowly turned, shaking now, turning to look up at the seven-foot-tall beast that had just walked out of the dark of my living room.

This thing had the great head of a wolf upon a man's muscular body, seven feet of brown fur, rage, and bulging muscle, with the angled legs of a wolf and a big, swinging, ten-inch-long circumcised cock between those legs. Oh, I was well familiar with this beast and the giant penis swinging between its legs. That huge dick had been brutally forced into all three of my holes, and I'd been hit in the face with it...multiple times.

I pissed on the floor right then, a yellow stream formed a puddle between my legs on the kitchen tiles.

I was that scared, terrified really, and that was new for me. I couldn't even think at that moment,

It let out a loud growl and advanced, swinging its huge right hand, deadly black claws on that right hand, those claws aimed right at my face.

"No, no, wait, WAIT!" I screamed.

It changed its target at the last possible second, hitting me with the palm of its monstrous hand. Its huge brown hand impacted against my left arm, knocking me through the air to where I slammed against my own fridge, the fridge rattling from the impact. I fell to the floor onto my bare butt and caught myself with my hands flat on the kitchen tile before my head could hit the floor, and even though I was tougher now that I was a lycanthrope, that blow had still hurt like fuck.

It advanced on me again, the black claws on its toes clicking across my kitchen tile, and I was crying now, crying in complete terror, because this was it...I was going to die. I started babbling without control, saying anything I could to keep it from killing me.

I'm sorry, I'm sorry, I'm sorry!" I cried out as it reached for me.

It grabbed me around the neck and lifted me into the air to where my head was level with its huge head, and I clutched its thick wrist with both hands, trying not to suffocate in its powerful grasp.

"I'm...sorry..." I choked out in a gasping sob. "Whatever I did...to you...I'm sorry..."

It gripped my narrow waist with its left hand and then let go of my neck, only to hold me by the waist with both hands. I was like a little toy to it, or more aptly, a tasty burger for it to bite down into. I was already naked, so it's not like I had to waste time ripping off my clothes. No, it just got handed a Saoirse burger without the wrapper.

"I'm sorry..." I wept. "Please, stop...Just leave me alone..."

God, I felt so low for acting like a crybaby, but I was terrified. I had only been this scared once before, and that was the very first time I'd been attacked by a werewolf, but that werewolf had been Daniel, and this guy...I had no idea who this guy was. I did know one thing, though...He fucking hated me for some reason, and it wasn't hatred, no. It was a fucking hatred.

This thing's eyes were a deep yellow, but there was something in them that even Daniel had not possessed when he'd been wolfed out. There was a feral glint so primal and so wild in this new werewolf's eyes, that mercy did not seem like an option for it, but I tried anyway. It was my only option, even if it wasn't his.

"P...Please," I begged. "Please, don't hurt me anymore..."

It growled in my face, causing me to flinch, and then it took in a sniff of air, and then it sniffed again. It bent down to where its head was level with my stomach, took in another sniff, and then raised its massive head back up until it was level with mine. It narrowed its yellow eyes for a moment, and that ominous look caused me to tremble, but I didn't dare move. It bent down one more time, took in another whiff of whatever it had caught the scent of, and then lifted its head again.

"Y...You don't have to h...hurt me," I said in a shaky voice. "Y...You don't. I can be your bitch. I can be your bitch, I swear. Please, don't hurt me anymore. I'll be your bitch."

It tucked me underneath its muscular right arm and then carried me bodily into the living room. It walked toward my open bedroom door, walked in with me, and set me down, onto my belly, on my own bed. It growled down at me as I turned to look up at it, but I knew what that growl meant.

"Okay, okay, okay," I babbled out. "I'll be your bitch. I will. I'll be your bitch. I'll do it."

I got up onto my hands and knees and thrust my bare butt up and out. Daniel was going to be furious that this had happened again, but there was nothing I could do about it. I couldn't run, and there was no way I could fight this guy, whoever the fuck he was, so it was either this or get torn apart.

It, or he, rather, stepped onto my small bed, and its whole weight plus mine caused the mattress to sink in as it grabbed my butt from behind with both of its huge, clawed hands. Its long, thick cock slid into my hole a second later, and I gasped from the size of it as it spread me open.

"Oooooh..." I moaned as over half of it slid in.

I felt his massive jaws close around the back of my neck, and this locked my spine, preventing me from moving. I was well familiar with this little terrifying maneuver because Daniel had used it on me when he was in full beast mode.

"Please, don't kill me..." I whined. "Please? Please, don't kill me..."

It let out a low rumbling growl, vibrating my neck in the process, so I shut my mouth, too scared to say anything else.

He pulled his giant meat back, sliding back through me, and that caused me to tremble from the strange mix of pleasure and pain it caused. I was now creamy down below, and that was a good thing because my long wet tunnel was being put to the test again, being tested against this guy's huge beast-dong one more time.

He pumped into me after that, slowly at first, and then steadily faster, fucking into me so that the bed rocked back and forth, thumping the headboard against the wall of my bedroom. Having a dick that big inside you is difficult to describe, because it fills you up, hitting your cervix over and over again while stretching your hole wider than what's comfortable. It made me want to piss even though there was nothing in my bladder, and I could actually feel the impact of it up into my stomach. It was fucking insane.

But there was something else going on, something I'd missed the first time he'd ravished me. Actually, it was more like a ravaging, because Goddamn did he kick my ass that the first time. This time was more pleasant because he was not using the savage force he'd used the first time he'd done this to me, but it was also different because I could feel a wild pulse inside me, primal, untamed energy I had not noticed that first time, either. It made my whole body quiver with ecstasy, making me give in entirely, making me actually forget about my mate, Daniel, for that short time.

"Ungh...Oh...Fuck...Oh..." I moaned out as he pumped into me.

His huge furry crotch slammed into me, his huge dick bulging my belly with each thrust, and my eyes rolled up in the white as I helplessly took this primal fucking. It caused my fingers to curl and clutch my bedspread beneath me, causing my toes to do the same thing. I'd never felt anything like this before, not this raw power, nothing so unchecked in its wild sexual fury.

'Wha...What is happening?" I choked out. "I feel strange...What are you doing to me?

He thumped into me, his huge, furry, muscular butt moving back and forth, back and forth, mercilessly using me as his personal fuck toy. He growled again because of the question I had asked, his throat rumbling into the back of my neck, and I could feel that vibration throughout my head. I pissed again, but this time it was a pre-orgasmic squirt, a shot of clear cum from my pee hole that stained the top sheet of my bed.

"Mother...fucker..." I gasped. "What...the fuck?"

I felt it deep inside me, a raw fury, a rage unbeknownst to me, and this pulsed through me in time with each thrust of the huge cock spearing me.

My big pink nipples hurt as they grew hard, like solid rock, and my clit, that incredible little sex organ filled with a huge package of pleasure nerves, heated up like it was radioactive. This weird, infinitely- strange pleasure then spread out in lines from my nipples up the soft bulbs of my swinging breasts, and an even stronger sensation spread throughout my entire pussy in waves, right out from my tiny little pleasure button, that magic little head of nerve endings that I had stroked many, many times in the past.

My vision darkened as the world transformed around me. I could see the Lady in the Moon reaching out for me, her giant hands reaching out to try and grasp me, and I reached out for her as well, but I was pulled backward into deep darkness, so dark that I felt lost in some kind of ancient hell. I shook in this darkness because there was someone else there with me, someone I did not have any desire to face.

I snapped out of this vision from the steady pump, pump, pump of the huge piece of meat inside me, but that waking nightmare had left me shaken, even more so than the threat of imminent death currently fucking my stretched-out hole. I felt poisoned somehow, envenomed by the creature desecrating the temple of my body.

'Why?" I breathed out in a high-pitched, meek voice. "Why are you doing this to me?

The beast above me and inside me growled again, a signal for me to shut up, but my brain was in a fog from the dark poison that was flowing throughout my most sensitive parts.

My nipples and clit beat out a rhythm of insane pleasure, a twisted pleasure that was difficult to resist, so difficult that it took everything I had, every last drop of will to keep from giving into those shadowy tendrils of bestial lust and animal passion. My throbbing, swollen cunt gushed out heavy white cream as I was pounded, and then all ten inches of cock were inside me, over and over again, my cum-flushed twat supernaturally expanding to ease in and fully cover that giant, bestial shlong.

"What is this?" I asked again, my voice still quiet and subdued. "What are you doing to me?"

WHAM! WHAM! WHAM! The beast pounded into me in a savage burst, digging the huge head of his cock into my cervix, causing me internal pain, but it also triggered a buildup of orgasmic pleasure so powerful that I nearly passed out. It was that powerful darkness pumping into me that made me panic, that ominous presence of night and shadow threatening to overwhelm me, overwhelm my soul. I didn't want to cum, not like this, not with this poison inside me.

"Uh, uh, uh, uh, uh, uh," I squeaked out in that humiliating, mousy voice. "Oh, oh, oh, wait, wait, wait, no, no, no, NO, NO, NO, WAIT, WAIT, WAAAAIIIIIT!"

I screamed as my whole body shook in his jaws from the nuclear orgasm that temporarily shut down all thoughts running through my head. My overly-swollen pussy gripped his long, thick beast-meat over and over again as I pissed out clear cum all over my bed. Hot, creamy, twat-gel squirted out of me to slosh around his massive cock and his huge brown balls, soaking my hairy cunt and his furry crotch with that rich cunt sauce. The muscles locked inside my arms and legs, and I could feel every part of me at that moment, even my big pink asshole as it winked reflexively next to the savage warmth of his lower belly.

He growled, a low rumbling sound, and then his burning seed filled me, pooching out my belly while stroking me with a liquid heat, transforming me into a living boiler. He then released the back of my neck, causing me to fall to my face in my own bedsheets, but my ass was still in the air, which, he took sadistic pleasure in injuring.

I felt one long black nail on the soft skin of my left butt cheek, and he ran that inhuman nail along that skin, tracing out something only he could see. My breathing picked up as I realized that he had some kind of hostile intent, so I begged once more, though I did not want to.

"No, please, wait! Whatever it is you're doing, I'm...Ah, ah, ah, AH, AHHHHHHHHHH!" I screeched.

He sliced into the soft skin of my beautiful bottom, cutting in a red line with that wickedly- sharp nail. He did this for a few seconds, a few seconds of agonizing, screaming pain, and then he stopped, pulling his thick cock from my wrecked twat without a hint of warning. Part of my pussy came out of my stretched hole for a second and then slithered back in, but the sensation was not pleasant. He then left me weeping in my bed, exiting out my open bedroom door. My keen ears picked up the opening and shutting of the backdoor in the kitchen, and I knew he was gone.

I tried to control my own sobbing as I pushed myself up off my bed, intent on staggering through the living room, down the hall, and back to the bathroom. I staggered and stumbled because I could not walk straight from the savage fucking I had just suffered through, and my ass hurt, burned like an open flame, something I was afraid to even look at it. I could feel blood running down the back of my left leg, so I struggled to get to my bathroom, and after what seemed like an eternity, I finally made it there.

I flipped on the light and was met with a nasty surprise. I'd made a partial change somehow, though not much of one. My eyes had turned that distinct golden color of the wolf, the underneath of my nose was a dark brown that was bumpy and moist, and my canines had sharpened into points within my mouth. My beautiful pink nipples were now swollen and brown, much larger, as was my most prized possession, my pink clit, now brown, so large that it poked out from between my huge, swollen, hairy, lower lips like a tiny penis. I looked disgusting, like a woman whose feminine parts were bloated with abnormal sex, but I somehow knew this would pass, and I'd be normal again by morning.

But it was my bloodstained bottom that needed immediate attention.

I slowly turned to inspect my ravaged ass, and it was covered in blood. I whimpered in pain as I soaked a washcloth in warm water and wiped off the blood, but I was not happy with what I found. Scratched into my left butt cheek in deep cuts, each cut a terrible two- inches length were the capital letters L.D. I didn't know what L.D. stood for, but this drove something deep inside me to the surface. It pissed me off that this invader of my home and body had done this to me, and coupled with that strange, wild rage, I could not control myself.

"God...DAMMIT!" I screamed as I turned and punched the bathroom mirror above the sink, punching it with the full force of a wild animal.

The mirror caved in as it shattered, damaging the plaster of the wall behind it.

Well, shit. Dad was not going to be happy about that.

*****

I opened the basement door, shut it, flipped on the light, and walked down each wooden step, one careful step at a time. I had taken a minute to strip again before entering the basement; I always did before coming down here, just in case Lance decided to get feisty. It made fucking me easier for him...Less ripped clothes.

I had ushered Lance into the house and into the basement after leading him out of the van, but it was the middle of the night, so no one was around outside to witness his hulking, feral shape in the dark. It was time to question him, though, because he had some explaining to do too little ol' Megan.

I stepped into the circle of light at the bottom of the stairs and walked forward until the basement light flipped on due to my forward motion. Lance arose from his sleeping spot to face me; he'd moved back next to the furnace after Sam had moved upstairs with me.

"Come here," I said unhappily, a distinct frown upon my pretty face.

Lance pawed forward, moving his bestial shape into my personal space, and then he started sniffing directly into my belly button. This was extremely unusual for him, and that piqued my curiosity in an instant, making me temporarily forget the admonishment I was going to bring down on him.

"Lance, what in the hell are you doing?" I asked, noticeable irritation in my sweet voice.

He backed up from me and growled, his muscled, furry arms out with hands and claws extended. Believe it or not, I understood him, understood why he was so agitated, but I was not frightened, no. Believe it or not, I was ecstatic over this news.

"Are you sure?" I asked in growing excitement.

He growled again, a terrible rumble filled with both rage and even stronger outrage.

I nearly fainted at this news. My heart swelled with joy as I jumped up and down, clapping my hands, letting out a little squeal as I did. Lance, on the other hand, was not as enthused as I...Not...at...all.

Lance started to lunge at me, but I bopped him on the nose with one quick hit, and he cowered and whined in return of my swift reprimand.

"Don't you dare," I said firmly. "Leave it alone...Like you wanted any of your own, anyway."

He growled at me again, but I wasn't sure I believed him this time. Besides, I knew how to handle his little tantrums.

"Oh, really?" I sighed as I rolled my eyes. "You could have fooled me...If that's true, then, well...that's what Sam is for. That's one of the reasons I brought her into our little pack. Besides, you know I still love you. It's your jealousy I have a problem with."

Speaking of Sam, she was going to hear about this. She was going to be so excited for me. We'd probably celebrate by going out to an expensive restaurant, my treat, and then find someone to torture, kill, and feed to Lance. It was going to be perfect. Even so, I still had to deal with the immediate unhappiness of my current male lover over this news.

Lance growled at me yet again, but I expected that result. However, it was time for me to go on the offensive, as he still had some explaining to do.

"That's enough of that," I said firmly. "You have some explaining to do, anyway...You had one simple job, one simple little task, and that was to bring Saoirse to me. How do you think I felt when you came back emptyhanded and smelling of sex, hmm? And you expect me to just accept the fact that you had a romp with Daniel's whore, and then you didn't even do what you were supposed to do, hmm? How do you think that makes me feel? Don't you dare complain about the gift I got from Daniel."

He whined again, but I wasn't interested in his excuses.

"Well?" I asked. "Do you have an actual reason this time, or are you going to give me another excuse?"

He looked up toward the top of the stairs, that huge wolf's head staring off into the distance for a moment, and I knew that his yellow-eyed gaze was far and away, as was his feral mind, both of them far and away in that little cabin in the woods. He lowered his head and sniffed around my belly button again, and then he backed away, a subdued look in his primal gaze.

I raised my right hand to cover my face as this juicy little tidbit of news struck me in its entirety.

"Oh...Oh my God...Oooooh, no...Oh, ho, ho, ha, ha, ha, ha, ha!" I laughed in open shock. "Oh my God, this is so much better than I could have hoped for! I hadn't even thought of that possibility!"

I lowered my hand, my face red with mirth, and stared him directly in the eyes.

"Are you sure?" I asked again on bated breath. "Are you positively sure?"

He whined again and then backed away into his corner near the furnace. I'm pretty sure he thought I was going to be angry over his little deposit, fly into a fit of rage, but no... I was ecstatic yet again, overjoyed, almost as much as I'd been at my own gleeful news.

"Oh, this is so delicious!" I said as I jumped up and down, clapping my hands again. "Oh, I hadn't even thought of that, Lance! Oh, you are such a good boy. Wait..."

Lance whined again but gave me a hopeful look, but that did not concern me. What concerned me was the fact that I could smell her pussy all over him, but I could also smell her blood, so that made me wonder...

"Did you leave her alive?" I asked.

It was a valid question. He had been super pissed at her for what she'd done to me in my own kitchen. It would not have surprised me if he'd lost what little control he had and pulled her apart like taffy.

But Lance didn't answer me this time. He just stared far and away again, back toward that little cabin in the woods, but I knew what that meant. She was still alive, in one piece, though I was sure he'd roughed her up a bit, that didn't matter. What mattered was that my plans had dramatically changed.

"Well, this changes everything," I said with a wide grin, a sparkle in my eye. "Now I can tell Sam that we don't have to skin that little bitch. Now we just let time do what it does best...Daniel's little whore is going to be so surprised!... And not in a good way...She'll wake up soon with tender breasts...having to piss a lot, be tired all the time...maybe some nausea...Oooooh, Daniel's not going to be happy about this, and that makes me extra happy..."

Lance charged forward, extended his arms and hands with claws out, opened his huge maw, and roared in my face, blasting my short blonde hair back across my head while forcing me to close my eyes from that angry monster shout.

"Oh, hush," I frowned as I gave him a stern look. "You should be happy, my love. Now we both get what we want."

Oh, things were definitely going to change for the better soon, but best of all...I had finally won this little war.

THE END

OTHER BOOKS BY AUTHOR

Karmic Love

Beginners of Nowhere

Undercover

Eternal Love

Undying Lust

The Good Taste

Offence and Justice

A Model for Murder

Lethal Legacy: Thrill of The Hunt 1 & 2

Beginners of Nowhere

Paranormal Club

Wildflower: First Edition

Wildflower: Second Edition

Mystic Agent

Dark Angel

Enchanted Soul